Welcome to Your Life

BETHANY RUTTER

HarperCollins*Publishers*

HarperCollins*Publishers* Ltd
1 London Bridge Street,
London SE1 9GF

www.harpercollins.co.uk

HarperCollins*Publishers*
Macken House,
39/40 Mayor Street Upper,
Dublin 1
D01 C9W8
Ireland

First published by HarperCollins*Publishers* 2022
This edition published 2023
1

A catalogue record for this book is available from the British Library

ISBN 978-0-00-846998-6

Set in Bembo by Palimpsest Book Production Ltd, Falkirk, Stirlingshire

Printed and bound in the UK using 100% Renewable Electricity
at CPI Group (UK) Ltd

This book is produced from independently certified FSC™ paper
to ensure responsible forest management.

For more information visit: www.harpercollins.co.uk/green

For anyone who's ever held themselves back

1

Hiding out in a branch of Harvester on a roundabout, a huge glass of wine in one hand and one of those long ice-cream spoons in the other, is *not* how I thought I would be spending my wedding day. But today hasn't really gone the way I planned at all. The problem isn't the wine or the ice cream – those are fine – the problem is that it's 12:15 p.m. and the ceremony is meant to start in fifteen minutes. Not only am I not there right now, I'm not *going* to be there.

I fear I am fucking up very badly. I just don't do this sort of thing. It's so not Serena Mills.

The dream I had last night was probably the start of it. Or at least, the start of it *today*. I dreamed I was in a car with my fiancé Alistair and the car had crashed off a bridge and it was flying through the air in slow-motion. I had time to open the door and jump out, but Alistair was holding my hand and telling me not to, that it would all be okay if I just waited it out. So I stayed in the car and braced for impact, and just as we hit the water I woke up. On my wedding day.

I'm not really one for reading too much into dreams. They're just the subconscious' way of working things out. I know that. I tried to tell myself when I woke up in that hotel room that the water didn't symbolize our marriage – that it symbolized liberation. Or maybe it symbolized *nothing* and it was just water. It was just a bad dream. I gave myself a few minutes to recover, just staring around the hotel room, basking in the warm late summer light coming through the blinds, the way it hit the silky, blush-pink dress hanging on the back of the door. My wedding dress.

9:05

'I'm getting married today,' I said out loud to the empty room. But it still didn't sound real to me. It felt so improbable. But a lot of things felt improbable – it felt improbable that Alistair and I had been together for ten years. It felt improbable how handsome he was, how tall and gently muscular, how sharp his jawline was, how green his eyes were. It felt improbable that he was so reliable when the girls at work all complain about flaky men ghosting them on dating apps. It felt improbable that I'd managed to fall into such a stable, secure life with him, without really trying.

A text came through from my sister.

Are you SURE you don't want me to do your make up?

Melanie kept trying to find excuses to do *wedding things* with me – she thought I wasn't being wedding-y enough, but I thought I was being just the right amount. I quite like doing my own makeup – so there was no need to interrupt her morning routine with my sweet little niece. And my sister always manages to wind me up; I love her, but she's uniquely gifted at getting on my nerves. Always overstepping. And besides, my sister and the rest of my family are staying in a completely different hotel, marginally less fancy than here.

I started wondering what Alistair was doing right then, at home a few miles away. I could picture him perfectly, the way he combs his silky, voluminous hair in front of the mirror, the way he angles his face to shave. I didn't need to be there to know exactly what he was doing. I know him too well. Absolutely no mystery there after ten years. But that's to be expected, right?

I had a couple of hours until I needed to be at the venue – this beautiful old stately home outside a nearby village – but I knew that time would slip away from me if I didn't get a move on with my various grooming tasks. I rang down to reception to order a room service breakfast. Since today was . . . was meant to be . . . a special day, I decided it was allowed. Before I hung up, I remembered to book a taxi to get to the venue for twelve, which, let's be honest, was probably a request I should have put in last night. God, the idea of ringing my parents or Melanie and asking if they could come and pick me up was too mortifying. It was enough to contend with their disapproval that I hadn't booked some extravagant vintage car with a ribbon tied to the front.

10:20

After a shower and a hair-wash, I put on a sheet mask and watched a member of a girl band making meringues on a cooking show until my breakfast arrived. I should probably have interrogated more deeply the thought which went something like, 'Ah, this is so nice. I wish I could do this all day.' But I didn't. I ate my eggs Benedict with great joy, before realizing I had made a mistake with the black coffee which was undoubtedly going to stress me out even more. Not that I was stressed. I wasn't stressed at all. I was fine, I told myself. But even if I *wasn't*, maybe it was okay that I was feeling a little, let's say, highly strung. You're not meant to be relaxed on your wedding day.

OMG Serena are you even awake?????

Another text from Melanie, which, alas, I couldn't avoid replying to.

YES I'm awake! I'm doing my own makeup so please don't worry about coming all the way over here with Coco, I'll see you at the venue.

I instantly worried that I hadn't been sufficiently festive so followed it up with a bride emoji and turned my phone face-down on the bedside table. *Everything is fine*, I told myself. *And I am getting married today.* Which meant I needed to get on with my makeup.

The wedding has been a great excuse for buying a ton of nice makeup. As I buffed the blusher into my cheeks and shaded my eyes with varying degrees of taupe and brown, I felt pretty satisfied with my ability to make myself look nice. The thought of someone flapping around me this morning was unbearable, even if they would have been able to apply false eyelashes for me – truly the pinnacle of event makeup (and well beyond my skillset). Until the ceremony, I just wanted to be on my own. I wonder if that was some sort of warning sign.

11:15

It was time. I decided I must put it on. The Dress. My wedding dress. The dress in which I was going to marry Alistair. It's a really fucking nice dress. I struggled to find something I liked, something that felt right, something that wasn't too depressing among the few plus-size bridal options. Then my friend – well, my and Alistair's friend – Irina sent me a link to the pattern for this one. And I put all my dressmaking knowledge, all my time and energy and brain power and fine motor skills into making it.

It's a floaty-sleeved maxi dress with a deep, plunging V-front and I really do look (at least) a million dollars in it. It's blush, rather than white, which, according to my family isn't 'very bridal', but it's the twenty-first century and what can I say – I'm an evolved modern woman.

I slipped it on carefully, making sure not to drag it over my makeup, and looked at myself in the wardrobe mirror. Yes. This was indubitably a look. My blonde waves had air-dried in the most perfect way and rested elegantly against the fine georgette fabric. My makeup had come together beautifully, down to the rosy pink lipstick. And the dress.

The controversial thing about the dress is not just that it's pink. It's that it fits me. It fits the body I really have, not the body my family (more specifically my sister) assumed I would have by this specific date. My decision not to do a mad wedding diet was . . . well, let's just say it was *noted*. Not just because I was opting out of a great bridal tradition, but because, to their minds, I'm refusing to confront the fact I've gained weight in the, God, decade that I've been with Alistair. As if I don't

5

know that. Newsflash: I'm not a teenager any more. Am I aware I could lose weight? Yes. Did I do it? No. If I'm honest, it's more that I left it too late for it to make a difference than that I made a conscious choice not to diet. My body image is . . . well, it's a mysterious, ever-shifting beast. I wish more than anything that I could say I feel amazing and hot and sexy a hundred per cent of the time, but I don't. It's not like I lie awake at night worrying about it but, equally, it's *there*. This little bee buzzing around my brain and sometimes the buzzing is deafening. But today? I look fantastic.

As I was gathering up my lipstick and room key and phone and cash to pay the taxi driver (realistically I probably don't need my Boots Advantage card at my wedding but, you know, just in case), I caught another glimpse of myself in the mirror and realized that between the tumbling blonde hair, the muted lipstick and the slightly nineties-cut dress, I looked like a fat Sarah Jessica Parker circa *Sex and the City*. Like I said, a look.

11:59

The hotel phone ringing snapped me out of my trance. I walked round the bed, nearly tripping on the hem of my dress which would have been absolutely the last thing I needed.

'Hello?'

'Miss Mills? Your cab is here.'

'Thanks so much, I'll be down in a second.'

I hung up, my hand still on the receiver. I breathed in, held it, breathed out. I'd been doing that a lot lately. Feeling kind of dazed and with a sensation that all of this was happening to someone else rather than me, I picked up my clutch bag and headed downstairs.

This is it. It's go time, I remember thinking.

Before I could leave the room, I heard my phone vibrate which made me jump, which then made me realize I was maybe more nervous than I thought. It was, of course, another text from Melanie.

Are you en route?

I replied saying I was just leaving, which was plenty of time. It was like she thought I wasn't going to turn up, like she needed to hold my hand through the whole thing because I couldn't manage it myself. Turns out she was right.

So I made my way down and nodded politely at the receptionist, and I went out to the front of the hotel and there was a ruddy-cheeked, stocky middle-aged man in a grey polo shirt leaning against the car, checking his phone.

'Are you here for me? Serena?'

'Serena Mills to Audley Hall,' he said cheerily, looking up from his phone and slipping it into his pocket.

Ever so carefully, I got in the car, making sure I didn't trap the bottom of my dress in the door. And away we went.

I think this was when things started to go really, really wrong.

We sat in silence for a moment, which was nice. But then the driver noticed the silence and turned the radio on. It had just passed the half-hour and the tail end of the news blared out. The weather reporter said it was going to be a beautiful day – twenty degrees in early September. I couldn't in my wildest dreams have expected a more perfect day for my wedding.

'Off to a wedding?' He looked back at me in the rear-view mirror.

'Yes,' I said, with a cheeriness I didn't really feel, without adding that it was actually my own wedding. I should have been jumping at the chance to talk about it, bask in the glory of my 'Special Day'.

'Feel like I spent half the summer driving people to and from weddings there! Audley Hall's beautiful, especially on a sunny day like today. It could still be summer now. Your mates have got great taste in venues. Some of them around here are a bit expensive for what you get but that's a really lovely spot.'

'Mmm,' I said. He seemed like a nice man, but I just couldn't relax. I worried he thought I was being cold. 'I'm looking forward to it,' I added, as cheerfully as I could manage.

'You should have a walk around the lake if you get a chance,' he paused. 'Beautiful.'

I nodded, weakly, wondering why I hadn't outed myself as The Bride, why I wasn't saying that I knew the lake well, having been there on at least two occasions for viewing and planning meetings. 'It sounds lovely.'

A moment of quiet. 'I love a wedding, me,' he said warmly, which broke through my nervousness a bit and made me smile.

'Are you an old romantic at heart?' I asked.

'Old? Me? Never!' he scoffed. 'But yeah, you could say that. I've been married to my wife for forty-one years. Barely spent a night away from her in all that time.'

'Wow!' I said. 'Forty-one years. That's . . . incredible.'

'We were pretty young when we got married, but I just knew. I just did. And turns out I was right.'

'How . . .' I began, my mouth dry. 'How did you know?'

'You just do, you know? You'll know it when the time's right. You'll know what I mean.' He paused for a second, staring

8

straight ahead with his hands on the steering wheel. 'I suppose it was because I was always excited to see her, you know? But like I could count on her. Safe, you know? And nothing's changed. I still feel excited to see her.'

'That's important, isn't it?'

'What?'

'The excitement?'

'Well, yeah,' he said, furrowing his brow. 'It's not about big romantic gestures, though. That's not what I mean. What I mean is that when I come home after driving people around all day, I'm excited at the thought she'll be at home in her slippers watching *The One Show* and I'll get to make her a cuppa and chat to her. It might not be, you know, *exciting* all the time but having that feeling that you are *excited*. I think that's one of the best things about being married.'

Ten years is a long time to spend with someone, especially someone you met when you were a teenager. Relationships grow and change with time, I know that. It would be stupid to think it would feel the same now as it did ten years ago. But all of a sudden it felt like I couldn't breathe. Because I knew this man I'd only just met was right and I knew more than anything that I hadn't felt like this about Alistair in years. *Whole years.*

But what if I never meet anyone else? What if I never again meet someone who loves me, who wants to spend the rest of *their* life with *me?* What right do I have to be ungrateful for Alistair? And do I really want to face the fucking *brutal* world of dating as a fat woman?

Jesus. That is *not* a good enough reason to get married!

I stared out the window, watching the hedges go by, the fields beyond them, completely shell-shocked. If I'd understood this six months ago, or even a year from now, that might have been okay. That might have been manageable. But not *today*. Not on my wedding day.

I knew, not even that deep down, that this was more than pre-wedding jitters. This was full meltdown territory.

The opening of 'Everybody Wants to Rule the World' by Tears for Fears started playing on the radio.

'You all right, love?'

I snapped out of my catatonic daydream. 'Yes. No. Could you let me out here, please?' I said, sensing my moment. We were coming up to a roundabout with a Travelodge and Harvester off one of the exits.

He looked concerned, peering over his shoulder at me. 'Are you sure? We're only about halfway there. Do you want me to wait if you're not feeling well?'

'No, that's all right.'

I rummaged around in my clutch for the cash as he pulled into the car park in front of the Harvester. 'I'm so sorry for messing you around,' I said, my breathing ragged as I realized what was happening: I really was running out on my own wedding.

I pushed the money at him over the back of the passenger seat and thanked him profusely, although I didn't specify that I meant for changing the course of my life rather than driving me to this car park. He looked confused and a little worried but let me go anyway, leaving me in the little car park. I didn't know what to do next. I had no idea who to tell or where to go. All I knew was I was not getting married today.

I stood under the too-warm-for-September rays for a moment, in my blush-pink dress and my heels, heart pounding, scared to death of what I was doing but mostly feeling absurdly free. I turned my face up towards the sun and let myself have those seconds, before deciding on the small matter of what to do next.

My phone vibrated in my bag.

Where are you?

Obviously it was Melanie again.

I hate that she had known all along that this was a possibility. I hate that she knew me so well. Surely this was why she was trying to keep an eye on me, make me account for my movements. I didn't reply. Instead I walked into the pub, feeling absolutely absurd and incredibly self-conscious in my slinky dress compared to everyone else wearing normal clothes for a casual Saturday. I sat down at a table and I looked at the huge laminated menu. Even though my stomach was turning somersaults while my heart was going a million miles an hour, when the pretty waitress came over I rather impulsively ordered a sundae. Or a 'Rocky Horror', as per the menu. Sounds a bit like my relationship.

'Anything else?' She tucked her pencil behind her ear and surveyed me properly, sitting alone in this booth in formalwear in the middle of the day. 'Sorry if I'm overstepping but you look kind of . . . stressed.' She quickly added, 'But well-dressed.'

'I assure you,' I said, my voice shaking a little, 'I am both of those things right now.'

'Sure you don't want some wine?'

'All right,' I conceded, nodding my head resolutely. 'I'll have some wine with my ice cream. Any white wine. I'm really not fussy. Thank you.'

She gave me a little salute and walked off. I decided to wait until the sundae arrived to reply to Melanie. Give myself that little reprieve in . . . dealing with things. This was all just so unlike me. I do everything right. I do everything the way you're meant to. I met Alistair in freshers' week. We moved in with a group of uni friends in our second year, stayed there in our third year. He got a job at his family's estate agents in a quiet, quiet town on the outskirts of London so I've lived there with him, commuting to the various jobs I've held in the seven years since graduating, in a nice little house that he owns (and it felt like I owned too but, let's be real, I did not at all), and now we were about to do what people do. Get married. Except we're not. We're not getting married. It's like I've been swept along on a current my whole life and this is the first time I've been able to control my direction of travel. I just wish it was in a slightly less dramatic way.

The waitress returned with my extravagant ice-cream arrangement and a *very* large glass of wine. I caught a glimpse of her badge. Lauren. I realized then that I had no idea what my taxi driver was called.

'Thanks,' I said. She winked at me, her mouth set in a wry smile of solidarity.

I took a big gulp of wine then a large spoonful of sundae, letting the ice cream mingle with the sauce and the cream and the nuts. I picked up my phone.

Melanie . . . I'm not coming. I can't do this. Please tell Alistair I'm so so sorry. Tell mum and dad I'm sorry too. I'm just sorry. But I can't get married.

2

Hey, where are you?

What's going on?

Are you okay?

What happened?

WHERE ARE YOU????

My phone won't stop lighting up with texts and calls from . . . pretty much everyone I know. The only person not blowing up my phone is Alistair. And that's because, oh God, he has just walked into the pub. He is surveying my empty ice-cream bowl and wine glass and wedding dress and profoundly ashamed face. I knew he would be here soon. I thought I owed it to him not to turn off the Find My Friends app. It seemed like the least I could do. You know, given the circumstances.

Tall and dashing in his visibly expensive suit, the sight of him makes my stomach lurch, not just out of guilt but at the dawning realization that I can absolutely *not* do better than him. Right now, his bloodless face carries a particularly painful mix of hurt and confusion and raw panic. Not the look of pure heart-softening adoration that's meant to emerge on the face of the groom

13

when the bride makes her first appearance. I realize now that I hadn't thought about what his face would look like when he saw me at the altar. I had never got that far in my mind. Never allowed myself to get that far, I suppose.

I hurt because I'm hurting him. I'm the cause of his hurt. This is all on me. I've done the absolute worst thing I could do to him.

'Serena . . . *what* is going on?' He doesn't sit down at first, his face pale, his voice shaking. 'Is this really happening? Are you actually doing this?'

I open my mouth, not knowing how to answer him. No words come. My head is in my hands. I know I look pathetic. I feel pathetic.

I glance up and see him check his watch.

'There's still time . . .'

I shake my head, feeling sick at his capacity for self-delusion. 'I'm so sorry,' I say again. 'I can't believe I'm doing this. I can't believe it at all.'

As Alistair realizes we're not about to imminently leave for the venue, that this hasn't all been some huge misunderstanding, the door to the pub bursts open. Melanie. She's holding my niece Coco, and trailed by her husband Matt. And then, horror of horrors, my parents. They enter, looking completely bewildered.

It's the full family offensive.

'Serena, what is going on!' my mum wails. 'I know we said we'd stay outside, Alistair, but I just had to see her myself. Serena, what is this all about?' She's looking at me as if she expects an explanation that will allow us all to get back to what we were doing, clear up all this mess and get on with the wedding.

'Mum, I'm all right,' I say, defeated. 'I'm sorry.'

'I can't believe this is happening to me!' Mum says, wide-eyed, possibly already wondering how she's going to explain this to the women at her choir.

My dad is red in the face. He looks less concerned, more furious. 'What the *hell* is going on? What on earth are we meant to tell people?' Yep, furious. And who can blame him?

'I think I'm going to faint!' cries my mum, putting the back of her hand to her head, very dramatically. Dad pulls up a chair and she theatrically flops down. The rest of them crowd around the booth. Coco starts up crying and I wish that was me. I wish I could just wail out loud and tell them all to leave. Melanie shifts Coco from one hip to another before thrusting her over to Matt and leaning on the table.

'You know you don't have to do this. You don't,' Melanie says insistently, and for a moment I think she's on my side, that she's telling me I don't have to go through with the wedding. 'Everyone gets cold feet, but they don't cancel the whole thing. You're just being ridiculous! And immature!' I can see decades of older sister resentment seeping out of her as she speaks.

'Listen to your sister!' howls my mum who is now weeping into a tissue. She's always had a flair for the theatrical but at this moment I really can't deal with it. 'Why?' she cries. 'Why now?' She slumps in her seat, eyes closed and grimacing, like, well, someone died. My dad has a hand on her shoulder and stares, just stares, at me.

'Look,' Matt says, crying Coco wriggling in his arms. 'This isn't helping, we should have stayed outside, come on. Let's leave them to it. We can see she's alive and well, and the rest of it is between her and Alistair.'

Of course the voice of reason would come from outside the family.

My mum sighs, my dad scowls, Melanie opens her mouth to say something then closes it again. Mum stands and bends weeping into my father as he puts a supporting arm around her shoulder. Everyone turns to go, and I mouth, 'Thank you' at Matt, who smiles ruefully. Throughout all this, Alistair is just standing there, wordlessly. Thank God his parents didn't burst in as well. I don't think I could have survived that, since they never seemed to like me much anyway.

'Fuck . . .' I say, swallowing hard. 'This is such a mess. I'm so sorry.'

'You keep saying that.' He slides into the booth next to me at last.

'I know, I know . . . I'm sorry. I can't tell you how sorry I am.'

'But why? I just don't understand any of this. It's like it's come out of nowhere . . . and why did you have to do it *today*?'

'I get that . . . I know it must seem really sudden. But I think maybe . . . I did know a while ago—'

'How long ago? How long have you been feeling like this?'

'Well . . .' I say, not really sure how to answer. Because obviously I never felt this earth-shattering certainty before today. But I did feel a bit sick when we got engaged a year ago . . . I thought that was normal! You know, feeling nervous at the idea of committing to someone for life.

'Look, I can't say for sure. It's not like it happened overnight. It just sort of crept up on me. Over months. Maybe even a year.'

'A year?'

Yes, I think, *a year*. It's a long time to sit with something like this in the back of your mind, too scared to think about it too much in case that might lead to you wanting to *talk* about it which would be unthinkable.

'I know it seems like the absolute worst possible timing—'

'You can say that again,' Alistair says, his head in his hands.

'But, you know . . . divorce is expensive . . . and messy.'

'Like this isn't? Maybe if you gave it a chance it wouldn't be as bad as you think?'

I sigh, sadly, almost crushed by his willingness to pretend none of this has happened and just press on. Keep calm and carry on, or something.

'Alistair . . .' I reach out and put a hand on his shoulder. I feel like I'm going to be sick. I can't believe I'm doing this, it feels like my whole body is vibrating with nerves and adrenaline.

'Jesus,' he says, shaking his head. 'Just listen to me. I can't believe I'm trying to twist your arm into getting married to me. It's clearly the last thing you want. I just can't believe you never said something sooner.'

'Neither can I. But I couldn't have . . . I wasn't sure until today.'

'What a day to choose. What the fuck am I going to do now . . .? What am I even meant to do? How can you do this to me? I just can't . . .' and he trails off, numb with shock.

It hurts. We don't fight. We barely even have 'heated disagreements' any more. But it hurts to see him like this. It makes me want to protect him, to take it all away, make everything better. Oh God, am I really doing this?

But it's too late. I am doing it.

'I know . . . I feel completely ridiculous. I'm so ashamed,' I say, and finally I start to cry. I can't believe I've done this to Alistair, to my family, to his family, to our friends. This isn't

17

something I do. I get up and I sit on the train into Marylebone and I get off and I walk to the office and I do my job and I eat lunch at my desk. Maybe once in a while I'll meet a friend after work or have drinks with colleagues, but most of the time I just get back on the train to Little Grayling and go home and Alistair's already there because he's an estate agent for the local villages so can be home earlier than me. On the evenings he has viewings I make dinner instead, and it's not as good as when he makes it, and then on the weekends we'll see his family or occasionally drive and drive and drive down the motorway to see mine, or we'll go for a walk with one of his estate-agent friends and their girlfriend, and that's just how it is, forever and ever amen.

Just thinking about that makes me feel like I'm going to suffocate. There was no way I could have gone through with it. A sharp blade of relief cuts through everything else and makes my tears come even faster.

'I'm guessing . . .' he begins, not looking at me. 'I'm guessing it's not just that you don't want to get married. Or that you don't want to get married to me . . . I'm guessing that this means you don't want to be together at all.' I hate that he even had to ask this. That he's even holding onto a glimmer of hope, when all I'm doing is delivering one humiliation after another.

The rise in his voice as he says this almost pushes me over the edge into full meltdown. I can't believe I'm doing this. It feels so hard, so brutal, even though I *know* it's right.

'Yeah . . . no . . . it's all over,' I say, trying to dab under my eyes with the edge of a napkin, but to be honest I'm not sure why I'm trying to keep my makeup intact. No one's going to see it now. The waitress appears from round the corner to collect my bowl and glass, but takes one look at the scene in front of her and does an about-turn without even stopping.

'Shit . . .' Alistair says.

'Yeah.'

'I can't believe this. I really thought we would be together forever. I can't believe this is how it ends,' he says, angrily.

Finally, anger.

'I can't believe you'd do this.' The bitterness is better than the despair. 'I really thought we were *it*, you know. Done. Together forever.'

'So did I,' I say, insistently. I might be breaking his heart right now but, my God, I don't want to completely shatter all his belief in love. And I really did think we'd be together always. But I thought it without thinking about it. I took it for granted, which is really the worst thing you can do. We're only together because we never broke up. I know that sounds obvious, even a stupid thing to say, but it's different to being together because you're so in love that you can't face the idea of *not* being together. Waking up every day and thinking, *Yes, this is the person I'm meant to be with, all of this makes perfect sense*, is different to waking up every day and thinking absolutely nothing at all. I feel like maybe I've spent much of the past decade thinking absolutely nothing at all. Sleepwalking all the way through my twenties.

'I really need you to go now,' he says. 'If this is really what you want to do.'

'Where do you want me to go?'

'I don't care.' His face is pure exhaustion, like he's given up on everything. 'I can't be around you any more.' He's looking down at his hands, resting on the table.

I stand up and awkwardly shuffle my way out of the booth. 'I'm so sorry.'

'You keep saying that but it doesn't seem to help me at all.'

'I know. I just don't know what else to say. I'll tell my family to, you know . . . . pass on the message to everyone. We've already paid for everything so I guess . . . if they want, people can just sort of . . . have a party without us.'

'Yeah . . .' he says, weakly. He looks up at me, his green eyes tinged with red. 'What about Thailand?'

Fuck. The honeymoon. Which we're leaving for in two days' time. Were.

'I mean . . . we've paid for that as well . . .'

'What a waste.' He shakes his head.

'Please go. Just go without me.'

'What?'

'There's no point in it going to waste, obviously I don't deserve to go but why don't you give yourself a break?'

'Fuck knows I need it now . . .' He pushes the heels of his hands into his eyes and rubs them back and forth like he's hoping when he opens his eyes again everything will be different. It won't. Do I wish I was going to Thailand for two weeks? Yes. Do I deserve to go to Thailand for two weeks? No. Should Alistair have something to show for this absolute farce I'm putting him through? Yes. 'All right. I'll go.'

'I'll stay in the hotel tonight and then when you're away I'll pack my stuff up and move out. Does that sound okay?' I can't believe we're already talking logistics. Or maybe I can, and that's part of the problem. That's . . . well, that's so Alistair.

'Yes, it sounds fine . . .' I don't blame him for not being particularly bothered what I do from now on.

I swallow, breathe deeply and brace myself. 'I'm going to go now.'

'All right.'

'Bye, Alistair.'

'I . . . guess I'll see you around.'

'I'm sorry. You really didn't deserve this.'

What a ridiculous thing, me trying to reassure him. *You know, sorry I don't want to marry you and sorry I'm humiliating you on your wedding day and sorry I'm throwing away our decade-long relationship on what seems like a whim, but I promise you that you're an all right person really.* Ugh.

He shrugs without even looking at me. 'Thanks.'

Before I leave the pub, panda-eyed and frazzled, I go up to the counter and push a twenty-pound note into the waitress' hand. She starts rummaging around in her till for change, clearly trying to think of the right thing to say.

'No, it's okay,' I tell her. 'Keep the change. You just witnessed the biggest moment of my entire life.'

She beams at me. 'Congratulations!'

3

Having to explain to basically *every person I know* that yes, I did jilt my fiancé as close to the altar as you can get without actually being *at* the altar . . . that's not been the *best* time of my life. Especially because I know what people *want* from me is some kind of explanation – a reason, a fact – something incontrovertible that I can point to and go, *This is why I did it! You see now, you fools! This is why!* Like, I was living a double life and had another boyfriend in another city, or was siphoning off his money and planning to do a runner to Costa Rica. Some single, compact answer that makes sense. Rather than, you know, the truth, which is that this felt like the last possible moment to call an end to a relationship I'd felt distant from for years.

I wonder if people would be so shocked if it was the other way around. It seems like something a man does to a woman, and this way round kind of freaks people out. Especially because I know everyone thinks Alistair is suspiciously good-looking in a way that places him 'out of my league'. *Make it make sense!* is probably the line that's flying around group chats of our acquaintance, people we were in halls with at

Nottingham. I even had to Google whether you still say 'jilted' when it happens to a man because I wasn't sure. It turns out you do. I am a jilter.

Obviously everyone we invited to the wedding was deeply concerned and also close enough to us to actually deserve an explanation from me. Which I've been doing (endlessly, it feels) by text for the past seven days. But word gets around, and soon enough people I haven't heard from in ages are sliding into my Facebook inbox to 'pass on their sympathies' /get the full juicy deets. And who can blame them? It's absurd! Who does that? And a woman! Women are meant to be crazy for weddings, *especially* their own. At least I didn't have to email my old boss, Patrizia, and tell her actually I didn't need to take the two weeks of annual leave I'd booked for my honeymoon. I'd managed to time the end of my contract with the wedding so now I am free of bosses, free of work. Except that work would be good right about now. I need to distract myself from the fact that my life has blown up and I am squarely to blame.

Not that I can really forget about it. This afternoon I had to walk to Tesco because I ran out of food and bumped into Jackie from the jeweller's, who made our wedding rings.

'So, how's married life?!' she asked as I shifted uncomfortably from foot to foot in the cereal aisle, the handle of the basket digging into my hand.

I smiled politely. 'I wouldn't know,' I said. 'It, um, didn't happen.'

She gasped and held a hand to her mouth. 'Oh, you poor love!'

'No, no, it was my choice,' I said quietly. She didn't know what to say to that. 'It was for the best,' I added.

'Well . . .' she said, looking me up and down, as if the right thing to say was written somewhere on my body. 'I'm sure you knew what you were doing.' She didn't sound convinced.

And now on a Saturday night at home, with Alistair gone, I have to focus properly on the incredible tedium of going through the little house figuring out what's rightfully mine and what I should leave for him. I have to focus on packing, not to mention the fact that in a week I will have nowhere to live. I ruminate on whether to text Melanie and ask if I can stay with her until I figure it out, but I know that would end in one of us killing the other, and I don't really want to impose on her while she has a baby to look after. But also, it would be somewhere between 'free' and 'incredibly cheap' which is what I need right now – paying half a mortgage in a little town outside of London has left me ill-equipped for the realities of renting. After half an hour of trying to establish the bare minimum quantity of kitchen utensils I need to survive (I've accepted I only deserve the most scratched-up roasting tin and the baking tray we could never get fully clean), I flop on the sofa with a large glass of wine. *Extremely* large.

I lie down, only semi-propped up enough to sip my wine, and balance my laptop on a cushion on my stomach. It's Saturday night and nothing's happening on the internet. I watch a makeup tutorial on YouTube and decide that a new eyeshadow palette will solve all my problems. It could just be that in this new phase of my life I *need* to embrace cool-toned nude eyeshadows. I let it autoplay on to a video of a very rich and very thin influencer agonizing over which undistinguishable-to-the-naked-eye shades of Farrow & Ball paint to use on her living room (bitch, you know you're going to choose Wevet just like your best mate did), eyerolling so hard my eyes might fall out of my head. My wine glass is empty and, just as I'm about to resign myself to another bout of packing, a WhatsApp notification pops up.

DARLING!!!

Lola's face stares back at me in tiny icon form, her trademark bold lipstick standing out against her dark skin and her otherwise makeup-less face. I haven't spoken to her in months . . . it's amazing how that can just *happen* now, even with friends you absolutely adore. Some of us stayed in Nottingham but the rest dispersed across the country – Alistair and me to Little Grayling, and Lola, among others, to London where she took her fashion design degree to the next level with a master's at Central Saint Martins. Even though I studied history, it was through Lola that I learned how to make clothes, bent over her sewing machine until I decided it was time to buy my own.

Hello you, I reply.

I'm not going to beat about the bush . . . I heard. Are you okay?

As a busy busy fashion bee, Lola was away for work during the wedding-that-wasn't, which was a source of great sadness for both me and her, but clearly word has got round to her about What Happened.

I'm alive. And I'm very unpopular with a large number of people. I think my family are just about ready to forgive me. I'm not sure Alistair ever will.

God, I'm so sorry, what an absolute nightmare. We should get a drink soon – it sounds like you need it.

That would be amazing, I'll let you know once I've moved.

Where are you off to?

I send a shrugging emoji.

Are you in need of a place to live?

Yeah, I can't stay here, weirdly enough!

How fortuitous. I'm looking for a new flatmate right now.

My heart starts beating a little faster. What is this serendipity? But then I think it through. I know Lola lives in a flat near the Arsenal stadium. That's not going to be cheap.

I know you live the fancy lifestyle . . . is it £££?

OMG no, not for you anyway. The mortgage is basically nonexistent, I don't even really need to have a flatmate, I just like having people around.

I didn't know she owned that flat, but . . . it's not that surprising, really. I knew she had gone to boarding school. I mainly remembered her tales of the overt racism she experienced there, which had transformed into something more sly by the time we got to university. While I'm thinking it over, she sends another message.

Lol I'm so lonely since me and Cinzia broke up.

And another.

Lol. Not lol. Very not lol.

Maybe it would be good for us to live together, both post-breakup. Maybe this is exactly what I need right now. Maybe it would be amazing to properly live in London. Is this really happening? Am I about to move to London for the first time in my life? To be living *and* working in London? Am I about to give myself the gift of the tube to work rather than tedious and erratic trains? Am I going to let myself do this? I take a deep breath, but not like the deep breaths I take when I'm trying to control my stress, more like a deep breath before jumping into a swimming pool.

Okay! It seems too much like fate for me to turn you down.

And within twenty minutes we've figured it all out. Like a gift from heaven. As well as being *extremely hyped* about having a place to live, I'm actually kind of excited to spend time with Lola. She was always the cool one of our friendship group. Like she always had somewhere more interesting to be. I thought maybe that was projection on our part, but also she's now the creative director at a very up-and-coming indie designer, so maybe it wasn't.

It's like a weight has been lifted. A place I can afford to live, with someone I actively like, in London! Actual London! I don't have to wake up at the crack of dawn any more! I can do fun things on the weekend! I can do . . . whatever I want. Whenever I want.

Not that I couldn't before. But you know the way it is when you're in a really long-term relationship. Your world narrows a bit. You get into routines and you never break out of them, and then your world narrows a bit more. The thought of being anonymous and unaccountable in a big city, no one knowing where I am or what I'm doing, does make me feel a bit sick. In a good way.

Fizzing with an excitement I haven't experienced for a very, very long time, I attack the rest of the evening's packing with renewed vigour. I stomp around the little house plucking books off the shelves, rummaging through a dusty row of DVDs and extracting my copies of *When Harry Met Sally*, *Gentlemen Prefer Blondes*, *Cabaret*, *Meet Me in St. Louis* . . . and that's about it, because who watches DVDs these days anyway? I contemplate taking the fancy Le Creuset pot but figure I should probably leave it as some kind of jilting tax.

I put my beloved sewing machine back in its box and try to mentally catalogue all the nooks and crannies of the house into which I've stashed various rolls and squares and offcuts of fabric. I look down the back of the sofa bed in the spare room where I have been known to squirrel things away. And there, wilting like a dead flower out of the top of a Liberty carrier bag, are the fluttering remnants of the fabric I used to make my wedding dress. The fear of the first cut of the blade, slicing through the material. The hours spent after work, squinting in the bad evening light at seams and hems, meticulously pressed, fitted to perfection. A waste. Like all of it.

That's sort of inescapable. The guilt. The shame. Yes, I'm excited about moving on. I feel like I'm on the brink of my new life starting – who wouldn't be excited by that? A new beginning! But the guilt is still there. It's really there. Sitting there in the pit of my stomach, waiting to manifest as beads of sweat and a tight chest when I think about Alistair's face, about his sheer disbelief that *his* life was imploding before him on what was meant to be the happiest of days. I can't run away from that. I can run away from my home, my partner, my life. But the guilt is very much following me. Not to mention the uncertainty. I wonder if I'll ever be able to shake that nagging *what if.*

★　★　★

Later, I lie in the dark, starfished across both sides of the bed. The only light is from my phone, held inches from my face, as I open Instagram and tentatively, grimacing, check Alistair's profile to see if he's blocked me yet. He hasn't. But he has posted a photo of himself on the beach in Ko Lanta, tanned and topless with a frozen cocktail in his hand.

Never thought I'd be here alone but fuck it! Happy honeymoon to me! Cheers from Thailand. 🍸

I brace myself and read the comments. The first one is from Alistair's brother Jack.

Her loss mate.

Next one from Cara Clarke who was in our halls at uni.

OMG what happened?!

Next up, his colleague Pete who never seemed to like me much.

fk her you're probably having a better time without her anyway.

Yikes! Why not say what you really feel, Pete! I decide I've had quite enough of that for tonight. I don't really know what I was expecting to find. I get it: I fucked up very badly and I hurt Alistair, who has friends and family who want to protect him. If he had done the same to me, I would probably want exactly that kind of support and reassurance. It still sucks, though. You know, having to see it. Like I'm not a person. I guess it's new to me, being the subject of a lot of discussion and interest. I've floated through life a bit. No fame or drama, no real friction with the world. But now all of a sudden I have become A Thing.

Did I ever want to be A Thing? No. Especially not somewhere that everyone knows my business. So I guess there's no better time to start over. And start over somewhere new.

Roll on my new London life.

4

The view from Waterloo Bridge when you're on the top deck of a double-decker bus.

The smell of freshly baked bagels on Brick Lane.

A busker murdering 'So Long, Marianne' in the long tunnel at Tottenham Court Road tube station.

An overpriced cream bun on a pavement table outside Maison Bertaux.

Being able to walk into the National Gallery off the street and just see, for free, Holbein's *The Ambassadors* right there in front of you.

A single perfect char siu bao in Chinatown.

When a theatre is changing productions and the huge back doors are open and you see the auditorium from the stage.

Noticing the mosaics on the platform of every stop on the Victoria Line as my tube pulls in and out of the stations while I'm exploring.

My relationship might have ended but love is here to stay. I am being romanced by London.

Ever since the Saturday morning when I hired a van and drove my stuff from Little Grayling to Lola's flat off Holloway

Road, I have felt so charmed. It's not like I haven't been here before, many times, but it was always fleeting visits, tied up with work or some other kind of purpose, and a last train to catch. To be completely at liberty in London and with all the time in the world? That's new.

I feel charmed even as I'm shimmying ungracefully out of my own bedroom window, balancing a full glass of wine. This particular window, you see, is the only way to access the 'roof terrace'. 'Roof terrace' might be pushing it as it may or may not be structurally sound and may or may not just be a piece of flat roof. But that's Lola's flat all over – a little ramshackle but essentially delightful.

My bedroom isn't huge. And it was weird trying to condense my stuff – all of those nebulous *things* and *possessions* – into one room, when previously I'd been able to sprawl across an entire house. Vases I said I would repair and never did. Cooking utensils I decided were absolutely essential but never used. Clothes from . . . well, *before*, that I kept telling myself I would fit into again. These all had to go. But it's okay because my sewing machine lives on.

Despite its small size, my room is kind of perfect: the big sash window which I am currently climbing out of, a comfortable double bed, a wardrobe, bookshelves, a desk which I'm using as a sewing table, dark wooden floorboards. It's more than enough for me. I walked up to Archway within a couple of days of moving in so that I could go to the garden centre and buy plants to make it more homely. I didn't even think to take any when I moved out and I can't really ask Alistair if he can keep them alive for me. I've been finding various pretexts on which to contact him just to see if he's okay. Sometimes he replies, sometimes he doesn't.

It doesn't stop me wondering, though. Either way, I couldn't steal the plants. So now I have a new string of hearts trailing down my bookshelf, as well as a lush green monstera in a red plant pot next to the bed. Between that and a fuzzy faux-sheepskin rug, it's already looking more lived-in. Here's some free advice: the three easiest ways to make somewhere feel cosy are plants, soft furnishings and lamps. They don't completely cure the homesickness for my old life, but they help. It's not that I wish I was back there, but it's just a big change, all at once.

'It was nice of you to give me the room with the . . . uh, balcony,' I say to Lola, when we've finally wriggled our way up there, my glass of white wine sweating in the dying but still-warm sun. An early October heatwave has made my arrival in London feel even more romanced.

'Oh darling, it's nothing. I'm glad you're settling in — you're so good at nesting, I can't believe you've already got greenery in there,' Lola says. She looks resplendent in her bright head-wrap, holding her own glass of wine in one hand and pushing her angular Linda Farrow sunglasses up her nose with the other.

The evening is verging on hot. It has an energy to it, like the city is palpably alive, even though it's a Sunday night.

'To be honest, it's just so nice to not be on my own any more. Obviously I miss Cinzia because I thought she was the love of my life, but I also miss her because I am, fundamentally, a social creature.'

'It was weird enough for the two weeks that I was in our old house without Alistair. Just knowing there's another human body in my home is very comforting.'

'To human bodies,' she says, raising her glass. She's wearing a silk jumpsuit that looks like pyjamas which, on her, is unutterably cool and on anyone else would be ludicrous. This is *precisely* why she works for a fashion designer. 'Speaking of which.'

'Yeeeeees?'

'Are you going to get back on the horse?'

'Which horse?'

'The dating horse.'

'Mate,' I lower my heart-shaped sunglasses. 'Are you kidding?'

'No! Why?!'

'I was with Alistair for ten years and I've been single for like . . . a month? One month!'

'Are you really trying to tell me you hadn't been thinking about it for simply *ages*?' Lola sighs.

'Well, I don't know, maybe?'

'Maybe?!'

I frown. I'm still undecided on exactly how long I knew, subconsciously, that the relationship was wrong.

'The truth is I hadn't been actively *thinking* about breaking up with him.'

'Oh,' Lola replies. 'I suppose I thought it had been building up for a while and it just happened to come to a head at the last possible moment.'

'No! It really did just happen the way it happened! When I woke up that morning I really thought I was going to get married. Really,' I say, feeling a little hollow in my chest. The place for the thing that I lost.

'Huh. Well, apologies. Cinzia said she had been thinking about breaking up with me for months, but she never felt like she could do it because our cat died so she just . . . sat on it.'

'She stayed in a relationship she didn't want to be in because your cat died?'

'You see what I mean? An outrage.'

'Well, I did not do that. I assure you. So this is all very fresh. Very . . . raw. I'm like human sushi right now.'

'A fine piece of bluefin tuna sashimi. That's what you are. But you are a *single* piece of bluefin tuna sashimi.'

'For the first time in ten years.'

'Which means it's time to add a dash of wasabi to your life . . .' Lola raises her arched black eyebrows over the top of her sunglasses.

'But really?! So soon?'

'Oh, absolutely! Why not?'

'Like I said! Ten years!'

'I'm not suggesting you meet the love of your life tomorrow, I just think it would be good to resume, you know, the habit of having fun. Because I can't imagine your life with Alistair was all fun and games, a decade in,' she says, drily.

Lola didn't take a dim view of Alistair just because he's a man, although it wouldn't surprise me, since she seems to find all men at best faintly ridiculous and outright nefarious at worst. I think she also found him specifically boring. She always seemed faintly disappointed in our relationship, like I could have done better, which is obviously a nice thought when you're recently broken up, but also I've never been sure if it's true.

'You would imagine right,' I grant her.

'So! It's time for a cheeky bone or two! Get back out there!'

'I hadn't even thought about it,' I say, the corners of my mouth twitching at her use of the word 'bone'. Delightfully un-Lola. 'Like, not once in the past month.'

'And here I am to help you think about it.'

I fan myself with Lola's forest-green fabric fan with

LONDON REVIEW OF BOOKS' printed on it ('the best hand fan money can buy,' she claims, sagely, 'you can't even get them any more. They're *rare* now') and look out across the rooftops of the Highbury–Holloway hinterland. I feel a little bit sick at the thought of being with someone who isn't Alistair. Truly, honestly, hand on heart, I swear: it hadn't crossed my mind. Trying to meet someone I like, who likes me, the idea of getting undressed with them, exposing myself to them. Someone who doesn't know me. It feels exhausting just thinking about it for about eight seconds.

'Wouldn't it be . . . disrespectful?' I ask, haltingly.

'To who?'

'Alistair, I guess . . .'

'Let me explain things to you,' she says, gently, before raising her voice. 'YOU! BROKE! UP!'

'Oh I'm *well* aware of that. But . . . it *is* quite soon.'

'It's not like you're crying yourself to sleep at night,' she says, before shooting me a sideways glance from behind her sunglasses. 'You're not, are you?'

'No, Jesus, no. I mean, yes I feel guilty. Really, really guilty. Like I don't deserve happiness, let alone romantic happiness. So, no, I'm not, like, crying myself to sleep or whatever, but it's not like I did a good or morally neutral thing.'

'Sweetheart,' Lola says, reaching out with her long, slim hand and squeezing mine. 'It wasn't great, let's not sugar-coat it, but it happened. And there is literally no good in beating yourself up about it forever. Punishing yourself. You not dating doesn't help Alistair move on. It just doesn't. Those two things are completely unrelated.'

I breathe in deeply. 'I've literally not been single since I was a teenager. A teenager! Isn't that absurd? I know you and Cinzia were serious but at least you've been single as an adult before.'

'Isn't it *exciting,* though?' she urges me. 'The possibility! Anything could happen!' She throws her arms wide, a little wine sloshing over the side of her glass.

I feel a lurch in my stomach. *Anything could happen.* For the first time in a decade. Before all of this absolute madness, I knew what life was going to look like, I knew its contours, its geography, the limitations. And now . . . all of that certainty has evaporated and, well, Lola's right. Anything could happen.

'Ha!' I laugh, a sharp, compulsive bark, before covering my mouth with my free hand. 'I hadn't thought of it like that. I guess you're right,' I say, a smile creeping across my face.

'This is why you said yes to moving here! Because you *can.*'

'Yeah! I really can!' I can do whatever I want. I can be wherever I want to be at any time of the day or night. I'm not sleepwalking in a sleepy town in a sleepy relationship any more. 'But maybe I should get through my first week of my new job first.'

'Any excuse!'

I'm not necessarily *nervous* about starting a new job but I don't want anything new distracting me when I have so many distractions already. Like the fact that Melanie is constantly 'checking up on me' in a way that suggests she's expecting – nay, *hoping* – for me to turn around at any moment and announce she was right and it was all a mistake.

To be honest, I still can't be sure it wasn't. I wish, more than anything, that you could live two lives, running on parallel tracks, and just flit between them. That way you would never have to give up or risk anything.

And of course, there's the thing I'm not saying. The other thing. The thing that Lola could never really understand. It's not just about Alistair. Or dealing with the fallout of our *dramatic* breakup. My reservations are not just out of guilt and loyalty. They're self-preservation, too. Because the thought of joining an online dating site and putting myself out there is scary. Really scary.

When all the women of London are laid out before you like the 'new in' section on ASOS, why would someone choose me? Alistair chose me, but that was a long time ago. I'm different now. And I know how it is for fat women. I read the same books and watch the same adverts as everyone else. I know how much we're hated, ridiculed, ignored if we're *lucky*. So, yeah, the thought of exposing myself to that kind of rejection is puke-inducingly scary.

'Look,' Lola says, trying one more time, lowering her sunglasses. 'At least download an app. Just one app. What harm could one cheeky app be, nestled in there with your podcast app, your bus times app, your taxi app? At least fill out your profile. You don't have to meet anyone, just let the thought of a little rebound fun into your heart.'

'It's not my heart I'm interested in right now,' I say in a mock-seductive tone.

'You're thinking about it, aren't you?!'

Even though the whole thing is legitimately terrifying, I can't help but feel sort of curious about who's out there. Where I fit into this whole . . . ecosystem of dating and, yes, maybe even sex. What my future might one day hold. Who would feasibly go on a date with me.

'Yes . . .' I concede, slipping my phone out of my pocket.

Maybe it would be good to prove to myself this isn't all a huge mistake. To prove to myself that I am desirable, to prove to myself that Alistair isn't the only man who will ever love me. Or even, to prove to myself that Alistair isn't the only man who will ever fancy me. To prove it *is* possible for someone to fancy me, just the way I am. But the bottom line is that it's *scary*. It's scary to put myself out there like that. Open to criticism, open to rejection, open to finding out how completely undesirable I am to men beyond the one I've just lost. The thought of voluntarily exposing myself to all that is overwhelming.

'You should get—' Lola starts, but I hold up my phone to show I'm downloading precisely the app she was about to recommend. 'Huh! You're a natural!'

'Well, that's about to be determined . . .' I say distractedly, furrowing my brow as I put in my signup details. 'Help me! How to sell myself . . .'

'Come now,' Lola says.

'No, for real!' I protest. 'You cannot imagine the extent to which I've never done something like this before.'

'But you're excellent! You're, first and foremost, extremely hot,' Lola shrugs and holds up a finger. It's sweet of her to lead with that. 'Secondly, you're a really hopeful person and always find the fun in things. Optimistic, you know? Thirdly, you have great taste in films and apparently men like that. Fourthly, you're, like, highly competent at your job. Maybe even . . . a career woman,' she says, holding up a further three fingers. 'Oh! And how many people can say they literally make their own clothes? Hardly *any*. Do not undervalue yourself!'

'I suppose,' I say, feeling a little warm glow creep over me.

As one of the most striking and stylish women I know, I can't pretend it doesn't mean a lot to hear Lola talk like that about me. 'Okay, so . . .' I look down at my phone. 'That's the, you know, the *textual* element of the situation sort of resolved. But obviously there's the photo element to deal with.'

'What's the big deal? Just upload your hottest recent selfie. Or *better yet*, take one now. We have the ultimate photoshoot right here – sexy autumnal golden hour lighting, London rooftop, photogenic drink in hand.'

'Yeah, uh, I'll do that,' I say, shaking my blonde waves out of the high bun I'd swept them up into. But that's not really what I meant. And it's okay – I wouldn't necessarily expect Lola to anticipate my every thought. What I meant was . . . what are the politics of photos on these apps? What am I, with my particular body, meant to do? Am I meant to conceal or adver- tise the fact I'm fat? It's like the Bridget Jones knickers quandary, where a full-body photo is the skimpy knickers and a selfie-only profile is the sucking-in pants. You know what I mean. For now, I'll stick with the selfie. I settle my mouth into a gentle pout and hold the wine glass slightly unnaturally to get it in the frame and hold up my phone to shoot.

'Smile!' Lola urges.

'Really?'

'Yeah! You want to look, you know, approachable.'

'I thought I wanted to look hot.'

'Smiling doesn't make you not hot! Your lips are good anyway, you don't need to play them up.'

'Fine,' I say, and add a hint of a smirk, the corners turned up into a knowing smile.

'That's it!' She claps her hands together. 'More!'

Her enthusiasm makes me break out into a genuine smile. 'All right!'

'Yes! Proper teeth smile! Look at you! An angel! A magnificent angel!'

'Are you sure?' I ask, looking down at my phone, shielding the screen from the dying sun and examining each take.

'A hundred per cent. Flirty and fun and sexy. It's perfect.'

'I'm not sure I'm any of those things, isn't it false advertising?'

'No! And no more of *that*, either.'

Oh God, oh God, oh God, I just go right ahead and do it. A couple of clicks on my phone. Upload. The photo appears on my profile. And the crowd goes wild. No, literally. We live parallel to a pub so we're always very up to date on goals scored, etc., by way of the sound of roaring men. At least I have their approval.

As soon as the cheers subside I feel stressed because, you know, what if the fact I have high, wide cheekbones and a relatively sharp jawline, what if that's . . . misleading somehow? Like you can't tell I'm fat? God, I wish I had some kind of fat oracle to consult on this stuff. Helpful as Lola is, this isn't her area of expertise at all. I'm sure she'd give it a good go – she always does. But I need real, proper fat chat.

'Write this on your profile,' Lola says, taking the final gulp of her drink and setting the empty glass down on the creosoted roof. '*Blonde bombshell, new to London . . . show me a good time?*'

'Absolutely not!'

'Why?!'

'It sounds . . . too much! Not to mention that I am *never* going to refer to myself as a "blonde bombshell" in a million years!'

'Fine . . .' Lola pauses for a moment, contemplating. 'What about *Newly-minted Londoner, into books and looks. Ask me about the time I served Nick Cave a sandwich.*'

'Is that literally the most interesting thing about me?' I grimace.

'Look. I may be a lesbian but I know the kind of nonsense that men respond to. Nick Cave. Bruce What's-his-name. Bonny Bear.'

'Do you mean Bon Iver?' I interject.

'Whatever,' she says, waving her hand dismissively. 'And the guy who does those films. The ones with the dogs and the puppets.' She produces a cigarette from some obscure fold in her jumpsuit and lights it, crossing her legs dramatically and sitting back in her chair before inhaling deeply and looking at me with a gaze like a film noir heroine. 'And this is that nonsense.'

'Fine. I guess it has a call to action,' I say, realizing that copywriting is probably a transferable skill.

'Precisely. Smoke?'

'Never. Sorry. Maybe I should take it up, though. Part of my new London persona.'

'I wouldn't recommend it,' she says, before taking another drag.

'So,' I say. 'I now have a minimal profile and one single photo, but a profile and a photo nonetheless.'

'Let's get swiping! I'm going to get us another drink . . .' Lola lifts herself out of her folding chair and somehow manages to shimmy into my bedroom window while holding a cigarette aloft.

Alone on the roof, I do as she said: I start swiping through the men of London. I swipe 'no' on . . . pretty much all of them. One because he has the air of an estate agent and I can't go back *there* again. One because he's too good-looking, one because I don't like his top, one because he isn't wearing a top at all, one because all his photos are with the same woman, one because he's posing with a tiger, one because he's blurred out his mates' faces in all his photos and that looks creepy as hell.

'How are you doing?' Lola cranes her head through the sash window and holds out the two drinks for me to take as she hoists herself out again, cigarette still dangling from her lip. The sun is setting on this perfect early autumn evening and I can feel the hum and buzz and clatter and roar of the city all around me. Within this busy, bustling world, I feel cocooned up on the roof of Lola's flat. I feel part of something.

'Not . . . so good?' I tell her. 'I just have no idea what I'm looking for.'

'You're thinking about it way too much, I can just *tell*. We aren't looking for the next Mr Serena Mills, we're just looking for . . . fun.'

'What about him?' I ask her, holding up the phone on a tall guy with a shaved head.

'He has the cold, dead eyes of a serial killer. Next!'

So I keep on swiping as Lola tells me about a rumour she heard at work that featured the dreaded word 'restructuring', but in classic Lola form she is refusing to engage with it until it's confirmed. And in no time at all, the swiping becomes instinctive, rather than logical. I'm not just swiping past people because they *specifically* look like they're too into horsey polo, I'm swiping past them because they have the intangible air of someone I wouldn't be compatible with. It's amazing how quickly I've tapped into this way of looking at things. I swipe 'yes' to a couple of people on the grounds of Good Vibes, but don't feel particularly enthusiastic about either. Maybe it's been too long and I just don't know how to do this any more.

'My thumb hurts,' I say. 'I think I've got RSI already from all the swiping.' I hand my phone to her to take over. 'I trust your judgement, go forth and swipe.'

Lola gasps with delight like I've just given her a birthday present. 'Really?!'

But she's already swiping away with a look of intense concentration. 'Who . . . do . . . I . . . think . . . Serena . . . wants . . . to . . . fuck . . .'

'I appreciate how seriously you're taking this task, thank you.'

'Jesus,' Lola mutters.

'What?' I say, craning my neck to look at the screen.

'All these men are just . . . obsessed with how tall they are. If I read the words "six foot two, because apparently that matters" one more time I'm going to jump off the roof. You're also not allowed to be a redhead without referring to yourself as . . .' Lola grimaces. 'A "ginger ninja".' She mimes puking. 'All I'm saying is that I've never seen that on a ginger girl's profile. Men have no charm whatsoever.'

She pauses her swiping and seems to be actually focusing on a profile for the first time in several minutes. 'Although . . . take a look at this guy.'

She holds my phone up to my face. 'Huh,' I say, pleasantly surprised. Good glasses (why don't men know how to buy glasses?), decent beard, an array of photos, none of them too weird, appears to have interests other than naming his own height. I pause for a second. But is he *too* good-looking?

'I'm swiping right,' she says, flicking her thumb across the screen. Well that's that decision made for me, then.

'What happens now?'

'We wait and see if he swipes right on you, which, of course, he will.'

'All right, keep on swiping. You're not doing too badly.'

I'm calmly surveying the Islington skyline when I realize Lola isn't swiping any more, and is most definitely typing. 'What are you up to?!'

'You matched with that guy!'

'Already?!' I feel my face grow hot. I wasn't expecting something to happen so soon.

'Yeah! I'm writing him a charming message.'

'Lola!' I reach out for my phone but she holds it away from me.

'It's for the greater good!'

'It had better be. God, I feel so *exposed*, you know? Just like . . . so open to judgement. Everything from my looks to my personality to my ability to be likeable on the internet. Well, I guess it's more *your* likeability on the internet.'

'And I am being very likeable indeed. Who knows, maybe Steven from Bow is your next bone.'

'That's the guy with the beard, right?'

'Right. But he's more than just a beard! Many of them are not, I am discovering.'

'What are you saying to him? Or rather, what am I saying to him?'

'Just charming general chat . . . Oh and he wants to know if you're up for a drink on Friday evening?'

'Friday?! The most precious night of the week?'

'No darling, it's been demoted now, that's Saturday. Second-most precious.'

'The *second-most precious* night of the week?' Something above Lola's head catches my eye, a strange levitating dot moving in a way I can't immediately fathom. I realize it's a spider, descending on its thread from the gutter above. 'Lola,' I say, very steadily, knowing that Lola can handle absolutely *anything* – except for spiders. It's possible that the only reason she could tolerate Alistair at all was that he once elegantly disposed of an absolutely enormous one scuttling around her shower in halls. 'Don't freak out, just stay still, I'm going to get rid of it for you, but there's a . . .' I say, getting to my feet and reaching over, wondering if this is going to mark the end of our delightful evening.

'Oh, is it a spider?' Lola says, turning to look at the area my eyes had been fixed on. She sees it hanging from the thread, and moves her chair out of the way so it can make it to the ground unimpeded, should it so desire. No frozen body, no look of terror, no hyperventilating. No fear.

'Who are you and what have you done with my friend?' I say, narrowing my eyes at her. Surely this is some kind of body-swap scenario.

Lola clears her throat and sets her shoulders proudly. 'I am a changed woman. I'm no longer afraid of spiders.'

'But how?!' I ask, remembering one particular trip to a farmhouse in the Nottinghamshire countryside to celebrate a friend's twenty-first where Lola refused to enter the games room to play snooker with the rest of us all weekend because she'd seen a spider scuttle in there.

'Exposure therapy. I'm not even joking. I decided I needed to get a handle on it and I went for it. I just . . . well, I suppose the phrase is that I felt the fear and did it anyway. I even had to *touch* one. Can you imagine! Me! Lola! Touching a spider!'

'My God . . .' I say, shaking my head. 'I honestly can't believe it. I'm proud of you! I'm really, truly, so proud of you.'

'You know what? I'm proud of me too.'

'Maybe that's what I need to do with dating,' I say with a smile.

'That's *exactly* what you need to do with dating.'

'I was joking.'

'I wasn't,' she shrugs.

'Are you for real?'

'Why not? It would be the perfect way to find out that . . . I don't know . . . that even if it's all a bit scary and intimidating at first, these are just dates, just men. What even are dates anyway? It seems like you've got a lot of anxiety wrapped up in the idea of dating so why not just charge at it, head on?'

She sounds convinced. And convincing. Maybe she's right. Maybe this is how I should tackle it. If it worked for Lola and her spiders, then truly, it can work for anything.

'Let's say . . . one date a week, yeah?'

'One a week?! Are you serious?'

'What else are you going to be doing?'

'One a week though . . .'

'Think of it as a good way to see different bits of London, get to know the place.' I can see right through her! She's trying to make it sound like a fun little escapade, baked into my exploration of my new home!

'Sure, but one date a week just sounds like . . . a lot.'

'It's meant to be a stretch! If it was easy then you wouldn't need to make it into a challenge!' She slaps her thigh resolutely. 'Let's call it a new life's resolution. People make resolutions just because it's the beginning of a new year! That's just *time*. What about the beginning of a new life!'

I throw my hands up, willing to give it a try, to give into her enthusiasm. 'Okay!' I say, laughing, feeling slightly hysterical at the prospect. 'One date a week! Let's do this!'

Lola holds out her elegant hand. I shake it, firmly.

'Shall Steven be the first?' She raises her eyebrows at me expectantly. I sigh. But I'm smiling. I can't help smiling at her.

She's already typing out a reply before I can make my mind up. 'Yes, let's do Friday.'

5

Taking the bus to work almost feels like cheating the system. Like I'm not playing the London game properly if I don't commute to and from work on the underground. The 43 cruises down Holloway Road, crawling past Highbury Corner and slowly slowly along Upper Street before turning off at Angel and sloping through City Road towards the Old Street round-about. And that is where I descend to do an honest day's work.

Another of Lola's doings – she heard on the grapevine that one of her Central Saint Martin's buddies was looking for a copywriter for Ophelia, their small but growing jewellery brand – emails, product descriptions, website copy – very much my comfort zone. Is Lola my guardian angel? Very probably.

While I don't need more than *one* guardian angel, I would definitely like the chance to spend some time with our university friends as A Single Gal. As I get off the bus I text Irina – who I first met when we wrote for the uni newspaper and was *meant* to see at my wedding – and tell her I'm in London now and that we should get a drink. It would be good to see her in person; I feel bad for everyone who came to the-wedding-that-wasn't, and what with all the mayhem of, well, *that*, and packing up to move,

I haven't had much of a chance to get in touch. Before I can even put my phone away, the little 'replying' dots appear.

I've been overzealous with my punctuality on my first day at this job, so I nip into Pret and buy my right to loiter there for a while with a filter coffee. When I get out my phone to pay with my contactless, I see that Irina hasn't texted me back even though she was typing before. I slide into a window seat and sip my coffee, opening our messages. The dots are gone. It just says 'delivered'.

On paper, my job at Ophelia is already the best job I've ever had. It's full-time, permanent and pays me more than any of my old jobs back when I had to take the weird little local train to towns around Little Grayling. And most importantly, it's a *London job*. Enabling my *London life*. But equally I probably shouldn't use that as a reason to buy coffee every day, otherwise I'll end up penniless.

I don't get a text back from Irina but I do get one from Melanie.

Hey Reenie, is it today you start your new job?

That's nice of her to remember. Suspiciously nice.

Yes! Just about to head there now.

Good luck! Not sure if you were planning on contacting Alistair any time soon but I think it's best if you keep your distance for a bit.

Something about this pokes at the 'impotent rage' cortex of my brain. What does she know about anything?

What makes you say that? Are you two hanging out or something?

Not hanging out

A pause, and then:

Just talking

Well can you not just talk please!!!!

Just like that it feels like someone's poked me with a pin and I'm deflating. Melanie and I might not be as super close as when we were teenagers – life's got in the way, I know that – but it hurts that she's taking so much trouble to check in with Alistair and hasn't even asked me how I'm doing. I can just see her now, all the way in Walthamstow, narrowing her eyes at her phone screen the way she does when she's annoyed, raking her fingers through her brown bob. I don't feel I'm being unreasonable in asking my sister not to get all cosy with my ex-fiancé but I'm sure she'll find a way to spin it so I'm absolutely crazy. I'm not. I'm just a bit lost right now.

This is a hard time for him! I just wanted him to know I was there for him if he needed me!

WHAT IF I NEEDED YOU? WHAT THEN???? Knew it would be too much to ask for you to take my side.

It's not about sides, really, is it? That's not a very mature way of looking at things.

Now I'm the one glaring at my phone. I'm going to ignore her. If she doesn't see that I might need the bare minimum of care and kid gloves right now, I can't spell it out for her. No more fuel on that fire. Just focus on my new job, my new home, my new single life. Breathe in and out.

I keep forgetting that I have a date on Friday. It's easy to forget because I had basically no part in snagging it, but I have committed to it nonetheless. I had expected more agonizing, more obstacles in my path before I got to a date with someone new. Like there should be a test or a form to fill in, something to register as 'Single' before qualifying as 'Ready to Mingle'.

But maybe just getting on with it is the way to go. Lola is quite good at that, I've realized. I keep checking Steven's photos to make sure he's sort of overall normal, but there doesn't seem to be a catch.

Once the time is right, I nervously press the buzzer to an office on a street round the back of the Old Street roundabout.

'Hello?' answers a disembodied voice.

'It's Serena . . . I'm new,' I say, tentatively. No one replies but I'm buzzed in.

The office is up three flights of stairs and I'm panting by the time I get there, which makes me feel incredibly self-conscious. I wait at the top of the stairs to catch my breath before opening the door, but of course I'm interrupted. A waifish blonde in a racerback jersey dress emerges, looking concerned.

'I thought you'd got lost!'

'No, no!' I say, breezily. And, indeed, wheezily.

'Well, come in either way.' She holds the door open for me and I follow her into the office, which is a tranquil oasis of white walls and plants. I'm actually taken aback by how small it is – the brand does a good job of appearing like a huge enterprise, but there are only five or six desk spaces here.

'OMG sorry, I completely forgot to introduce myself,' she says, smacking herself on the forehead and rolling her eyes. The

OMG is completely non-ironic. 'I'm Kirsty – I do operations and office manager stuff.'

'Nice to meet you,' I say, discreetly brushing a bead of sweat off my forehead. 'I'm happy you guys landed on me!'

'Yeah,' Kirsty shifts from foot to foot, incapable of staying still. 'Our last head of copy was a nightmare – she was very *prickly*,' she says, grimacing, 'very fashion.' It's interesting that she assumes I am neither prickly nor 'fashion', based on the brief interaction we've had thus far. I mean, I'm not, but she doesn't know that.

'Well, I'm glad I have such a high bar to clear . . .' I mumble.

'Let me introduce you to the others!' Kirsty claps her hands, deaf to my mumblings. I can only describe her vibe as intensely Goop, like she's addicted to yoga and quite possibly bought a jade vagina egg.

'The most important person is obviously Anjali,' she says, gesturing at a similarly elegant woman in a billowing oversized shirt and perfectly cut black trousers, and piled with tons of her own jewellery. (I spent long enough looking over the website with laser precision at the weekend to be able to recognize it.) 'She's the boss!'

'Aaah, you must be Serena!' Anjali says, walking towards me with arms outstretched. She's very tall and *very* thin, only half of which I can relate to.

'It's so good to meet you!' I allow her to envelop me in a hug. She smells absolutely incredible: woody and burnt and mysterious. And expensive. But there's such a warmth to her already that I don't feel intimidated by her aesthetic.

'You came extremely highly recommended by Lola, whose opinion on people I probably trust more than anyone else's!'

She leans towards me to whisper in my ear, 'Don't tell the others I didn't even bother to interview you.'

'I won't,' I whisper back. I can see Kirsty's looking put out at the furtive conversation. 'She told me you're the most chic person she knows – that's the word she used, *chic*,' I say, and Anjali is clearly delighted by this. Off to a good start with my boss.

'That's Duncan,' Kirsty says, regaining control of me and gesturing towards a figure in a black T-shirt hunched over a laptop. He springs into life upon hearing his name.

'Hi, nice to meet you!' he chirps. 'I take care of a lot of marketing stuff. We outsource a bit to an agency but I do the bulk of it. You're doing content, right?'

'Yeah,' I say, trying not to be too charmed by Duncan, who is, it cannot be denied, pretty cute.

'Great, well, sometimes there's a bit of an overlap so I guess we'll be calling upon each other's expertise in no time.'

'Oh, and there's Nicole, who'll be your deskmate, but she's at a meeting with a vendor this morning.' Kirsty manoeuvres me over to the other side of the small office. We're approaching a double desk, half of which is, indeed, completely unoccupied. The other half is brimming with papers, Post-it notes, trinkets (a pink china poodle? An empty vintage perfume bottle?) and a couple of empty cans of Cherry Coke.

I'd sort of forgotten the socializing element of work. The thought of it makes me a little excited: a (small, admittedly) room full of people who don't know anything about me, who can meet me as a single person. Their story of my life starts here. They don't need to know about the wedding. It's a strange and exhilarating kind of freedom.

'My desk will look like this in no time, I'm sure,' I say, setting my bag down on the tidy half of the table.

'Nicole is amazing at what she does so the mess is fine,' Kirsty shrugs her tiny birdlike shoulders. 'You'll like her, I just know it. You two will definitely get on.'

'Oh, great,' I smile, even though I'm wondering, once again, on what basis she's made that assumption.

'Now, let me show you where the kitchen is . . . and the toilets . . .' Kirsty's already marching off. 'They're in the same place. Not, you know, literally. Obviously.'

'Obviously,' I say, smiling.

After the thirty-second tour of the 'facilities', I'm returned to the office.

'Serena, why don't you get set up with Duncan? He knows what's what,' says Anjali, craning her neck like a meerkat.

Duncan's head springs up. 'Oh, sure!' He jumps to his feet and gestures for me to follow him back to my desk. He motions for me to sit down in the swivel chair and sits in Nicole's vacant chair next to me, wheeling it over awkwardly, his expensive-looking trainers dragging across the lino floor.

'I'm not actually IT support,' he says, while we wait for my laptop to start up. 'I mean, we don't even have IT support! But it sort of falls to me to sort out email addresses and logins to the content management system and stuff.'

'Got it.'

'Ophelia's grown *so* fast in the past year it's been hard to keep everyone's roles containable. Anyway, we'd be fucked without a copywriter so, good job you're here.' He gently nudges me with his elbow before moving his glasses from the top of his head to the bridge of his nose. I look at him out of the corner of my eye. I can't get distracted like this on my actual *first day*.

'So your login details are . . . these,' he says, purloining a heart-shaped Post-it note from my absent colleague's desk and scrawling an email address and password on it before sliding it to me as if it's got some astronomical amount of money written on it like in an American film. 'Anjali will send you the new products and trading topics every Tuesday. Stuff changes all the time but we like to keep up the pretence that Tuesday is the day we know what's going on.' He smiles at me conspiratorially, which is obviously the quickest way to make someone fancy you.

He walks me through the content management system which basically works the same as every CMS since the dawn of time – you've seen one, you've seen 'em all – and finally his work is done. I try to think of some questions to keep him there, but he's on his feet before I can come up with anything.

'Let me know if something goes horribly wrong. I guess as it's Monday and the new products aren't ready yet, you can just poke around the site and see if there's any copy you want to change or update,' he shrugs.

'Great . . .' I finally settle on something sensible to ask him. I want to lean into the conspiratorial vibes. 'Anything else I should know?'

He pauses for a second, like he's weighing me up. He makes his evaluation: 'Nicole can be a bit of a troublemaker. Just so you know, so you'd probably do well not to get too close to her.'

And with that he's gone. I'm left staring at my screen, a potent mix of attracted and curious. Curious about him (warning me off on our first meeting? That's most definitely A Lot) but more curious about this Nicole.

I do what he says and click through the different pages on the site, making notes on my fancy new notebook (illegal to start a new job without one, if you ask me) of stuff I want to change. Every so often my eyes flick up to Duncan's chair.

Yeah, he's hot. Sharp-featured, thick-haired, expensively dressed. Oh no, he's caught me looking because of *course* he has. Shit shit shit. Look away. Or don't look away, because then that'll be obvious that you *were* looking. God. What an idiot. But I don't have long to cringe because the doors have burst open and in walks . . . who is this ray of sunshine?

A young woman in a bright red satin shirt tucked into high-waisted, wide-legged white trousers and a towering pair of seventies-style boots. She has long, bouncy, balayaged hair that's been styled just right, immaculate makeup and huge sunglasses. She is fat. She is fat like I'm fat. She doesn't look like anyone else here. And I'm pretty sure that's why Kirsty assumed we would get on. Fat comrades. I'm not going to befriend her just because we're both fat, Kirsty. That's not how it works. I don't know anything about her, beyond the fact that Duncan doesn't like her.

She's greeted by a chorus of 'Hey,' 'Sup,' 'Happy Monday, mate' and makes her way to her desk.

'You're here!' Nicole beams at me as she sets her pink crocodile-effect handbag on the desk and wrestles out her laptop, pushing her sunglasses onto her head with one hand. 'I struggle without a deskmate. *Extremely* nice to meet you, I'm Nicole.'

'I'm Serena.' I realize I'm already hoping she likes me.

She's looking me over with a warm gaze, her full, pretty lips forming a kind smile. 'Cute earrings.' Her voice is kind of high and husky at the same time.

My hand flies up to my ear and I feel the metal daisies against my fingertips. 'Oh, thanks! They're not from here . . . I hope that's okay . . .'

'Get out. We demand a hundred per cent brand loyalty at Ophelia.' She fixes me with a hard stare which she holds for a few seconds while I panic that I've already committed a huge faux pas. 'I'm . . . obviously joking, sorry.'

'For a minute I was . . . actually not sure. God, I need to chill out.'

'No, I think the person that needs to chill out is, in fact, me. Apologies.'

We sit in awkward silence for a moment. I sense that I'm expected to make conversation. I wonder if I should or if I should just keep myself to myself. The silence increases in its awkwardness, and I cave. 'So what do you do?'

'Sales, mostly. We used to be direct-to-consumer but now we're in a few department stores so I spend a lot of time working with vendors making sure they have the right amount and variety of stock, blah blah blah,' she says. 'Not that I don't like my job! I do, I just know it's not as easy to explain to people as, well, copywriting. Which, by the way, desperately needs overhauling. If you ask me. Which you, uh, didn't.'

I'm about to open my mouth to say that I agree with her, but something stops me. 'I'll take a look at it,' I say instead, with a professional smile.

'I'm probably totally wrong,' she goes on, 'but I feel like we need to be more friendly in our tone of voice. Like, still aspirational, but warmer.'

She took the words right out of my mouth. Why am I trying to resist her? Because Kirsty said we would get along? Because Duncan said we shouldn't?

'No, that sounds bang on, I was thinking the same thing myself.'

'Oh, great!' Nicole chirps. 'By the way, you can ask me if you have any questions.'

I try not to check my phone too much on my first day, so that I look diligent and focused, but it illuminates on the desk next to me. A text from my friend Rachel. My *engaged* friend Rachel. She and I had got on particularly well when we worked together in the marketing department of a theatre after graduation, and even after she got offered a marketing job at the National Theatre we would still meet up every so often for dinner. It always felt like such a chore to sit on the tube and the train to meet her in central London after work. How times have changed! I should arrange to meet her, but it looks from the text like I'll be seeing her soon enough anyway.

What's your address? I assume you have a new one! Or did you stay in the house? Either way, let me know!

I spy a wedding invitation on the horizon. It's a funny thought, that I should be married by now. I can't help thinking of Alistair, and all the hopes I had that it would start to feel *right* before the big day rolled around. It would be extremely rude of me to ask her if she's sure, if she's really sure, just in case no one else has – and of course I don't. I text her back with my address and an explanation that I live in London now, then turn my phone over so I don't let myself slip into a back-and-forth texting situation.

Once Tuesday comes and goes and I write the week's product descriptions and understand the particular Ophelia Designs approach to emails, I feel like a pro. And that's partly because of Nicole's help. She knows every material, she knows the adjectives we avoid, she knows everything. And her outfits! Every day a new delight – red leopard print, a lilac broderie anglaise dress, a polka dot plissé jumpsuit. Clothes that I didn't really know fat women wore. For someone that can, and, indeed, often does, make my own clothes, she's really shone a light on how unadventurous I am. Everything I own is black, grey or navy. Chic, yes, but exciting, perhaps not.

Realizing that my work is perfectly manageable means I free up a lot of brain energy to focus on The Date. It's happening. By Friday, I feel . . . ready for it. I think? Well, not totally. Can you ever truly be ready for your first date in ten years? But I have to press on. It's too late for me to back out now, since I'm on my way to the pub. Have I been spending the last twenty-four hours hoping he'll cancel? Yes. Have I been spending the last twenty-four hours wanting to cancel? Also yes. But it feels too soon to engage in acts of romantic self-sabotage so quickly after the last.

I lean my head against the bus window then quickly yank it back when I realize I've just rested my clean hair against a large grease patch.

I cycle through the apps on my phone to distract me from my pre-date nerves, but given that I only did this little process five minutes ago, it doesn't yield much entertainment. I open my texts to see if there's anyone I haven't replied to, but instead find that my text to Irina remains unanswered.

We could do something on Sunday if you're free? I try not to feel any shame about double-texting. I'm a grown woman, I'm allowed to double-text.

God, I'm nervous. I'm just so nervous. Like I'm about to take an exam. I could be sick. Oh, God, it's my bus stop. I thought I had a bit more time. Turns out I'm not quite as much of an expert on London geography as I would like to believe.

Before I put my phone back in my pocket, I text Lola Why am I doing this?

Ah, just the person I was thinking about, she replies.

Really? Why?

Firstly, because of your date, which I think is going to go excellently.

I'm glad someone does!!!!

Secondly, because I have some . . . News

???

I really wanted to tell you in person but it's all happening so fast that I need to get organizing ASAP!! The ~restructuring~ at work has ended up with me temporarily being sent to the New York office and they need me to go like . . . now. Not RIGHT now but next week. Obv this doesn't really affect you beyond the fact that I'll be gone for a bit.

I already felt a bit sick about the impending date and this might push me over the edge. Not that I'm not happy for her but . . . I like our little living situation. I like having her around, no, I *need* having her around. Urging me to do things I otherwise might not. I'll miss her. I'm not used to being alone, unmoored, just sort of floating around with no one to account to.

But it's not about me! It's her life! I swallow down my anxieties and text her back, barely looking up from my phone as I step off the bus.

63

OMG that's incredible?! I'll have to come visit you! How long will you be gone for?

A couple of months, apparently. At least until Christmas.

Fuck. So I'll just be home alone for the foreseeable.

Wow! I can't believe you're going next week! I type, my heart beating fast at the bus stop near the pub in Hackney where we're meeting.

Yeah! It's so wild??? Now you have a bone palace to yourself. Perfect timing, right?!

Ha, yeah, perfect!!!!! I type, then delete the excess exclamation marks. I'm not a complete maniac.
So that's that.
Oh God, I really am so nervous.

I'm not interrupting your hot date, am I?

No, I'm waiting outside the pub and I feel sick. How am I meant to stand? Nonchalantly? Firmly?

Like a normal person I think.

I lean against the shutters of the shop next door, tentatively bending my knee and resting my foot on the shutter behind me. I instantly feel ridiculous and return the foot to the pavement where it belongs.

Do you think everyone walking past knows I'm waiting for a date?

Even if they do, what's to be ashamed about the pursuit of romance, my friend.

Argh! I keep STARING INTENTLY at random men that are just minding their own business walking down the road!

You need to project CONFIDENCE! Whatever you do you must NOT let him know you're nervous.

Sounds easy enough!! What if he's seen me from across the road and thought I was ugly and ran away?

I text her again without waiting for a reply.

It's 7:31 and he's not here am I being stood up?

I wouldn't have thought so! You have to give a grace period of . . . Well, more than 60 seconds.

Maybe it's not so useful externalizing every nervous thought to Lola. I drop my phone into my bag but, before I can even zip it up, it vibrates again. But not from Lola this time. Irina.

Look, you can't just pretend nothing happened. You fucked Alistair up really badly. I know you're my friend but so is he. I don't feel like I can just hang out with you like it's normal.

'Hey,' a man's voice cuts through my hot-cheeked nausea. 'Are you . . . Serena?'

6

Well, that was a disaster. Or maybe not a *disaster* because that would imply something actually happened – a cataclysmic event, for instance – rather than a couple of the most extremely boring drinks in a pub that I'd ever had, while part of my brain was elsewhere, panicking about Irina's text. I'd worked myself up so badly and put so much pressure on it that I hadn't actually considered it might simply be boring. No chemistry. Nada. Nothing.

Picture the scene: we exhaust the *getting to know you* chat so quickly that within about half an hour I'm panicking there's nothing else to talk about, when I'm suddenly struck by the divine inspiration to ask him what TV shows he watches. Maybe we can get a cool five minutes out of discussing our favourite episode of *Seinfeld*? Instead, he says his favourite show of all time is *Game of Thrones*. Not my cup of tea, but fine, whatever. Not so! When our good friend here discovers I've never seen it, I'm then treated to a twenty-minute-long explanation of the plot, the *whole* plot, from series one to eight, plus an extended account of why the ending sucked. When he asks if I'm going to watch it now, and I have to gently explain to him that not only has he told me every major plot point, he's also explicitly told me it's not worth watching to the end, he then treats me to another twenty minutes of explanation of why it's so *amazing*. Look, I was grateful for something to stimulate the conversation, I just didn't realize it was going to be quite so one-sided.

At least this was Lola's poor judgement – once I start meeting guys I've chosen myself, maybe things will look up. Come on, they have to. They have to.

Not least because that date prompted me to text Alistair. Just to check in, just to say hi. (Just to check I had made the right decision? To check my feelings?)

> Hey! How are things? Not too unbearable to go back to work after Thailand?

> Can't lie, it's pretty unbearable :) Hope your first week went well.

I don't blame him for not really wanting to talk. I have to admit: it's a weird time. I was on such a high from all this new stuff – moving to London, the exciting prospect of dating, a new job, and now I just feel kind of . . . deflated. Almost as if doing loads of exciting new things doesn't change the funda-mental truth that I ended a ten-year-long relationship.

I had an emotional goodbye with Lola on Monday. Emotional in that I felt incredibly sad and anxious but pretended I didn't.

It's going to be weird just rattling around her flat without her, with no one to chat to when I get home from work. I've never had that before.

But I've decided it's a good thing. It's exactly what I need right now. A kick up the bum. Radical reflection. Throwing myself into dating, shaking my life up, sorting my life out. And no more Alistair. I need to stop thinking about him, to properly draw a line under it and not wonder if I did the wrong thing. I know people are thinking it, and they're probably saying it, too. Irina can't be the only one who feels like that. Should I text her? Maybe I should text her, explain myself, make her understand how I was feeling by the time the wedding came around. But what would I want to say? Would I be apologizing? No! I'm not going to apologize to her. The only person I need to apologize to is Alistair.

But Alistair . . . I can't talk to him, even if he wanted to talk to me, which he doesn't. No contact at all for, let's say . . . three months, to get it all out of my system. Melanie said he wanted me to keep my distance, anyway. No Alistair for three months. And a whole new life in a year. Genius. It's a numbers game! Surely there's got to be some cute guys out there in this big, sprawling city? With the zeal and optimism of a religious convert, I unfollow him on Instagram. No creeping for me! Gone! I don't go as far as blocking his number but if the urge to drink and text gets to me then I might have to.

It's Friday, and with half my brain I'm worrying about what I'm going to do with my first Lola-less weekend – how to maximize my time now I've got my eye on the Big Life Change prize – and with the other half I'm doing some competitor analysis of rival jewellery brands' website copy. Nicole flicks a paperclip at me from her side of the desk.

'Psst,' she hisses, 'hey, wanna eat lunch with me today?'

She's wearing a long-sleeve leopard-print shirt buttoned up to the neck and tucked into a flared, lime-green suede mini skirt. Daring? It most certainly is.

'Sure!' I say, feeling embarrassingly delighted that she's asking me to hang out with her. Despite what Duncan said, I've found her nothing but kind, warm and friendly. She's kind of chatty, sure, but 'troublemaker'?

'Meet me on the comfy chairs at one?'

'I'll be there,' I say, trying not to sound too keen, when in fact I am possibly more keen for this social contact than I have been for anything in a long time. I have a feeling Irina isn't the only person who's keeping their distance from me in the wake of the wedding. That feeling of aloneness keeps prodding at me. I don't want to let it in.

One o'clock rolls around and we reconvene with our lunches. 'So,' she asks, 'how's it going?'

'In a professional capacity?' I say, opening my cute little lunchbox which contains a halloumi and wild rice salad I made in a bid to not spunk so much money at Pret.

'Yeah, or not, you choose,' she shrugs. Nicole has gone down the 'spunk money at Pret' path and has a frankly delicious-looking duck wrap.

'I'm happy to be here and I feel like I'm kind of finding my feet,' I say. 'Like, I get what the tone of voice is now, I'm figuring out what the purpose of the emails is, all of that. It helps that the product is actually, you know, *nice*.'

'Good!' Nicole says, beaming. 'I'm glad.' She has such a *warmth*, like she's just ready for the world, not always wondering how she's going to be received or judged to be inadequate. How does she do it?

'And more generally, yeah, I'm okay,' I lie. Half lie. I'm not *not* okay, I'm just not properly loving life right now, that's all.

She eyes me with suspicion as she says, 'Sounds fake but okay.'

And I just know that I'm going to tell her everything. I just know that she's someone I can talk to. I don't have to hold back, wonder what her reaction will be. I just know.

'No, it's just . . . my flatmate has moved abroad for a bit and I feel weird about being on my own after all this time, and I tried to have my first date in, like . . . ten years last week and it was a real letdown and I'm a bit like . . . oh did I make a mistake, should I have got married and stuck with that?'

Nicole is looking at me, slightly open-mouthed, like when she asked me to have lunch with her she had no idea she had a tale of this magnitude coming her way.

'Back up; that was a lot of information you just imparted in one go there.'

She repositions herself in her seat now that she knows a story's coming – like she knows how to listen – and looks at me expectantly. So I tell her. About Alistair. About all of it. About how now I just feel a bit lost.

'So that's that,' I say, when I've taken her through it all.

'Huh,' she says. 'Wow. Well, first of all may I congratulate you on extricating yourself from that relationship in the nick of time. And for moving to London. And taking a new job. It's a lot!'

'It is, right?' I say, surveying my salad to make sure I'm not going to be left with tons of rice and no halloumi at the end. I'm very much in this for the halloumi.

'So yeah, you should definitely cut yourself some slack.' Nicole rolls up the sleeves on her leopard-print shirt. (Extremely cool.)

'I'm not very interesting, though. Tell me about you? Do you have a partner?'

'Mate, you can't tell me you did a vanishing act on your

wedding day and expect me to believe you when you say you're not very interesting. Where's your self-esteem?!' Nicole laughs and shakes her head. 'But in answer to your question, no, I do not. I am single as hell,' she says, throwing up a peace sign.

'Are you, like, dating?' I ask, feeling delighted that she thinks I'm interesting.

'Maybe a little bit,' she grins. 'No, I'm kidding, yeah, I'm dating if you want to call it that.' There's something so effortlessly casual about her. I don't get it. I cannot comprehend it at all. I'm looking at her and I'm looking at me and we're basically the same size. I don't get how she can be so easy and chill about the prospect of dating.

'Oh, that's cool, like app stuff?'

'Yeah, mostly,' she says. 'Are you going down that route?'

'Yeah, that's where I met the guy last week but I'm wondering if it's just not the one for me.'

'I wouldn't extrapolate too much from one bad date,' she says, sounding extremely wise. 'Just . . . let yourself be open to the idea of it, at least. The whole idea. Not just apps and stuff, but the idea of meeting someone.'

'It just feels so high-stakes. I know it sounds insane but I've really never been with anyone else except my ex,' I say. 'Do you think guys will be able to sense it?!'

She raises her eyebrows but otherwise keeps her reaction in check. 'I mean, yeah, I see why it would feel like a lot of pressure for you. But do they need to know?'

'I guess not.'

'I have this theory about vibes. When you're in a relationship you give off a vibe that you're in a relationship and then when you're single you give off this single vibe, and so you end up meeting more people to have sex with. It could just be it's some primal shit, some animal attraction thing, or maybe it's because when you're in a relationship you're not looking at the world as, like, potential sex partners. The way you do when you're single, you know.'

I can't say I do know.

'Sex! God, I don't know if I'm there yet . . .' I say, grimacing. The idea of getting naked in front of someone I don't know is A Lot. 'But I'm trying to exposure-therapy my way out of my fears.'

'Yes! It's good to rip the plaster off sooner rather than later and find someone nice to bone.'

'Bone?' I repeat, in slight disbelief that this is the favoured terminology of both Lola *and* Nicole.

'You heard me,' she says, smiling naughtily. 'Bone. Find a nice man to bone. Then you won't be so stressed about it.'

'I'm not *stressed* about it . . .' I lie, taken aback that we've strayed into such intimate territory so quickly. 'But I'm . . . trying to change things,' I say, decisively.

'Tell me more, my dude?'

'I'm trying to really . . . shake up my life, I guess. I feel like the next year is vital for me, like I need to bring about some kind of huge reset.'

'Reset, eh?' she asks, intrigued.

'I'm giving myself a year to sort myself out. Put the past behind me. Become the person I'm meant to be or something . . .'

'And who do you think you are right now?' Nicole asks. 'Just so I have some perspective on this.'

'Good question,' I say, shifting a little uncomfortably. 'I guess . . . I'm just a little lost. I feel like I haven't really been in control of my life, like it was just happening and I was there but not really participating. Sort of dragging my heels, hanging back. So I don't know exactly who I am in lots of ways. But I know it would be good for me to meet some people. My housemate, she set up this plan for me, she calls it my new life's resolution, to go on one date a week for the next year, do some dating, so I'm going on a date a week for the next year.' It sounds ludicrous when I say it out loud but Nicole is an enthusiastic audience. 'Or at least, as long as I can stand it!'

'This sounds quite intense, and I'm into it!' she says, delighted, clearly not a stranger to intensity herself. 'A very fun plan.'

'You can keep me accountable. Help me on my merry way,' I say.

'Deal,' she says, nodding decisively. 'And who is the person you're meant to be? The person you think you'll be when you've had ... I guess, fifty-two dates? Are you allowed to stop if you meet someone you want to be in a relationship with?'

'I hadn't really thought that far ahead . . .'

'That's okay. So answer me: who is the person you're meant to be?'

I pause for a moment. 'I'm meant to be confident and adventurous and assertive. I'm meant to be someone who knows what I want, and if I don't know, I'm brave enough to explore. And I'm not that right now. At all.'

She nods, eyeing me thoughtfully. 'You can get there.' I want to ask her about her dating life, get some gory details, some inspiration for my own dates, but before I can, she asks, 'So, any exciting plans this weekend, since it's the beginning of your new life?'

My stomach drops a little thinking about the planless expanse

74

of my weekend. 'Not really . . .' I say, a little embarrassed that I don't have something bigger to tell her about. 'I might see my sister and her husband and my niece . . . or I'll be mindlessly swiping on my various apps . . . I'll probably watch a whole series of *Real Housewives* . . .'

'Sounds like the world is your oyster,' Nicole says, kindly.

'You know what?' I say, clapping my hands together decisively. 'I'm going to make a new top. That's what I'm going to do with my weekend. I haven't used my sewing machine since I got here.'

'You sew? That's genuinely very cool,' she says, which makes me feel warm and fuzzy inside because *she's* cool, goddamnit! 'Are you any good?'

'I made this dress,' I say, shrugging, gesturing down at the black cord smock dress I'm wearing with black tights and Adidas Superstar trainers.

'Fuck! That's proper genius-level shit!'

'How about you?' I say, a little self-conscious about taking up all the conversational oxygen. 'What are you going to do this weekend?'

'Tonight I have a date,' she says, smiling coyly, 'then tomorrow I think I'll just chill at home, do some cooking, and then on Sunday I like to go to my exercise class, get my sweat on.'

'Oh yeah? What's the class?'

'It's a spin class but it's at this stupid fucking fancy expensive place and it's *really* hard but you feel like such a badass when you finish it.'

Huh . . . she works out. I guess I should probably do that. Not that I particularly want to do an exercise class that's being described to me as both incredibly expensive and incredibly punishing.

'I have a free credit to bring someone to a class if you want to come?'

'I haven't really done any exercise for years . . .' I say, cautiously, thinking of how many times I've started and then abandoned Couch to 5K.

'Oh, who cares! It'll be fun!'

'One day,' I say, smiling tightly, hoping to stall for . . . well, a good while.

'I'll hold you to that,' she says, closing one eye and pointing a long, French-manicured acrylic nail at me.

But I desperately don't want her to think I'm brushing her off. I want to be her friend. She's fascinating to me – a wild mix of incredibly kind, warm and comforting. And I'm so utterly curious about how confident she is in her body and her life. Everyone talks about how hard it is to make friends as an adult, and it feels like Nicole has been thrown in my lap. I shouldn't take that for granted.

'Look,' I say, 'I might need warming up on the whole spin class thing, but I do like a little pint every now and then.'

'Who among us doesn't, my dude?' she says, wisely.

'Do you want to get a drink after work sometime?' I ask, a little self-consciously, suddenly possessed with the fear that she's going to say no.

'Literally always.'

Before we know it, lunchtime's over and we're slinking back to our desks. I spend the afternoon writing some copy for our paid search ads, but also wondering what I'm going to do with my weekend. I pick up my phone and do a little swiping. Maybe I can conjure up a Friday night date to keep me on my weekly target. Date number one wasn't a goer, and I've accepted that.

But I just have to keep moving. Nicole has given me a little spring in my step and I'm determined to keep on track with my goal. Time to find next week's date!

Date Number: 2

With: Jamie aka the Chemistry-Free Zone
Where: The Sun & 13 Cantons, Soho
When: Monday night

Him: So . . . what do you do for work?
Me: I work at a jewellery brand. Doing copywriting.
Him: That's interesting. I didn't know you could copyright jewellery.
Me, brow furrowed in confusion: Oh! No, I mean . . . writing copy. For emails and the website. Not like, um, intellectual property.
Him: Right. Though I am sure larger brands do copyright their designs.
Me: I suppose so? How about you?
Him: Supply chain fulfilment.
Me: That sounds interesting. What exactly does that involve?
Him: It is centred around FMCG.
Me: FMCG?
Him: Fast-moving consumer goods.
Me, still not understanding: Of course.
[Awkward silence]
Me, desperate for something to say: Have you watched the new true crime documentary on Netflix? About the backpacker murders?

Him: No. I don't have much time for television. When I do, it's mostly sports.

Me: Oh . . . what kind of sports?

Him: Formula One.

Me, racking my mind for Formula One related chat, so what have we got . . . Lewis Hamilton, Monaco, Damon Hill . . . end of list.

Him, filling the void: Are you into Formula One?

Me: No, unfortunately not.

Him: Didn't you say you were from Sussex? Anywhere near Goodwood?

Me, desperately wishing I could contribute to this conversation in any way: No. No, alas, not. The other side of the county, unfortunately.

[Extended awkward silence]

Him: So . . . how will you get home?

Me: Oh, um, there are a lot of options . . .

Him, nodding sagely: Yeah, same . . . I'll hop on the District. But where I live is also serviced by National Rail. So if I'm on the South Bank I can take a train from Waterloo or Vauxhall and be home in fifteen. I guess you've got options too. The Victoria or the Overground. And there is a National Rail too, if I'm not mistaken. Yes, Moorgate to Welwyn Garden City.'

Me: Yep, lots of options. I really like taking the bus when I can.

Him: I don't like the bus.

Me: No? But I guess that's one of the good things about living around there. The options.

Him: Islington's a borough, yeah?

Me: Yes . . .

Him: How's their council tax?
Me: Okay? I think. I don't really have anything to compare
it to?
Him: [nods]
Me, looking around: Well . . .
Him: Yeah.

Date Number: 3

With: Peter aka the Interrogator
Where: The Reliance, Old Street
When: Friday, post-work

Peter pushed the date to six o'clock. Which is way too early
in my books – I don't want to bring that straight-from-the-
office look, that just-finished-work energy, so I end up popping
into a neighbouring pub to do my make up in the toilet. That's
one thing I've decided about these dates: however nervous I
am about them, I will always arrive looking like I've tried.

Alas, my date didn't get that memo. I find him at the back
of the bar on a battered faux-leather couch, in a plaid shirt and
jeans that look less artfully scruffy than just generally scruffy.

'Are you Peter?' I ask, almost hoping that he isn't.

'Hey, sorry, one sec.'

He's on his phone and doesn't look up. I sit across from him
and wait while he texts, growing increasingly embarrassed at
being so blatantly disregarded like this.

Finally he puts the phone down and says, 'Serena? Hey,
good to meet you. You've got a drink? Sweet. Sweet. Are you
nervous?'

'Oh . . . er, no,' I say quickly.

'Great, great, I just want you to feel comfortable, Serena,' he says. He's so comfortable and laid-back he's almost horizontal on the couch.

'Well, that's very considerate of you,' I say, trying not to sigh out my disappointment. I wonder when I can leave. I think Nicole was staying late tonight to finalize some new point of sale graphics. Maybe she's still there. It's not even like we're BFFs, but I know she would show me a better time than this.

Peter sits up, like he's ready to do business.

'So,' he says, clapping his hands, 'Serena . . . Se-re-na.' And I wonder if he's about to ask me what I do for work or where I live or if I've been on Tinder long. 'Given the choice of anyone in the world, whom would you want as a dinner guest?' And yes, he really said whom.

Not what I was expecting in terms of question, though, so I'm game. 'Hmm,' I say, thinking. 'I feel like the expected answer is, you know, David Attenborough or Louis Theroux . . . but I'm going to go for Dolly Parton.'

Before I can ask him for his answer, he's moved on to the next question. 'Would you like to be famous? And, if so, in what way?'

'Oh . . . um . . .' I say, trying to think through my answer. 'I don't think so . . . I think it seems like a lot of effort and kind of stressful. So no. Would you?' I ask, hoping I can at least learn something about this man.

'Before you make a telephone call, do you rehearse what you are going to say?' It's this question that makes the penny drop.

'I . . .' I say, realizing where I've heard all this before. 'Is this the list of questions designed to make someone fall in love with you?' I can't help smiling at how funny and weird it is. I remember this *New Yorker* article doing the rounds on social media a few years ago, it had this list of thirty-six questions that are apparently meant to lead to love, and clearly Peter took this very seriously.

'Would it be so bad if it was?' He raises his eyebrows at me suggestively.

'I mean . . .' I say, not knowing exactly how to articulate the feeling that you can't force someone to fall in love with you by asking questions.

'You see, Serena, romance is important to me, so I'm trying to, you know, beat the system. Find the *one*, you know?'

'And you think these questions are the way to do it?'

'We didn't even get to *Of all the people in your family, whose death would you find the most disturbing and why?* So I can't accurately judge you as a potential partner yet,' he says, shrugging.

'Have you memorized them?'

'Of course! Like I said, I take this seriously.'

'Wow . . .' I say.

'So?'

'So what?'

'Of all the people in your family, whose death would you find the most disturbing and why?'

'I'm not sure I can answer that.'

'Why?'

I offer him a diplomatic shrug.

'I'm going to level with you and be completely honest, Serena,' he says, leaning forward on the battered sofa, cupping his pint with both hands. He picks it up and drains it in a few huge gulps.

What is going on?

'I always try to be straight up, I'm not a game player and that's something I pride myself on. The reason I pushed our date earlier is because I've . . .' he scrunches his face faux-awkwardly.

I'm sure whatever he's about to say is going to be good.

'. . . double-booked another date for eight and, cards on the table, I kind of wish it was the other way around because I don't know about you but I feel like this is a *connection*. But yeah, I am going to have to shoot but, pending how the next date goes, I would really love to get to know you better.'

And with that he jumps to his feet, plants a kiss on the top of my head, and leaves.

Very bemused by what's just happened to me, I text Nicole, asking if she's still at work. More and more these days I find myself wanting to hang out with her. It's like she's simultaneously a stabilizing force and just very good fun. We've gone for post-work drinks a couple of times over the past two weeks and, I have to be honest, it's nice to have a reliable female presence in my life with Lola away.

Just leaving, have you met the man of your dreams? If so stop texting me.

Omg no in fact the opposite. Do you want to meet me for some chips at the Reliance?

Always

Chips are always good, aren't they? I order at the bar and get myself another glass of wine, plus a pint for Nicole, and take Peter's place on the sofa.

'Tell me everything,' Nicole says, flopping down next to me. 'Oh my God, thanks,' she adds, noticing the waiting pint before sipping from it with great enthusiasm.

'Was the meeting okay?'

'It was fine, continue,' she says, waving away this considerably less interesting topic like it's a bad smell. So I tell her about the date, and before long she's shaking her head in disapproval. By the time the chips arrive it's like we've forgotten all about this Peter character. After a bowl of chips and another drink and gossiping with Nicole, I'm ready to head home. Write this one off. Hope the next date is better.

On the way to the bus stop, I check my phone. A voice note from Peter. Oh, God. I'm never happy to see a voice note, let alone from a random man I just met who gave every impression of being rather all over the place.

With great trepidation, I press 'play' and hold the phone to my ear as I sit down on the bus.

'Hey, Serena, she was not the one so, hey, if you're up for it maybe we could pick up where we left off . . . I mean, I'm free right now if you're still in the 'hood or if not then I could come to you. Whatever works. I didn't realize we were going to have such a connection and I don't want us to lose that.'

I don't reply.

And the messages pile up through the evening, complete with *Arrested Development* memes of Will Arnett saying, 'I've made a terrible mistake.'

Before I go to bed, another voice note appears.

'Listen, real talk, I've been going through some shit at work lately and it's clouded my vision, and I can't shake this feeling that we had something special. Talk to me. Let me in. Let me get to know you. Let me break down your barriers.'

Finally, when I wake up the next morning, 'Serena, just let me know you're all right. I'm worried.'

My chest feels a bit tight with panic when I ask myself, did I *really* leave Alistair . . . for this?

7

On Saturday morning, I walk up the back streets off Holloway Road until I get to Seven Sisters Road. There I find what I've been looking for: a fabric shop.

I run my hands over the rolls, feeling the material under my fingers. I know what I'm looking for — black linen — but it doesn't stop me admiring the bold florals, the candy stripes, the silky, jewel-toned satins. I buy a couple of metres of the least-scratchy black linen they have and stroll back home. In no time at all, I've cut out and stitched myself a new top, just a plain T-shirt-style little something, with neat French seams. I try it on and congratulate myself on a couple of hours well-spent, before realizing it hasn't taken up much of my day at all. Next time I'll have to make something more time-consuming. I think about a style of dress that I keep seeing on Instagram, a kind of prairie dress with a high neck and ruffled sleeves. Obviously all the mainstream brands are making them in their thousands for women they deem an 'acceptable' size. I track down a pattern company doing a version of it. But of course, that's not in my size either. Thwarted.

In the absence of anything else to do, I flop on the sofa and

I swipe. Too tall, too clever, too handsome, too muscly are a handful of reasons why I avoid several men who are presented to me. I even forlornly swipe left to reject a guy because he looks too much like my celebrity crush Seth Rogen and him not matching with me would feel *too* horrible. Instead I try to be more . . . tactical? Of course, I'm not swiping right on the men that look like *complete* duds, men I would have absolutely nothing to say to, but somewhere in the middle. Somewhere that – at least to me – feels realistic. Because next week – which means another date if I'm sticking to my goal – is going to come at me whether I like it or not and I've got to find me a date, so I'd better focus.

And then my swiping is interrupted by a little Lola face popping up on my screen, because of course I've fallen down a furiously swiping rabbit hole and forgotten it's time for my FaceTime catchup with Lola on my Saturday afternoon, her Saturday morning, squeezed into a rare moment where she isn't working her butt off or socializing effusively with her new colleagues and acquaintances, going to gigs and gallery openings, fashion parties or hot dates – and whatever else the Lolas of this world do. She tells me they've already asked her if she can stay past Christmas and into January. So, the bachelorette lifestyle is to remain on the horizon for some time.

'Any post for me?' she asks, deathly afraid of missing something important like a planning application to turn next door into an explosives test site.

I walk to the hall where I've been collecting a little pile. 'It's mostly junk mail, stuff from charities, a bank statement. You should go paperless.'

'I wonder how many trees I've sacrificed by forgetting to

tick that box,' she says. I scan the pile and notice, among the letters for Lola, there's something addressed to me.

'What's that?'

'It's for me,' I say as I wrangle it open with one hand and show it to Lola. 'I've been invited to a wedding.'

'How fun! I love a wedding.'

'I do too, I think,' I say, smiling. It's from Rachel and I'd somehow forgotten I was expecting it. 'A good excuse to whip up an outfit.'

'You should do something with that,' Lola says.

'Something like what?'

'I don't know . . . just *something*. I don't think we should all turn our hobbies into side-hustles, but you really are so talented. And meticulous.'

Her belief in me is incredibly kind, but I can't see anyone paying money for what I make.

I feel restless after my FaceTime with Lola, unsatisfied even though I've received a wedding invitation *and* literally made a whole top that didn't exist this morning. Like a moth to a flame, I'm drawn back to the fabric shop where I buy enough lightweight black cotton canvas to make a chic midi skirt with an elasticated waist. That's how I spend my Sunday morning, making sure the pockets are in exactly the right place and big enough for my phone, ensuring the hem is meticulously even, perfecting the gathering around the waistband before trying it on with the top I made the day before. A perfect pair.

As I examine myself in the mirror in my newly made outfit, undeniably chic but undeniably, deliberately anonymous in its monochrome, matte fabrics, I can't help but think of the rolls of patterns, colours, textures, there for the taking. Maybe next time.

Date Number: 5

With: Adrian aka the Monologuist
Where: The Duke of Edinburgh, Brixton
When: A Friday night, unfortunately

Monologue
Noun

(from Greek: μονόλογος, *from* μόνος *mónos, 'alone, solitary' and* λόγος *lógos, 'speech') a long speech presented by a single character, most often to express their mental thoughts aloud.*

'Do you know how many weddings I'm going to this year? Seven. *Seven.* I'm not kidding. All my uni gang are getting hitched. And five of those weddings are abroad. Alice is getting married to a Danish guy in Copenhagen, Mark is having his in Macedonia, there's Charlie and Ruth in Tuscany. Can't wait for that. *Love* Italy. You get the picture. I am going to be completely broke and I'm worried that by the time it's my turn they'll all have settled down and had kids and won't be able to come to mine because my dream is to get married in Thailand. *Love* Thailand. There's this place there. Ko Po Da Nok. No one knows about it. Paradise. Heaven on earth. It's impossible to get to but a pal of mine lives out there. Stevey. And he took me to this beach and . . . oh my God. I knew as soon as I saw it that this is where I was going to get married. Is that weird? Planning my wedding? I know that a lot of guys don't do that, that it's more of a girl thing but, hey, I guess I am kind of weird then. I really want to have the kind of marriage my parents have.

They've been together for, like, ever and I want that for myself. Family is so important to me. I need to be with someone that's family-oriented. I'm so close to my parents and if I'm being completely honest I've never let them meet any of my girlfriends because if you ever meet my parents, for me that is like you are becoming a part of the family and my problem is I always end up being friendzoned. That really sucks. I don't want to be your friend! Well, I do, I want to marry my best friend!'

End scene.

Date Number: 8

With: Chris aka the Comedian
Where: The Coach and Horses, Soho
When: What I thought was going to be a sedate
Sunday evening

He's already finishing a drink when I arrive. It's a slight red flag but who am I to judge? He downs the last of it and says, 'Somebody stop me!' Yes, that is correct, like Jim Carrey from the movie *The Mask*, which came out in 1994. He made a decades-old comedy reference. This is fine.

He hops off his stool and says, brightly, 'I'm Chris. What can I get you?' I'm pretty sure he didn't have an ironic twiddly moustache in his profile photos, but what can I do about that now, eh?

'A pint of . . .' I survey the indistinguishable cool branded labels on the taps and decide on the one with an orange label. 'That one.'

'Commendable choice, methinks,' he says, miming tipping his hat at me. He is, of course, not wearing a hat. He returns with our drinks and says, 'One pint glass of amber gold for the maiden. As you might perchance have perceived I am rather, how do you say, bonkers. *Prost!*' We cheers. And as much as I can immediately, unquestionably, irrefutably tell this is a romantic non-starter, I am . . . entertained.

'So . . . from where do you hail?'

'I live just off Holloway Road, sort of up from Highbury and Islington station,' I say, grateful for the shift into more neutral territory.

'That's near Finsbury Park, isn't it?' he says, hopefully.

Sensing he needs it for one of his bits, I say, 'Kind of, I guess . . .'

'What what? There's a park where they bury the good people of Finland? I hope they're dead first. I jest of course. I myself harken not far from the land of which you speak. A little place up the road. You see, I happen to be a father. A father of daughters. A multitude. And so I thought it only fitting we moved to their spiritual home. Seven Sisters.'

There is just something so compellingly stupid about what's going on here. I'll take it. I laugh.

'Once more, I jest. Let me state outright for the record, I am not a father. Perchance may I enquire . . . are you?'

'Am I . . . a father?' I say, a little perplexed but mostly just overwhelmed with how ridiculous this man is.

'I mean, do you have children?'

'None that I know of,' I say, winking.

'I say . . .' he says, and then he goes into an Austin Powers, 'Yeah baby!' This man is clearly on a different planet. Or at least sent from a different decade. But, for better or worse, I can't stifle a big laugh so he continues, this time moving on to Doctor Evil. 'Throw me a frickin' bone here!' And then he takes a handful of crisps and yells, in the immortal words of Fat Bastard, 'Get in my belly!' before shoving them in his mouth. I can't even be embarrassed about the people at the next table staring at us.

I sigh, completely overwhelmed with his ludicrous behaviour. 'You do the best Austin Powers I've heard in . . . twenty years.'

'Why, thank you. So where are you from originally, assuming from Finsbury Park you are not born and raised?'

'Haywards Heath.'

'I don't believe it!' (Yes, in the exact style of Victor Meldrew from *One Foot in the Grave*.) 'I'm from Crawley. We are *literally* neighbours. Oh, wouldn't that be perfect. A local boy and girl come good in the big smoke. Wouldn't it make the old folks proud! Me sees not mead inside your tankard. Let us fill it with haste with two more pints of the palest ales of India.'

He dashes off back to the bar, leaving me completely dazed and nearly hysterical at this brilliantly, boldly, daringly, unforgettably terrible first date.

8

A wedding *the weekend* before Christmas? WHO DOES THAT? Honestly, tell me, who? The one redeeming quality of this festive ceremony is that it doesn't require an overnight hotel stay but . . . still. This is precious calendar real estate!

I had high hopes that my shiny new life would arrive overnight, complete with tons of socializing and handsome men, but the past few weeks haven't exactly been filled with amazing dates and old friends getting in touch. To be honest, it was nice to be asked to this wedding. I was *surprised* to be asked, especially after I didn't exactly give them a great experience at my own non-wedding wedding.

People joke about how many weddings you go to in your late twenties and early thirties, but this is only the second wedding I have in the calendar for this year, including my own. I only hope it doesn't absolutely *fill* me with regret and send me pining over Alistair.

I swipe red lipstick over my lips – Pat McGrath in Elson, my most decadent beauty purchase and one I could not live without, which makes the final step in my wedding prep routine. *Muy glamorosa.* I'm not sure why I'm making so much of an effort for this, since I'm going solo and don't think I'll know a single person there except the bride and groom, but it's nice to scrub up once in a while and if not for a wedding, then when? I can't imagine I'll stay that late, which is fine because . . . well, because of the low barrier to entry. Who cares how long I stay? Who cares whether I look devastatingly beautiful or not? It's just down the road from me! I might as well!

And I've made a whole new dress for the occasion. The decision-making process went a little bit like:

Me: Hmm, I wonder what I'll wear to this wedding next weekend.

Nicole: Something sexy?

Me: Sexy sounds scary.

Nicole: Sexy sounds sexy. You would look fire in a slip dress.

Me: I've never made a slip dress before. I don't know if I could even find a pattern in my size.

Nicole: Found you one. I'm ordering you a PDF pattern right now. That noise was the pattern arriving in your inbox. Don't make it in black.

So, duly beaten into submission by Nicole, off I trotted to the fabric shop to find the perfect satin. And there it was: not black, but a gleaming sapphire, perfectly suited to a slinky dress. (I also picked up some leopard-print faux-fur in a moment of madness because they were selling it off, but I'm unconvinced that's ever going to see the light of day.) I've got to admit: I am not a hundred per cent on the thought of me in a slip dress but I decided to face my fear and do it anyway. And I *think* it's paid off? I'm realizing that, broadly speaking, Nicole knows what's good for me. Over the past few weeks, our post-work drinks have become more and more frequent (when she can fit me in around her hot dates, not that she's ever made me feel like an afterthought), and I'm finding her friendship to be a bright spot in this strange, uncertain world I'm living in.

As I hop on the bus (look, I know I *could* walk, but just because you *can* doesn't mean you *should*) I check my phone and see a text from my mum. A photo of our elderly dog, Jackie, asleep on the rug in front of the fireplace with her legs in the air. Cute. Mum sends me photos of Jackie a lot these days. I think it's her way of checking in with me, to make sure I'm okay, without looking like she's prying. As a family, we're not amazing at talking about our feelings. Except for Melanie, and that's more *opinions* than feelings anyway. But my parents? Not so much. And I think the post-wedding fallout was hard for them. It must have been. I should make more of an effort with them. I know I should.

I text back, feeling that little tug of guilt at putting my parents through the stress and worry of blowing up my life the way I did. And another tug of guilt at how little time I'm spending there over Christmas, but I think it's for the best this year.

She's such a princess, can't wait to squeeze her (and you!) in a couple of weeks!

I arrive at Islington Town Hall only a few minutes before the ceremony is due to start, which is not an error of judgement on my part but rather a strategic move to spend as little time as possible awkwardly standing around, not talking to anyone because I don't know anyone. I look at the screen in the foyer and head to the right room in the building for the

Hall–Johnson wedding. Up a carpeted staircase and into the Richmond Room, a beautiful wood-panelled space with dramatic red curtains and carpets, and blue chairs laid out in rows – to my horror, almost all occupied. I make a quick dash for a seat in the back row, out of the way, sitting next to an older couple, and within minutes the opening bars of 'God Only Knows' by the Beach Boys start blaring out of some speakers. Okay, I admit it – I cut it a *little* too fine. Luke is already standing at the registry office equivalent of the altar.

When Rachel glides down the aisle in her figure-hugging fishtail ivory wedding dress, she's truly breathtaking. All slim and toned and curvaceous. The kind of body that men *specifically* look for in a woman. Long, straight brown hair cascading down her back. Radiant with all the warmth and love of being a bride. I wonder what I would have looked like on my wedding day if I'd have made it this far. Would I have been able to conceal it? Made myself look as serene and happy as Rachel? Or would I have looked like a deer in headlights? A man to the scaffold? I sigh, a little too loudly, but I pass it off as a swoon of admiration for the blushing bride.

'Doesn't she look beautiful?' the lady sitting next to me asks.

'She really does! Incredible,' I whisper back.

'We've lived next to her parents all her life – I remember when she was little, she used to love playing dress-up and she *always* wanted to be a bride!' says the woman gleefully, but our conversation is cut short by the celebrant clearing her throat and welcoming us all to the wedding in a voice so quiet we have to strain to hear her.

The ceremony is over in no time at all, as they always are in secular services, and then it's time to shower the happy couple in confetti on the steps of the town hall. The photographer makes me feel self-conscious – I wasn't before his lens was turned onto me. There's something about a camera, about a photo, that makes my skin crawl, like I'm one photo away from a full self-loathing meltdown. I'm conscious, as he snaps a series of photos, that I'm the biggest person here. I don't know when I started looking around rooms, gatherings, meetings and scanning the participants for their fatness or thinness, but it's a *thing*. I don't exactly know how it makes me feel. But right now it just makes me feel a little self-conscious. Although maybe that's also because I'm flying solo.

When we shuffle down Upper Street to the reception venue, I say a silent prayer that my heels don't start killing me, and as if by magic, I hear a woman say next to me, 'I *love* your shoes!'

'Oh, thanks!' I say to her, taking in her sharp, elegant jewel-toned velvet suit over a silky camisole. Utterly chic. 'I feel like reading my sister's magazines when I was a teenager definitely gave me an inflated sense of how often I would actually be wearing heels in my adult life . . .'

'Ha!' She throws her head back in a generous laugh. 'So true!'

'I'm Serena, by the way,' I say, making sure I walk in step with her, keen to hang onto my newfound friend.

'Zara,' she says, holding out her hand, nails short and rounded, painted a glossy black, not a chip in sight. I shake it. She's elegant. Poised. Cleopatra fringe, heavy eye makeup, lipstick so pale it almost blends in with her skin.

'So, how do you know the bride? Or groom?' I ask her.

'Went to university with Rachel, now I live round the corner from them in Stokey,' Zara says. 'How about you?'

'We worked together in my first job out of university,

actually,' I say, thinking about how *long* ago that feels, how I'd already been together with Alistair for, what, three years by that point. 'Before she got the job at the National.'

'Yes, she's certainly climbed the ranks there,' Zara says over her shoulder as we push open the door to the pub.

Rows and rows of glasses of prosecco are standing to attention on the bar, quickly evaporating with each person that enters. We make a beeline for the alcohol.

'But if you ask me, the less said about Luke the better . . .' Zara says, sipping on her prosecco, as if we had just been talking about him. I'm a little taken aback at how forthright she is with her opinion of Luke at his own wedding but, wanting to glide smoothly through the conversation like a knife through butter, I say nothing.

'He's all right . . .' I say, even though I do think he's boring. I can't suppress the smile that's creeping across my face at Zara's naughtiness.

'All right should not be good enough for someone like Rachel!' Zara protests.

I sigh. 'True. Well, they're married now so we should probably keep these thoughts on the downlow. Let's drink to that,' I say, as we clink our glasses together.

'*Na zdrowie,*' Zara says. I'm starting to like her.

There are a lot of people here, milling around in the bar area before we head upstairs for the meal. I don't know any of them, exactly as I predicted. I wonder exactly what level of cool you have to achieve before you wear an emerald-green velvet suit to a wedding and where Zara managed to acquire that cool. We're so different physically that I don't even feel . . . I don't know, *threatened* is the wrong word but maybe . . . embarrassed to be standing next to her? She's all angles and severity and I'm this fluffy blonde Cabbage Patch Kid in a navy blue satin slip dress and a fur stole. Chalk and cheese.

We stand around chatting in the absence of anything else to do while Rachel and Luke are having their photos taken. 'So,' Zara says, 'you didn't get a plus-one?'

'Nope,' I say.

'I've developed my own policy on that.'

'Hit me.'

'I think if the person you're inviting knows three or more people at your wedding, they don't need a plus-one even if they've been with their partner for ages. If you wouldn't invite their partner on their own, they don't get to be there. You save the plus-ones for the people who *won't* know three or more people at your wedding,' she says, casting her gaze over the crowd of guests in the bar.

'You know what?' I say. 'That's actually pretty decent logic.'

'Just one of my little bugbears as a perpetually single person in a sea of couples. It's a couple-centric world out there.'

'Huh . . .' I say, wondering if I've thought of it that way myself. I guess the world does feel a little different now that I'm not one half of a two-person unit. I don't have a default *person* to do things with. Cinema, holidays, even a takeaway. I've had to acquaint myself with cooking for one, halving recipes (sometimes . . .), I've started going to the theatre on my own sometimes. But all of that just feels like *freedom* to me. Maybe it won't a couple of years down the line. Maybe being able to cook with mushrooms won't seem like such a fun little novelty after all.

'Not that I have anything to complain about,' she says. 'I have a few old uni friends here so it's fine for me. But even if I didn't, it's a lovely wedding and I wouldn't miss it.'

'I haven't been to a wedding in a while, actually,' I say, wondering if I'm about to disclose the reality of my situation. It might be a fun little anecdote to share with my new best friend Zara.

She drains her glass, sets it down on the bar and reaches over for another which she swipes elegantly. 'It's funny, last time I saw Rachel she was telling me about this wedding she went to in the summer,' she says before taking a sip and shaking out her glossy, sleek hair.

In that intervening moment I manage to develop the power of foresight. I know exactly what she's about to say.

'Oh yeah,' I say, hoping I'm wrong but knowing I'm not.

'The bride *literally* jilted the groom at the altar. All the guests were *there*, in their seats, waiting for the ceremony to begin, and she just didn't turn up?'

I try to swallow down a mouthful of prosecco but it feels bitter and dry in my throat. 'Oh . . .' I say. I don't want to sound too interested, give her any ammunition with which to continue.

'Isn't that insane? Like, have you ever heard of that happening?' Zara is more animated than she's been the whole time I've been talking to her. 'You have to wonder what goes through someone's head, right? Like, did she *know* she was going to do it? And why did she leave it so late? How much do you have to fucking *hate* your fiancé to humiliate them like that?!' She throws her head back in a coarse laugh like it's the funniest thing she's ever heard. 'I wonder what he'd done – Rachel said she had no idea but it must have been *something*, right?' Zara pauses for a second, looking at me, waiting for a response.

I smile, weakly, even though I feel hot and sick and embarrassed, like I'm in a bad dream and I've just been pushed onstage at the O2 Arena in my knickers to give a performance when everyone's expecting Rihanna. 'Yeah . . .' I say. 'It must have been something.'

I hoped that would be enough but clearly Zara isn't done yet. 'Obviously the money is one thing – don't get me wrong, that's bad enough in itself – but just how fucking *brutal* is it to do that to someone, you know? I mean, I'm not exactly a teddy bear but I can't imagine doing it to someone who thinks I'm going to marry them!' She shakes her head in disbelief. 'Horrendous.'

'I . . .' I mumble, needing desperately to extricate myself from this conversation. 'I'm just going to pop to the bathroom,' I say, setting my empty glass down on the bar without waiting for a response.

So much for a new best friend.

I mill around trying not to make eye contact with anyone in case they see I'm about to burst into tears, but I can't figure out where the bathroom is. I'm worried if I open my mouth to ask someone the floodgates will fully open. Eventually I find it on a mezzanine level between the bar and the dining area upstairs. I push my way into a stall and lock the door behind me before sitting down on the closed lid.

The thing is, I don't *actually* want to cry and have a meltdown about this. But I can't pretend it doesn't hurt. Knowing that this is what people think about me is *weird*. It doesn't feel like me. But it *is* me. I am the person who threw their happy, relaxed life away in the worst possible fashion. And what do I have to show for it? A handful of dates with men I hardly care to remember? Well, except for mad Chris the jokester. Who could forget him. It makes me wonder if being married to Alistair really *would* have been worse than all this.

But now I'm away from Zara and her cold, hard, dismissive words, I just wish I had someone here who knew me. Someone I could tell, and who would say, 'Oh my God, what a bitch! You didn't do anything wrong, don't worry,' and it would make me feel, you know, normal again. Basically, I wish Lola was here, or at least waiting for me at home to listen to me tell this anecdote and give me a little sympathy.

But she's not. I'm here on my own and I just have to suck it up, because Lord knows I can't get a reputation for running out on *other* people's weddings as well as my own, now, can I?

It strikes me how much I'm missing Lola. I drop her a WhatsApp.

Thank you for rescuing me when I needed it. Really wish you were here today!

A little bit more sentimental than our usual messages. Normally I'm updating her on, say, a new Palestinian restaurant opening on Holloway Road or the fact I broke one of the pint glasses she's had since she stole it from a pub when we were at university. You know, the little things.

You drunk? 😜 she replies instantly.

No! Just feeling pathetic, that's all 🙍

You're a lil sweetie, I miss you too! 💔 I'm at a brunch in deepest Queens and I'm going to have to spend about $70 on an Uber home!!!! I feel sick! Mama does not need this many mimosas or expensive cab rides!

Poor baby 😶

It's not my usual style to wear my heart on my sleeve but Lola's really been there for me when I needed somewhere to go. Even if she hasn't been, you know, *actually here*. It feels good to tell her that.

I leave the stall and head over to the mirror, taking my lipstick out of my beaded clutch bag to reapply over the sink. I felt so good when I left the house and now, looking at myself in the mirror, I'm struggling not to regret this slinky dress, this uncompromising shape, concealing nothing. But I'm here now, I'm wearing it; however much I might regret it, I just have to own it. What would Nicole do? She wouldn't be feeling self-conscious right now, would she?

As I'm putting the finishing touches to my (frankly very juicy and beautiful) lips, I hear a bell ring to signal that it's time to eat. Because I'm already one floor up, I end up being one of the first people into the main dining room, which is full of big, round tables covered in white tablecloths with beautiful dark floral centrepieces.

Before the room fills up, I manage to find my table and my name card. I take a look at the name card to one side of me – Susie – and then the other. Zara. Nope. No thank you. I quickly switch it for a name on the other side of the big round table. Henry, whoever he is, will be my new seatmate. I hope either him or Susie have good chat. I don't need both. Just one would be fine with me.

I take my seat and text Nicole so I don't look too desperate for company.

Do I have a story for you on Monday.

Wedding drama? she replies almost instantaneously. I worry I'm a bit too boring for Nicole, so it's reassuring to know she's at least intrigued by the promise of gossip about my life.

Kinda! It's like wedding drama Inception! Wedding drama about wedding drama!

Can't wait . . .

I'm about to reply when the scraping of chairs around me makes it apparent that the table is filling up.

'Hi, I'm Susie, nice to meet you,' a pretty blonde with immaculate makeup says, sitting down on one side of me. 'This is my boyfriend, Jake,' she says, gesturing towards a handsome, stubbled man on her right.

'Hi Susie and Jake, I'm Serena,' I say, offering a hand to both of them.

'There you are!' says Zara, taking her seat on the far side of the table.

'Here I am!' I say, gamely, hoping she doesn't undo all my good work and insist on coming to sit next to me. But just at that second, the chair to my left is pulled out and the moment is gone. My plan has worked, I am free of Zara and her inadvertent gossip about me! I feel like the smartest girl in the whole world.

'Hi,' I say, turning to my left. 'I'm Serena.'

'Henry,' says the man in the seat next to me, and, *well*, what's that I'm feeling? The bottom falling out of my stomach . . .

9

Have you ever met someone and instantly, *instantly* known that you're about to become completely obsessed with them? Well, I couldn't say I had until this very moment.

'Pardon?' I ask. I have no idea why. I heard him perfectly clearly. His low and gentle voice. Those playful, kind brown eyes behind glasses that are neither too obtrusive nor unfashionable. A thick head of ginger hair wrangled into a neat side parting and a slightly darker beard that's neither out of control nor obsessively groomed. A solid, stocky build dressed in a tidy but not excessively formal charcoal tweed suit.

'Henry.'

'Yes, Henry.' Look, I was just feeling a little discombobulated, that's all.

'How do you know Luke and Rachel?'

'Oh, uh, I, erm, I . . .' Yes, I admit, this was a moment of fully fledged tongue-tied rom-com fluster. I paused a second to pull myself together. 'I used to work with Rachel . . . years ago,' I say. 'You?' I'm desperate to know every little detail about this guy.

'Um . . .' Henry says, furrowing his brow and looking a little awkward before smiling. 'I'm never sure how to put this exactly but, I sort of saved Luke's life?'

'What?! That was you?!' I gasp. I remember when Luke had his accident – I didn't work with Rachel by then but I knew about it through social media and a tearful dinner with her a couple of weeks later. Luke had been hit by a van turning left while he was cycling to work, almost crushed by his own bike and left bleeding in the street, but a random stranger had moved quickly, pressed his scarf down against the wound and called an ambulance while everyone else around him just stared, panic-stricken.

'Yeah . . . that was me. After that, you know, once he was out of hospital and back on his feet, we started meeting up for a drink every now and then.'

'Fuck,' I say, genuinely impressed, barely able to take my eyes off him as a waiter comes around filling our glasses with champagne for the toast. 'I mean, you know, well done. Good on you for saving a life. Excellent work.'

I know. I am sounding completely mad. I need to tone it down. 'It's really cool that you stayed in touch.'

'Yeah,' he says, nodding pensively. 'We don't really have anything in common but we always manage to have a good time. It was hard at first, I don't think he really knew how to, I suppose, deal with *me* as a person. It was as if he couldn't get his head around the . . .' he casts around for the right word, looking reluctant and embarrassed, 'magnitude, I guess, of the whole thing.'

'Of what you did for him,' I fill in.

He shrugs, as if it really is no big deal. 'Right.' Just then Rachel's dad taps his fork against his champagne flute.

'Wow, well . . . cheers,' I say, picking up my glass.

'A toast, to Rachel and Luke,' Rachel's dad booms from the top table. 'We couldn't be happier to see Rachel married,' he says. 'And to finally have another man in the family! Cheers! To Rachel and Luke!'

'To Rachel and Luke!' we all chorus, jumping to our feet and raising our glasses. As I take a sip from my champagne flute, I glance at Henry. I've never fancied a ginger before! Not out of any kind of prejudice but . . . there aren't that many around, are there? God, he's cute! Not, like, model hot, in a way that would make everyone look and be like, *Oh my God, that guy is soooo hot*, but . . . just . . . somehow completely irresistible to me.

I feel stressed out and alive! I flip through my mental archive of questions that would help me find out more about this guy without coming off *too* intrusive. Too interested. Or should I play it cool? Fuck, what to do? I have no idea how to play this! No idea at all!

I feel so out of practice of fancying someone, of figuring out if they could possibly be interested in me, of believing they *could* be interested in me, and then seeing that through to actually having sex with them. This is a nightmare. Only a few minutes ago I had never met this guy before in my life and now I'm completely obsessed with him based purely on what? Some animal instinct? He might be a complete dickhead! Yeah, let's hope he's a complete dickhead. Even though he *literally* saved someone's life and then befriended them, potentially solely to help them come to terms with their own mortality. I am truly screwed.

We sit down again, and I find myself taking extra care to move in what I perceive to be an elegant and feminine way. I am careful of my posture, trying to make my spine form a straight line with my shoulders back at all times rather than lazily hunch like the goblin I truly am – too many hours at my sewing machine. I wonder if Henry is about to disappear in conversation with the woman sitting next to him, but she appears to have a date with her. Henry's here alone. A good start.

Please let him be single, please let him be single, please let him be single.

'So . . .' I say, trying to sip the rest of my champagne as elegantly as I can manage. 'Are you flying solo tonight?' Is that too obvious?

'I am indeed,' he says, shrugging off his jacket and turning around to hang it on the back of his chair. He doesn't say any more than that. No *Oh my girlfriend couldn't make it* or *My wife's at home with the children* or something. So far so good. 'And you?'

'Yep, same! I sort of thought this might be the singleton table but it seems there are some couples among us,' I say, looking around at the table of eight, made up of two couples, plus me, Henry, Zara and a woman in a cool pink jumpsuit sitting next to her. They appear to be deep in conversation. I suppose Zara is probably telling her new friend about this mad woman she heard about who ran out on her own wedding day. Who knew I would be such a compelling anecdote!

'I had no idea what to expect other than that last time I saw Luke he told me Rachel's family had coughed up for a *lot* of booze,' he says, raising his eyebrows.

'Oh, sweet!' I say, slightly too enthusiastically. 'You know, just because who *doesn't* like free-flowing alcohol at a wedding. Not because I plan on getting smashed off my face.'

'I wouldn't blame you if you did,' Henry says in a low voice, a smile of complicity forming on his lips. It's a nice smile. Of course it's a nice smile. He has a nice face!

We're served our starters – some delicious, flavourful tomato tarts. I cut mine up into tiny, delicate, ladylike pieces as I eat, mindful to the point of paranoia of Henry sitting next to me. Not wanting to talk with my mouth full, I let us eat in peace. As I eat I wonder what happened to the food for our wedding. I hope the staff at the venue ate it. Or at least I hope it didn't go to waste.

'What are you thinking about?' Henry asks me as he sets his knife and fork down on his empty plate. He looks amused.

'What? Why?'

'Well, all of a sudden you looked very serious, like you were trying to find the meaning of life in those tomatoes,' he says.

'Oh! No, not at all,' I say, shaking my head. 'I was just thinking about Rachel and Luke and how I hope they have a long and happy life together,' I lie.

'I'll drink to that,' says Henry, picking up his glass of white wine.

'Well, Henry,' I say, picking up mine. 'It would be rude not to, now we know they've budgeted for it, right?'

We clink our glasses together and take a gulp of wine.

'Not bad,' he says, swirling it around in his glass and holding it up to the light.

'Are you a . . . wine person?'

'Ha!' he booms, joyfully. 'Absolutely not! I don't know a thing about it, only whether I like it or not.'

'Sort of like art,' I say, then worry that it was too much of a non-sequitur. 'You know how people say that about art?'

'Um . . .' Henry says, 'not exactly like art for me, I know a bit about that. But not wine.'

'Okay, let's try this again from a different angle. Are you an . . . art person?' I say, trying to exactly replicate my original cadence.

'Only for fun,' he says, shuffling his chair a little so it faces me more. I feel a glow of delight ignite in my stomach. Just that little display of attention. Just that small intimacy. I hope he's catching me from a good angle. I hope he's thinking about how cute I am. Can I dare to hope for that? I feel like normally I would be obsessing about how out of my league a guy is but there's just *something* about Henry that makes me feel . . . reassured? At home? Something about him just feels right to me. 'I mean, I don't work in art or anything,' he says, quickly, as if it would be a crime for him to mislead me.

'What do you do?' I ask.

'It's honestly too boring – my work is the least interesting thing about me.'

'I'll be the judge of that,' I say, which I can just tell he likes.

'I write for a trade publication about mining,' he says, raising his eyebrows expectantly, waiting for my face to cloud over with boredom. 'See?'

'Don't put yourself down! Mining is a very interesting field,' I say, although I have no idea whether it is or not.

'Well, I'm glad you think so, but I do try to sort of . . . de-centre work in my life. I know it's an easy question to ask someone and I don't blame you for asking it but I just feel as if it's not always the best way to get to know someone.'

I feel a little chastened, embarrassed of asking such a banal, stupid question.

110

'Oh . . .' I say, frowning. 'No, you're right.'

'Look, I'm sorry, I really didn't mean it to come across like that – it's just something I struggle to explain in a way that doesn't sound rude.'

'No, it makes sense!' I say, realizing that it actually does. 'I write about jewellery. I write descriptions of jewellery that we're selling and I write emails to convince people to buy the jewellery that I write descriptions of. I suppose that's not a very good indicator of who I am as a person.'

'Exactly,' he says, warmly. 'So . . . who are you, really?'

'Wow . . .' I say. 'What a question.' I realize that I could tell him that I've just come out of a ten-year relationship that I ended abruptly on our wedding day. I feel like you can probably learn something about me from that, but it's not really something I would want *him* to learn.

'What are you passionate about?'

I think for a moment. 'Being here. In London. I never lived here before the autumn and it's turned out to be the greatest joy.'

'Oh, cool!' He looks genuinely delighted for me. 'Where were you before?'

'A boring town outside of London. So it's not like I had never *been* before, but it just wasn't the same for me. It's really marked a kind of new freedom for me . . . I like the feeling of being able to just disappear into the crowd, not be known by anyone.'

He's nodding, like he's listening really intently. 'Well, welcome.'

'Have you always been here?'

'Yep,' he says, crossing his legs like he's making himself at home. 'I've never left for more than a few weeks, which is a bit embarrassing, isn't it?' He's looking at me expectantly, like he really does want an answer.

'Nah,' I say, brushing it off, 'I don't blame you. Lots of nice art here, if that's what you're into!'

'True,' he says. 'I do think about leaving sometimes, in the way you feel sort of compelled to when everyone's talking about how cheap it is to live in, oh, I don't know – Margate or Hastings. But I actually *do* London things so much that it would only make me wonder why I bothered.'

'That's a good point,' I say, turning to mirror his pose. 'I think you should stay.'

He blushes a little. So he does know I'm trying to flirt with him. Is that good or bad? I guess . . . good?

We're interrupted by the waiter with the main courses. He's consulting a little table plan, setting down the plates according to what we requested when we RSVPed. Except, I realize, I've messed things up by switching Henry and Zara's places . . .

'I don't *remember* going for the vegetarian option . . .' Henry frowns down at his plate. 'I mean, it looks very nice, but . . .' I look across the table at Zara, who's explaining to the waiter in no uncertain terms that she *did not* order the lamb. Oops!

'Zara!' I call to her across the table, wanting this all to get cleared up sooner rather than later so I can return to my chat with Henry. 'Did you order the vegetarian option?'

'Yes!'

'Yours is here,' I say, pointing at Henry's plate. 'And I think you have his lamb?'

'Oh! Well, that's easy enough,' she says.

Once Zara and Henry have swapped plates and he and I are sawing away at our lamb, I can't help but feel like the momentum has been lost a little. I rack my brains to think of something to say.

'Do you—' I say, at the exact moment that Henry turns to ask me something. We enter into an awkward verbal two-step of 'No, you go' and 'What were you saying?' Eventually we both back down and laugh at the awkwardness.

'I was just asking,' he says, 'if you had to travel far to get here. It wasn't a very interesting question, my deepest apologies.' Perhaps he had been scrabbling around in *his* brain for something to talk to me about, too.

'Oh! Um, I actually live up the road.'

'Really?'

'Yeah! I mean, it's like, quite a *way* up, past the roundabout and then Holloway Road, but it is, essentially, at least to my mind, the same road,' I say, shrugging. 'How about you?'

'I'm down south in Greenwich,' he says.

'Oh! I've heard such nice things about Greenwich and I've never been,' I say. 'I know that's such an annoying thing to say – what is it with people who never do the things they say they want to do that they could easily do, right? But I just feel like since I moved here all my time just' – I mime a magician's hand gesture – 'disappears.'

'It's a real thing! Also we literally don't have time to live fulfilled lives while doing forty-hour work weeks.'

'Tell me more?' I ask, swallowing down a mouthful of creamy potato dauphinoise.

'I mean that the forty-hour work week is predicated on the basis of a two-person partnership where it's one person's full-time job to do all the childcare, all the cleaning, all the cooking, all the household tasks, but we don't actually live like that any more. So now we're *all* working these five-day weeks, if you're *lucky*, and then beating ourselves up because our houses are messy or we don't have time to exercise or—'

'Or go to Greenwich,' I say.

'Exactly.'

'I like this theory of yours.'

'I mean, it's not exactly my theory, but it's something I believe in.'

'So is that your way of telling me your flat is a shithole?' I say, unable to keep a naughty smile off my face.

He puts his knife and fork down and looks at me. 'Why don't you find out for yourself?'

Bingo! But what? It wasn't meant to be this easy!

'Is this because you think it's the only way to get me to go to Greenwich? Because I promise you it's not,' I say, hoping I'm not pushing my luck.

'No,' he says. 'It's because I think you're cute.'

I want to flip over the big round table, punch the air and run victory laps around the room. I honestly can't believe it. This was almost *too* easy. Am I being pranked? Is that what this is? Was he planted here for some obscure reason? Is he going to murder me? What's going on? I realize I haven't said anything for a moment.

'Sorry, was that too much?' he asks, looking genuinely stressed out. 'I didn't mean to make you uncomfortable, fuck . . . I'm not normally like this . . . I'm usually very, uh, reserved . . .'

'No! No, not at all,' I say. 'I would love to.'

'Phew,' he says, mopping his brow with his napkin. 'For a second there I was like . . . does she just think I'm a fucking creep, did I totally misread those signals . . .'

'God, was I giving signals?' I say, a little mortified. I want to be a mysterious, unknowable lady, not some kind of pathetic horndog!

He shrugs. 'Just a little.' How has this made me fancy him even more? Gah, his eyes are so brown! His teeth so straight and white and neat! He looks like his suit actually fits him and he didn't just drag it out of the back of his wardrobe a few hours ago.

'Well . . .'

'Christmas is a bit of a weird time for it but if you're around between Christmas and New Year then . . . could be nice?' he ventures.

'It could,' I say, my heart racing at the thought of a hot date with Henry to get me through Christmas with my family.

'That's settled then. Give me your number and I'll text you nearer the time so we can arrange something?'

I read him my number and he puts it into his phone. As soon as he does, I'm consumed with the belief that, for the first time ever, I've forgotten my own phone number and given it to him wrong, or he took it down wrong, or any number of potential snafus. But no, I know he has it. I just have to stay calm, be chill, give myself over to fate. Good luck with that, Serena.

We're not sure what to say to each other after that. It's like now that part's done, we've forgotten how to chat, let alone flirt. He gets drawn into a conversation with the couple on the other side of him over dessert. I demolish my lemon tart and start fantasizing what it'll be like to see him in a couple of weeks' time. Already that seems too far away! Anything could happen between now and then! Ugh! Bloody Christmas. But more to the point, I wonder if anything could happen *tonight*. Maybe a little dancing after dinner, maybe a sneaky kiss before we part ways . . . maybe we *don't* part ways? I am living the bachelorette lifestyle after all, a whole flat to myself a bus ride away . . .

But after Rachel and Luke cut the cake and we all cheer, Henry gently lays a hand on my upper arm and says, 'Sorry, just wanted to let you know I've got to go now.'

'Oh!' I say, which comes out more disappointed than I meant it to, by which I mean it came out just as disappointed as it made me feel.

'Yeah, I've got to . . . uh . . .' Henry trails off in a way that makes me want to ask him *Yes, what, what have you got to do that's so important?* 'I had a prior engagement tonight but I told Luke I would be here too. I've got to dash . . .'

I realize I'm sort of frowning uncomfortably. 'Of course!' I say. 'Text me?'

'Yeah, I will,' he says, slipping his suit jacket back on and smiling. 'Don't worry about that.' He says not to worry, so why am I worried already? Riddle me that!

We say goodbye and I watch him make his way over to the top table to Luke and Rachel, who squeeze him tight and send him on his way. I wonder if he's going to look back over here before he goes, but I don't want to find out he doesn't, so instead I slide my way into conversation with Susie, even though I feel a little rude since I haven't really shown any interest in her for the whole meal. But it's good timing because now the cake is cut we can head downstairs where they've dimmed the lights, opened the bar and turned the music up loud for us to dance. Not that I have anyone to dance with.

I look at my watch as I stand alone, over by the bar, sipping a vodka and cranberry juice. Nine o'clock. I wonder if I should reattach myself to Zara, put aside my prior misgivings. But all the life has gone out of me. I don't know why, exactly. I was so buoyant at meeting Henry. But now some little crack of reality has shattered the fantasy and I don't like it. I need to just stop being sore at the fact that he had somewhere else to be tonight and remember, fuck, *I have a date with him!* That's some pretty cheering news, right? I met him, I fancied him, and now I'm going on a certified actual date with him. Someone I met in real life! No app required!

Date Number: 11

With: Sean aka the Men's Rights Activist
Where: The Crown and Shuttle, Shoreditch
When: Thursday night

A man looms – that's the only word for it – he *looms* over my table, and ventures, 'Se . . . rena?'

'Oh, hi! Nice to meet you,' I say, getting to my feet. We hug, but it's a little awkward. 'Sean, right?'

'Yeah, Sean,' he mumbles, passing a hand through his hair uncomfortably. He's kind of handsome, a little scruffy, but not so bad.

'Well, hi,' I say.

'Do you want me to get you a drink?' he asks, a little grudgingly.

'Oh, sure,' I say. It's not like I was *expecting* him to, I was just waiting for him. 'Can I have a glass of rosé, please?'

He looks like he's thinking about it. 'All right,' he says, finally.

When he reappears, he sets his drink down, hands me mine, sits in the chair opposite me and says, 'So,' like he's expecting me to know what to say next.

'Are you . . .' I venture, 'nervous?'

'Do I look nervous?' he says, jiggling his leg up and down. 'Are you?'

'Um, no – I feel like only one person is allowed to be nervous at a time and the other person then sort of has to . . . reassure them.'

'Right, right,' he says, drumming his fingers on the table like he has somewhere to be.

'I mean . . .' I say, kindly. 'It's always weird, isn't it? Meeting someone off the internet. I know it's sort of become more normal now but it'll always feel a little strange.' I rack my brains trying to remember something from his profile. 'So . . . you live in Hackney?'

'No, Clapton.'

'God, sorry, that must have been someone else,' I say, shaking my head as I realize that these men's profiles are all blurring into one.

He laughs, a little bitterly. 'Oh, is that how it is?'

'No, no,' I say, 'I don't really go on many dates.'

'Oh, that surprises me,' he says. 'That's meant to be a compliment, by the way.'

'Oh,' I say. Is he flirting with me? I honestly can't tell. I can't tell if he fancies me or hates me and wants to leave. 'Do you go on a lot of dates?'

He takes a gulp of his beer and shakes his head, grimacing. 'Dating fucking sucks if you're a man.'

'Does it? I sort of get the feeling that men treat women like they're a bit disposable on dating sites.'

'You would say that.'

'Why?'

'You're a woman,' he says, dismissively.

'I don't know if it's that . . .' I say.

'Everyone wants to talk about how hard it is for women but no one wants to acknowledge how hard it is for men,' he says, finally hitting his stride, loosening up a little. It's just a shame the thing that's relaxed him is, well, men's rights activism.

'Do tell me more,' I say, resting my elbows on the table and leaning my chin on my fists, the picture of intense concentration.

'I mean it,' he says, sensing my scepticism.

'Well, like I said, tell me more.'

'Women say they want to meet Prince Charming but really all they ever seem to go for is some guy who'll treat them like shit. These guys . . . they're all fucking . . . footballers and fucking astronauts and they're all ripped as hell and seven feet tall or whatever, and then women are surprised when they get treated like shit. Whereas guys like me? Nothing.'

'Sorry, I'm a bit confused,' I say, sipping my pint.

'About what?' he says, and once again I reflect on how unfortunate it is that he's a dickhead, because he's really not bad-looking.

'I can't figure out if you're like . . . saying this because you fancy me and you want me to fancy you? Because if so, this is kind of off-putting, you know? I'm just not really sure what your angle is with all of this.'

'Angle? I don't have an angle, it's women who have angles, trying to worm their way into your life, into your wallet.'

How did this happen to me?! Please, cosmos, I beg you, Henry cannot be the only normal man in London. Surely not? I don't deserve this! Or do I? God, is this punishment for Alistair? Is this some kind of cosmic justice?

I stand up. 'You know what, your profile made you look kind of normal but I think it's best if I just go now.'

The prospect of my date with Henry means I'm barely committed to this one as it is, let alone willing to listen to some diatribe from this angry man.

'What are you talking about?' he asks. 'We were getting on so well!' It sounds like he means it, which worries me.

'No,' I say, shaking my head. 'I've got laundry to do.' I don't know where that came from but it sounds plausible.

I dash out of the pub, feeling like a complete idiot. What a waste of time. Why the fuck did I think that was going to be a good date? Because he *did* look like a normal person in his profile! That's why! It's not on me! This is a *him* problem.

I've barely made it onto the bus home when a message pops up on my screen.

Not sure what just happened there but whatever it was clearly wasn't my fault so please transfer me £6.50 for your wine. My bank details are . . .

My date with Henry cannot come soon enough.

10

Coming to accept that Christmas is just not that exciting any more has been one of the cruel truths about growing up. It's just that every year it gets that little bit less exciting. I feel like you have to either fully lean into being a Mad Christmas Person who makes it part of their personality, or you accept it's a good excuse for some days off work but not much else. It doesn't help I've been alone in the flat in the run-up and it felt a bit weird and sad to decorate it just for me, so I haven't really *felt* the cosy vibes. I decided to only commit a few days to actually being at my parents' house because while my parents are one thing, sharing the house with Matt, Melanie *and* Coco is quite another.

Four nights of that air-raid siren wail punctuating my Baileys-soaked dreams is more than enough if you ask me. Although Coco is more pleasant to deal with than Melanie, who is resolutely unapologetic about cosying up to Alistair instead of me. At least I have my post-Christmas date with Henry to look forward to. True to his word, and despite my fears of flakiness, he did text me, yesterday, to arrange a date for the thirtieth.

I'm hoping this is the beautiful blonde in the blue dress from the wedding. If so, Serena: hope you're having a merry Christmas, and would you like to have a date with me on the 30th? If it isn't . . . please ignore this message.

So we've arranged a perfect-sounding first date – a walk in Greenwich followed by drinks and then dinner at his. *Please* let him be a good cook.

But, until then, I'll have to make do with walking Jackie with my dad. She's theoretically *our dog* but really she's *his* dog. It's him who takes her for walks, and him who she sits next to on the sofa every evening. I haven't spent any one-on-one time with my dad since the wedding so now feels like as good an opportunity as any. As we walk the streets around their house (our house? Is your childhood home still your house when you no longer live in it?), I realize that once we got the light conversation out of the way when I arrived on Christmas Eve, we're not sure what to say to each other. Silence swirls around the sound of our feet crunching on the gritted pavements.

'I just wanted to say . . .' I venture after it becomes too much to bear. 'That I'm sorry about the wedding.'

Dad doesn't say anything for a few moments. Then he shrugs. 'It's nothing to do with me,' he says, finally.

I sigh. 'I know that, but surely you have some kind of *opinion* on it, or some kind of *feeling*,' I say, recalling his red-face fury in the pub when my family tracked me down. 'I know you were angry about it.'

He stops in his tracks. 'Angry?'

'Yeah,' I say.

'I wasn't angry,' he says, furrowing his brow. 'I was worried about you. You wouldn't have done what you did if you weren't desperate. Of course I was going to be worried about you.'

'Oh . . .' I suddenly feel all hot and guilty. 'But you never said anything to me.'

'When would I have the chance?' We start walking again as Jackie's clearly intent on sniffing around a lamp-post. 'You disappeared to London so I just assumed everything was fine and under control,' he says, shrugging.

'So you weren't angry with me for ruining the wedding?'

'I can't pretend it was what I *wanted* for you,' he says, tugging on the beanie hat that's covering his shiny bald head. 'But the wedding itself was the least of my worries.'

I swallow. 'I guess I thought you were angry for wasting everyone's time.'

He shakes his head. 'It just felt like you had slipped away a bit. Like you couldn't talk to anyone about it. And then we hardly heard from you for ages. But I didn't want to pry or push you too much.'

I nod. 'I'm sorry about not talking to you and Mum more. It was bad of me, I know that.'

'No harm done,' says Dad, smiling. 'As long as you're all right now.'

'I think I am,' I say, filled with the hopeful, nervous confidence of my impending date with Henry. It's like having him on the horizon has made everything feel brighter, even though it's scary because I so very much want it to be good. It's made me feel better, made me feel as if I must be at least vaguely attractive, at least a little bit worth dating. Made me feel that maybe throwing everything away in the summer was worth it. Meeting all these men is a bit of a wild ride, if I'm honest.

Like, no, it hasn't been great, but equally . . . it's not really how I thought it would be going. I thought I would be meeting loads of people I fancied and worrying about whether they fancied me or were going to reject me because of my body. That was what I was anxious about going in. But that hasn't really been the problem at all. In fact it's the opposite: I haven't been interested in any of them. I guess there's a lot riding on *this* date.

Jackie barks at a labradoodle across the road and Dad raises his hand in greeting at the owner, who waves back. For the rest of the walk, I try to make up for lost time by interrogating him about his work, the ongoing redecoration of his and Mum's bedroom, and his beloved Haywards Heath FC.

That evening, alone with Mum in the kitchen, I can't help feeling she's got something she wants to say, this little unsaid sentence buzzing around us as we wash up.

'Did you . . .' Mum ventures delicately as I'm drying, the tea towel feeling increasingly damp in my hands. 'Did you wish Alistair a merry Christmas?'

There it is.

'No, I didn't,' I say, a little impatiently. 'Should I have done?'

'Well, did he contact you?'

'No,' I shrug. 'I wasn't exactly expecting him to, since we've broken up and all.'

'I'm *aware* that you've broken up . . .' Mum says, sighing. I feel guilty for being so defensive with her. I'm sure she's been worried about me, too. 'I was just wondering if you're in contact, that's all.'

'Not really, no. I mean, I could text him any time I wanted, it's not like I don't have his number,' I say. 'But I just try not to think about him too much.'

'Oh?'

I realize I phrased that wrong. 'I don't mean that I'm suppressing an urge to talk to him, it's not like that,' I say, shaking my head. 'I just meant that I'm really trying to put all of that part of my life behind me. It was a big part.'

'It was,' Mum says, sadly. I think back to how, at the time, I was so wrapped up in my own almost violent urge to get away from the relationship, that life, that path, that I didn't think how strange it would be for my family. I'd asked them to buy into this narrative with me, this belief that Alistair and I were meant to be together forever. And then for me to turn around and say, *Oh no, actually, that was all wrong so please adjust your notes accordingly*, that was probably a bit strange for them too.

'Do you regret it at all?' Mum asks, gently.

I think for a moment. 'No. I don't regret it. But I do miss the certainty in some ways. The security. Even though the thing itself was wrong.'

'What are you guys talking about?' As if she had just been loitering outside the kitchen and waiting for an opportune moment to show herself, Melanie emerges from around the doorframe in her *I'm a cool mum* dungarees and striped T-shirt, the bottom of her dungarees tucked into her thick woolly bedsocks.

'Nothing,' I say. 'Just me and Alistair.'

'Oh,' says Melanie, like that's news to her. 'I still don't see what was wrong with him.' She opens the fridge and pulls the carton of orange juice out of the door.

I sigh. 'There was nothing wrong with him. There's nothing wrong with Matt either but I don't want to marry him,' I say, nodding in the direction of Matt, who's come to join us in the kitchen with Coco in his arms.

'Why do I feel like I've walked into the middle of *something*,' he says, narrowing his eyes and looking around at us before walking backwards out of the room, kissing Coco on the head and whispering, 'Come on, let's get out of here . . .'

'Well I'm glad to hear you don't want to steal my husband, but it wasn't really my point,' Melanie rolls her eyes and pours the orange juice into a glass.

'What was your point?' I say, wearily.

'My point was that after all this time I still don't really get the whole thing, I don't get why the prospect of your life with Alistair was so horrendous that you had to back out in such spectacular fashion. Why you had to hurt him like that.'

'Fine, you don't get it, whatever,' I say, wanting to cut off this conversation sooner rather than later. I could let it descend into full-on back-and-forth squabbling for the next half an hour but, in the words of Slade, *Iiiiiiit's Christmas!* So I'll nip it in the bud since Melanie clearly won't. I just wish she was on my team a little more. I wish she had wondered what it was like for me, dealing with the guilt of it all, the huge upheaval. 'It's not your life. You don't need to get it.'

'Fine,' she shrugs, like she never really cared in the first place, and pads back into the living room where Matt and Coco are watching some baby cartoon with my dad.

Me and Mum wash and dry in silence. The empty home, the sleeping alone, the cooking for one . . . that's been hard to get used to. The end of a long relationship is like trying to end lots of habits at once. It's not *necessarily* about regret, it's just habit. But I'm hoping the arrival of Henry is proof I made the right decision. Melanie's just being difficult, as is her way, as has *been* her way for the past twenty-eight years. It's what older sisters are there for: to know better.

That evening, after leftovers and while everyone else seems to be napping to *It's a Wonderful Life*, I find myself idly swiping. There really is no one around here that I think would feasibly go for me. Slim pickings. But there is a guy in my inbox who I've been messaging back and forth with but failed to meet up with yet, and something about knowing Henry is on the horizon means that the date would feel pleasantly low-stakes.

Hey, I write, infused with the spirit of optimism at knowing I'll be back in London tomorrow, and also maybe slightly infused with a few glasses of my mum's sherry, if you're around in the near future want to get a drink?

Sure, he writes back, and then I get a bit panicky and check his profile again to check he looks at least relatively normal. He does. Marcus, thirty-four, front-end web developer because, well, that's just the job that all the men on my apps seem to do these days. Sandy blond hair, a little bit taller than me, nice brown eyes. So far, so normal. In the absence of anything to do on my first night back in London after Christmas, I arrange to meet up with him at a pub on Kingsland Road in Dalston, which I know to be cosy and potentially romantic. Might be good to get in some first date practice before I see Henry. Can't hurt, anyway.

★   ★   ★

Date Number: 12

With: Marcus aka the Let-Down
Where: Molly Blooms, Dalston
When: Weird Christmas–New Year dead zone

When I get to the pub, there's no one there that strikes me as my date. I take a seat, trying to fight my natural inclination to believe that I'm being stood up. I am punctual to a fault and it's still bang on eight o'clock, so it would be a particularly unreasonable assumption at this point. I scroll through my Instagram feed, double-tapping on everyone's holiday scenes, a couple of *boy done good* engagement ring posts. Good luck to 'em. After five minutes I'm starting to feel a little nervous, taking another look around the pub to make sure my date hasn't slipped in while I was knee-deep in photos of people going for walks. But no.

A text comes through: There in 5. No apologies, nothing.

Is that a red flag? No, I'm being too harsh. Five minutes . . . it's within the window of acceptability . . . I'll let him off. But when the clock strikes 8:11 – making this man over ten minutes late – my good bitch, you have earned yourself Strike One.

But then he arrives with a 'Hey, Serena? Sorry I'm late.' He has a sexy dishevelled thing going on and the apology seems genuine so I decide to retract my strike. Mostly because of the sexy dishevelled thing. He's kind of cute, actually. He orders a sparkling water. An unusual choice, but I respect anyone's right to not drink.

'Oh, that's cool,' I say. 'Do you not drink at all?'

'I wish!' he says, rolling his eyes.

128

'Oh,' I say, not really sure what's going on.

'I'm not going to lie. I have a stinking hangover. I have been a wreck all day. I am just so . . . tired. Just tired. You know when you just want to sack it off for the day and stay in bed?'

Strike One (again! What can I say, I'm a soft touch)! No date wants to hear you're tired and that you'd rather be in bed – I'm here for the romance, the seduction, a night to remember. Don't *tell* me you're turning up, essentially, against your will. Either come or don't come!

'So you had a heavy one last night?' I say, trying to entice some conversation out of him.

He shakes his head and laughs to himself, like it's a private joke. 'You can say that again. Oh my God, I am wrecked. But you look nice. Tell me about yourself.'

I want a conversation – repartee – I'm not going to give him a monologue. No more monologues!

I sigh. 'What do you want to know?'

'Oh I don't know . . . what's your favourite colour?' Strike Two. 'Sorry, I'm just really tired. It was my best mate's birthday last night and he took us to a gin distillery. I mean, sounds refined, doesn't it! But really, what the hell, gin is fucking crazy. And we're drinking it straight. It was so cool trying the different herbs but I swear I will never *touch* the stuff again as long as I live.' He shakes his head, ruefully, then winces at the motion.

And then he bolts from the table, runs to the bathroom and, as the doors swing in his wake, I can already hear the inimitable sounds of vomiting.

11

I get to see Nicole today! Thank God. It's only been a week since we were last in the office but it's honestly felt like a lifetime. We strategically volunteered to go into work on the same day over the holidays so we could hang out and chat.

I get to the office at 9 a.m. like usual but Nicole doesn't turn up until 9:30 and I feel silly for forgetting that it's the twenty-ninth of December and there's literally no one around to notice what time we arrive.

'I missed you, my dude!' She draws me into a tight hug. She smells of a new perfume, maybe a Christmas present. Otherwise it's that same old newfound familiarity.

'I missed you too!'

'Fucking cute dress!' she says, gesturing that she wants me to spin around.

I comply. 'I made it!'

'You're literally magic. Here I am spunking my money on clothes and you just whip them up out of nowhere.'

'It's not that hard,' I say, blushing.

'Don't put yourself down!' she urges. 'It's a fucking cool skill. Fact.'

'I guess so . . .'

'How was Christmas?'

'Meh. It was fine. Nice enough. Tried to navigate family conversations about the extent to which I've thrown my life away,' I shrug. 'Glad I only committed to being at home for a few days, not sure if I could do much longer without going on a murder spree. I came back to the flat because I had a date—'

'With Henry?! Why didn't you text me?!'

'No, not with Henry! That's tomorrow . . .'

'Oh! Okay, good, because if you hadn't texted me every detail I was going to scream my head off.'

'I appreciate the enthusiasm.'

'So who was the date?!' she asks.

'Ugh, just this guy from Tinder . . . I don't know, it was a moment of weakness. And boredom. And optimism.'

'Didn't go so well?'

'No, it was shit. I thought he looked, you know, decent enough from his profile but he was just hungover and pathetic the whole time. It felt so . . .' I sigh, '*lazy*?'

'Ugh, babe. You deserve better.'

'My thoughts exactly. If that's what my date with Henry is like I'll throw myself into the Thames.'

'It won't be. You know you have chemistry! That part is tried and tested!'

'True,' I say, hoping she's right and finally resigning myself to do some work.

We 'work' the morning away, which for me consists of interspersing doing the copy for the sale reminder emails with watching YouTube beauty tutorials. *What?* I'm determined to master the cat-eye liquid liner in time for my date with Henry. Nicole sends some emails to our freelance graphic designer ('So fit I make a note in my diary to wear something boob-y for our Zoom meetings,' according to Nicole) about next season's collections and then listlessly spins around on her swivel chair on her phone, then whistles a very tuneful rendition of the operatic number 'O Mio Babbino Caro' as she makes us coffees, before returning to some more emails.

'Fuck!' Nicole yells out of nowhere.

'What?!' I ask her, possessed with a panic that something is seriously wrong.

'I just found out Mary I and Mary Queen of Scots are different people! Fuck! Did you know this?' She looks at me, absolutely incredulous. 'Were you in on it?'

'I . . .' I say, frowning, a little confused. 'Yeah, I think I did know that. But I don't know how I knew . . .'

'Huh, I feel like this has been deliberately kept from me for twenty-eight years.'

'Should I take this to mean you're not working *particularly* hard this morning?'

She looks at the clock. 'Afternoon now. Lunch?'

'You know what's *so* fucked,' I say to Nicole as we eat together in the cosy little breakout area.

'Uhhh . . . London property prices?' Nicole ventures absent-mindedly, chasing a perfectly spherical tomato around her plate with her fork, failing to stab it at every attempt.

I look up from my phone where I've been swiping and clicking and profile-reading even though I know I'm only doing it as some kind of cosmic pretence so I don't *feel* like I'm putting all my eggs in the Henry basket.

'Yes, that. But also men's obsession with *youth*,' I say, rolling my eyes.

'Tale as old as time, my friend,' she says.

'I'm looking at these men on these apps and it's like . . . so transparent? It's not even an age gap thing, I honestly don't care about that, it's like . . . guys our age thinking they should go out with eighteen-year-olds. Men who are thirty-five and they've set their age preferences as eighteen to thirty.'

'Like an all-inclusive clubbing holiday.'

'Not a club I want to be in, to be quite honest with you. Like, truly, what do they have in common with someone who's eighteen that they don't have with someone who's thirty-one?'

'Exactly. I just don't get what these men would see in these girls *other* than the fact they're eighteen, you know? Like, what level of chat are they giving?'

'Are they in it for the chat . . .?'

'Anyway, so many of these guys have their *upper* age cut-off as twenty-nine! Like, literally once you're thirty you're just dead to them.'

'It's fucked.'

'Yeah, like I benefit from it *for now* but not for much longer! Thirty's on the horizon and then what? I might as well be dead.'

'You're so dramatic! I thought you were smart,' Nicole says, although I don't know what I've ever done to give her that impression.

I sigh. 'I wonder what Henry's dating profile would look like,' I say, sighing.

'We're not thinking about Henry, we're diversifying away from Henry,' says Nicole.

134

She's right.

'But I'm still curious. Like, would I have picked him out if I'd seen his profile online? Or was it really just a chemistry thing?'

'I think chemistry is real but I also think that you're going to have chemistry with men you meet online. It's not like it's one or the other, you know?'

'Ugh, I hope so.'

We're quiet for a second, eating our lunch in peace. 'It's so nice like this, isn't it?!' Nicole says, the quiet finally resonating with her. 'Don't you wish it was like this all the time?'

'I guess,' I say, furrowing my brow. 'The office is not so bad though, right?'

'On the whole, no,' she says, slowly. 'I'm just getting a bit . . .'

'What?' I say. 'You're not thinking of leaving, are you?!'

That would be, no exaggeration, the *worst* thing that could happen to me right now. What's the point of work without Nicole?! None! There is no point! Apart from money, but still.

'No . . . it's not that,' she says, shaking her head rapidly, like she's trying to dislodge the doubts. 'It's nothing.'

Part of me doesn't want to press her – we talk enough that if she *did* want to talk to me about it she would. But I feel protective of her.

'It doesn't sound like nothing . . .' I say.

She looks at me for a second, like she's weighing up whether to commit to the conversation or not. 'Is Duncan ever weird with you?' Nicole says finally.

'Duncan? Duncan who sits *there*?' I say, gesturing to his desk, as if there was another Duncan who sat somewhere else.

'Yeah.'

'No, not really. Why?' I ask, even though I can very much see where this is going.

'Well . . . I sometimes feel like he's sort of . . . *lying in wait*. Do you know what I mean?'

I don't really know what she means, but I sense it's not good. 'Lying in what for what?' I ask.

She shrugs, like she regrets bringing it up. 'I don't know. It's just a vibe I get, like he's watching me in a way that's not normal.'

'Like he has a crush on you?' I venture, stupidly, regretting it the second it comes out of my mouth. If it was just a silly crush thing she wouldn't be looking so serious. And remembering how he tried to discourage me from being friends with her. With hindsight, that was weird. And I feel guilty for even thinking about taking it seriously.

She smiles sadly. 'Maybe,' she says. 'Anyway, let's do a couple of hours of work before we bounce outta here!' She jumps to her feet and I drag myself up after her, bitterly regretting being flippant. The last thing I want is for Nicole to think that I'm trying to trivialize her worries.

'I'll keep an eye on Duncan,' I say. 'I promise.'

'Thanks, dude,' she says, pulling my fuzzy ponytail like it's a rope on the end of a church bell.

True to our word, we work until four o'clock before switching off the lights, setting the security alarm and locking the door.

As we're descending the stairs back down to the exit, Nicole says, 'You know, this dress is really, *really* nice. Do you ever . . . or would you ever make stuff for other people?'

'Oh!' I say, taken aback. 'I mean . . . I never have before, but

136

I guess I could, as long as they knew I'm literally just little old me at my sewing machine and not a pro?'

'Looks pretty pro to me,' Nicole says, shrugging as she holds the door open for me. 'Well, if you would consider it there's a ton of shit I want to wear that no fucker is making in my size right now. I don't know if, like, a pattern exists for the kind of stuff I want or if you can . . . I don't know, freestyle it or something. Bear in mind I don't know the first thing about sewing. All I know is that I love clothes and I'm a fat bitch and often those two things are incompatible.'

I laugh, delighted as always by Nicole's way with words. 'Let me think about it! Obviously I want to assist in your quest to be the most stylish fat bitch in London, but I hate the idea of overpromising and underdelivering.'

'I'll make it worth your while!' she says in a sing-song voice.

'No way, I'm not taking your money!' I'm actually mortified at the thought of someone paying me for making them clothes. I'm really *not* good enough for that.

'It's work,' she says, rolling her eyes. 'You should get paid for work.'

'Like I said, let me think about it?'

'Sure! Anyway, have fun on your date and you *must* let me know how it goes!'

I can't help grinning pathetically. 'I will!'

I put my headphones in and FaceTime Lola on the bus home. It feels like it's been a long time since she left and she's not back any time soon.

'Serena!' she yells joyously as she walks down a snowy street, the sky behind her a gunmetal grey. I know how time zones work, I'm not *completely* stupid, but it still surprises me that she isn't surrounded by the same darkness outside my bus window.

'How are you?! How was Christmas?' I ask. It's always a joy to see her face, which is objectively a work of art.

'It was fine! I spent it with some colleagues in their apartment on the Upper West Side. It at least *felt* like Christmas, you know? It wasn't all weird and discombobulating like Thanksgiving where I didn't really know what was going on or whether I was meant to be at work, you know?'

'I'm glad! What have you been up to today?'

'I just went to see some Kara Walker papercuts at the Brooklyn Museum,' she says, smiling. I know what that smile means.

'I assume you weren't alone?'

'You assume correct! What can I say, it's not hard to meet girls in this town . . .' she shrugs. 'How about you? Any excitement? Any Christmas drama for me?'

'Nah,' I say, shaking my head. 'But I have a hot date tomorrow!'

'Is it?!' she says, excitedly.

'Yep! I don't want to say too much but,' I can't help blushing and breaking out into a grin. 'You'll probably get to meet him soon.'

'So it's serious?!'

'Look, it's very, very early days, like not even an early day but maybe the dawn *before* the early days . . . but I think maybe it could be?'

'Wow! Well, I wish you luck! Hey, I meant to tell you, I've sorted my flights home. Fourth of March.'

'Great,' I say, 'so I'll plan the wild party for . . . March third?'

'Do what you want. It's your home, too!'

It's not, but I appreciate the sentiment. We chat until the bus pulls into my stop and we say our goodbyes as I hop off. So that's it, a couple more months until Lola's back. Will I have a confirmed new boyfriend by then? Can I abandon my weekly dates with the useless men of London? No more gazing at a guy across the top of a pint, wondering how he seems so different to his profile, wondering where that easy back and forth of messaging disappeared to, wondering why it seems so hard to just *meet someone I click with*. I guess I'll find out tomorrow. And part of me can't help but think this is going to be the start of something. Something amazing

12

The day arrives. December thirtieth. My date with Henry is finally really happening! Am I excited? Yes. Am I cautious? Also yes. Am I desperate for it to be better than that *depressing* drink I had with Marcus the other day? Yes, yes, a million times *yes*.

Hyped???? Nicole texts bright and early. Of course she's remembered it's today.

Hyped!

Run me through your romantique plans

Meeting him at Cutty Sark, going for a stroll by the river and then for a pint in a pub

Leading to possibly . . . . more???

Maybe 😈

DEFINITELY like why the fuck else are you going down there

Ugh I hope so!

You deserve it bb

What should I wear I'm so stressed I literally can't think what to wear. Last time he saw me in, like, sexy wedding clothes but the vibe is like chill cosy casual so I'm scared he's gonna be like . . . Wot

When in doubt just go for one of those Breton tops you always wear, dark jeans, lil boots and a nice coat. That cobalt blue one? Looks nice with your hair 👧

I feel instantly reassured. It's amazing how she just does that.

Unless you have a leopard-print one? Idk I always feel like animal print is a good way to get the MEASURE of a man, since they're so fucking allergic to it.

I don't but . . .

BUT YOU COULD MAKE ONE BECAUSE YOU ARE A GENIUS?

I look at the clock. It's still early. I literally could. I've got that stash of leopard-print faux-fur that I picked up weeks ago. I'm already Googling for an easy coat pattern.

I mean, I wasn't going to put it like that but . . . yes

You're the best

I am

What are you up to today?

Aside from sending good vibes into the universe for your date, I am taking my sister's kids to see some nonsense at the cinema AS IF I haven't done enough Auntie Nic shit over Christmas! I swear I spent more on their toys than I spent on makeup for myself in the past year.

142

God, I dread to think what horrors await me when Coco is old enough to know what toys are.

I sacrifice the bath I was going to take in favour of making this coat. Just an open, shawl collar, no time for buttons, but it works. Anyway, I feel like I've been taking a lot of baths while Lola has been away because I would otherwise feel guilty about occupying the one bathroom in the flat. Her return at the beginning of March is getting ever closer, and I'm looking forward to it. Even if I haven't taken full advantage of her absence by bringing lots of men home. I suppose I'd better spend all of January in the bath to fully make the most of it, or start concocting long, elaborate meals that necessitate dominating the kitchen and making a lot of mess, you know, bad flatmate stuff, just to get it out of my system.

After a few hours of dedicated sewing, I have produced a coat and, checking it out in the mirror, can't help but think how nice it would be to be able to introduce Henry to Lola as my boyfriend.

Would she think it's too soon? Is it too soon? It's only been a few months since Alistair . . . and I *was* with him for ten years . . . but that's all theoretical. Arbitrary.

I shave my legs, wondering if it's presumptuous, whether by shaving my legs I'm tempting fate – the fate of not having sex with Henry, aka the thought that has sustained me over the Christmas holidays. As I rake the razor over my foamy legs, I remember how taboo it felt, the idea that I could be unhappy with Alistair. It wasn't an acute unhappiness, something I could explain easily. It was just a *lack of happiness*. A lack of actively feeling happy.

If I really force myself to think about it, I was honestly too ashamed to talk about my unhappiness. I didn't want to be seen as disloyal. I know how it is – one of your friends tells you about something awful their boyfriend has said or done and you never forget it. Your mate tells you how boring her sex life is with her partner and then every time you see them you think, BORING. Well, that's why I never talked about Alistair to anyone. That's why it was such a shock to them. I guess, too, that I just didn't want to have the conversation with myself, either. If I didn't let myself go there, it didn't have to be true.

Once I've dried my hair, got dressed to precisely Nicole's specifications and done my makeup (natural but definitely there), I make the epic quest from North to South London, first taking the Overground then changing to take the mysterious, legendary Docklands Light Railway. Having previously had no reason to explore this mode of transport, it has developed near-mythical status in my mind, and it turns out to be a driverless monorail that swoops through Canary Wharf, glass towers looming over you, and through slightly grey residential areas. My nerves are increasing and increasing, as the train stop-starts, stop-starts at a multitude of deserted office stations. I feel all jittery when we finally pull into Cutty Sark station. I make my way out onto the street and follow the signs for the actual *Cutty Sark*.

God, it's kind of sweet around here – a huge, looming pirate ship and all the twinkling lights still up from Christmas. The sky is a clear, bright blue like it knows today is an important day for me and wants to dress accordingly. It's almost too perfect. It strikes me that the crisp, bright day and the beautiful surroundings are almost too much, too good – that it's all setting me up for a fall. If I'd slipped on ice on my way to the station or messed up stitching the lining on my coat or my DLR had been delayed, then maybe I wouldn't be so nervous. It's all a bit too good to be true. It's three o'clock and the suggestion of darkness is forming around the edges. I wander around the outside of the boat, trying not to let my nerves get the better of me but knowing that today is what two weeks of nerves and excitement and anticipation have been building up to.

'Hey!' I hear a voice from a nearby bench. I turn around and there, in a thick wool coat and surprisingly chic leather boots, is Henry.

'Oh, hey,' I say, like I'm surprised to see him there, like I haven't been waiting for this moment since we first met.

He stands up, and he's shorter than I remember. I mean, I'm pretty tall. And also I don't particularly care. And maybe it's all the defensively height-obsessed dudes of Tinder, but I actually find it a bit hot.

We hug, and I can't help smiling, even though my nerves keep bubbling up under the surface. He's smiling too.

'It's nice to see you,' he says in such a way that sounds like he really means it. His beard is looking a little less well manicured than it was at the wedding and it's pretty hot.

'It's nice to see you too,' I say. It feels like we already know each other in some sort of way, even though we've only met once before and only for the length of a meal.

'I love this coat!' he says, surveying me with great delight.

'Thanks,' I say. 'I made it, actually.'

'As in you . . . made this coat?'

'Yeah!'

'Wow,' he says, looking like it's the most impressive thing he's ever heard.

'I made that dress I was wearing at the wedding, too,' I say, relishing the opportunity to remind him of our meeting.

'Well *that* was . . . stunning,' he says, looking at me out of the corner of his eye to gauge my reaction.

I smile, as modestly as I can manage. 'Thanks. Just one of my many talents.'

'So . . . did anything dramatic happen at the wedding after I left?'

'Oh, only dancing on tables, a screaming row, infidelity . . .'

'I'll take that as a no, then.'

'You would be correct to do that.' We lean on a railing and look down to the Thames. The tide is up. 'I've never been here before.'

'I know,' he says, 'that's why I thought you should come.'

'I thought it was so you could spend more time with me,' I say, turning to look at him.

'Damn, you found me out!'

'I'm pretty perceptive like that. So, how was your Christmas?'

He breathes in, like he's weighing up what answer to give. 'Challenging?' he says, screwing up his nose a little. 'But it often is.'

'Oh yeah?'

'My parents are divorced and there's always some sort of . . . friction about who goes where on what day, and then it's all . . . having to navigate what each of them are saying about the other. I can't be seen to take one side more than the other. Petty stuff, but oddly time-consuming.'

'Is this a new thing?'

'Ha! No, absolutely not – they've been doing this for about twelve years now. They separated just after I went off to university so you can imagine what a weird year *that* was for me. Since then it's just been this sort of exhausting marathon of separation, moving out, divorce and then you think you've got to the end of it and then you find it's just going to be *there* forever. And never more so than Christmas.'

'Shit, that sucks, I'm sorry,' I say.

'God, I didn't mean to get so dark and heavy so soon! Tell me about yours?'

'My parents are decidedly un-divorced and decidedly un-dramatic. My sister is a bit annoying, but her husband and my niece are nice to have around. Maybe one year I'll suggest that she doesn't get invited so I can just hang out with Matt and Coco instead.'

'Coco is a sweet name for a baby,' says Henry.

'It is! Do you have any nieces and nephews?' I ask as we stroll slowly down the path that runs alongside the river.

'I do – my brother James and his wife have twins, which is *a lot* and contributed to the overall feeling of Christmas chaos.'

'Just having one kid is like . . . a headache. Two sounds like a nightmare.'

'They're cute enough but my *God* it never ends. Still, it's kind of nice to feel like there's a point to Christmas now. It's about making it fun for them, since it's basically impossible to make it fun for us.'

'That's one way of looking at it,' I say. We turn up a side street and then into an open gate, leading on to some huge, beautiful Georgian buildings. 'Pretty nice around here.'

'You ain't seen nothing yet,' Henry says, with a smile so sincere I want to throw my arms around him and kiss him. But I don't. He leads me along the path that divides the group of buildings on either side, and into one on the right, up a short flight of stone steps into an entrance flanked by the most enormous columns.

'Wow . . .' I say, taking it in. There isn't really anything more I *can* say. Wow just about covers it.

'Right?!' he says, delighted in turn by my delight.

'This is . . . stunning,' I say. The walls feel like they're a mile high, the huge windows arching up into the air. But it's the ceiling that's the main event. Absolutely gargantuan in size and completely covered in beautiful, richly detailed paintings.

'I mean . . . obviously it's all some celebration of British naval power which is always a bit . . .' he mimes vomiting. 'But . . . it's still a pretty compelling sight, isn't it?' He looks up, craning his neck. 'The British Sistine Chapel, I guess.'

'The real Sistine Chapel was too stressful for me, this one's much nicer,' I say, walking a little ahead of him. The huge, cavernous room is surprisingly empty for such an amazing place, only a few people dotted around.

'I've never actually been,' he says.

'The Vatican is weird, I went with my ex when we were in Rome on holiday,' I say before instantly regretting bringing up Alistair, or indeed any ex at all. It's not like I want Henry to think I'm a virgin, or never been kissed, but still, I can't help but feeling that talking about an ex is perceived as some sort of signal you're not really over them.

But Henry doesn't seem too bothered. 'I don't even really like Baroque paintings. So what I'm saying is I don't care for the context *or* the style, but I still find myself sneaking in just to see it because it's here and that feels sort of magic.'

'It does feel magic,' I say, with a sigh. Pure magic. After all the upheaval, the shaking up of my life, the dates, the men. Now, magic. Outside the huge windows the light is fading. I just want to be hanging out with Henry forever, seeing magic things and looking at his sweetly handsome face, the way he walks with his hands in his pockets, that deep red hair. We walk around the Painted Hall in silence, me taking in all the details for the first time, him still overjoyed by it for the fifth, tenth, fiftieth, hundredth time. I stop and look down at a plaque on the floor.

'Nelson, like the column,' I say, reading a plaque inlaid into the floor that states this was where his coffin lay in state.

'The very same,' Henry says, standing on the other side of the plaque. 'Hey,' he reaches out and squeezes my hand, an action that catches me completely off-guard. 'Want to get a drink?'

I look at him with such surprise at having been touched that at first his face falls. 'Do I ever!' I say, enthusiastically. I kind of want to kick myself at having been taken aback by him touching my hand, like I gave him the impression that was unwanted. I was just surprised, that's all.

We walk out of the hall and back down to the river. As we walk, we talk about our respective works, which mostly involves me gushing about how great Nicole is, and he tells me about the volunteer office admin he does for a migrants' rights organ-ization. I feel like I understand a little better now what he meant at the wedding when he said he wanted to de-centre his day job in his life.

'Oh . . .' I say, as we approach the Thames again, glistening in the fading evening light. 'I feel like that's a really cool thing to do.'

'I think people like the *idea* of saving the world but a lot of what goes into trying to . . . well, *save the world* so to speak is just a lot of quite unglamorous work. Email lists and admin and endless meetings with action points,' he says, smiling. 'And often alongside people you don't get on with as people, but you share this common goal so you just put that first.'

'I feel like maybe I have room in my life for something useful,' I say, thinking about how fundamentally frivolously I spend my time.

'Maybe you do,' he says, like it's not his place to tell me either way.

He pushes open the door to the pub and it's dark and cosy – the exact opposite of the Painted Hall we've just come from: all low beams and a sensation of everything being slightly on top of itself.

'What can I get you?' I ask him as we find an unoccupied table in a cosy corner.

'Oh, um, how about an IPA?' he says, slipping his coat off.

'Okay, great,' I say, heading for the bar. As the barman pours two pints, I can't help but feel like there was something more *direct*, more flirty about him at the wedding. Not that I really have anything to complain about right now – I'm really enjoying spending time with him.

'Cheers,' he says, when I hand him his pint. We knock our glasses together and I take a sip, trying not to stare at him too much. I'm just a little crazy about his face. His glasses, his wide mouth with his straight teeth, the kind, soft eyes.

'This feels more like the kind of date I'm used to,' I say, taking a sip. 'I don't usually get to see a huge ship and a painted Baroque hall.'

He smiles. 'Well, I'm glad you're enjoying your inaugural visit to these parts. Should I take that to mean you go on a lot of dates?' he asks, without any particular inflection.

'Not really a lot,' I say, quickly. He doesn't *need* to know about my weekly commitment. 'But some. You?'

Now he looks uncomfortable. Instead of answering he just drinks his pint and shakes his head. He doesn't add anything. Which, I must admit, makes me feel weird. I liked it when he was all straightforward!

'Okay,' I say, neutrally, but painfully aware that there's clearly *something* going on there, but I don't need to dig any deeper, don't need to disrupt the date and ask too many questions. I don't need to know.

'So,' he says, the intensity lifting a little. 'Have you seen Rachel and Luke since the wedding?'

'No, they're on honeymoon, aren't they?' I say. 'I've seen some fancy Mexican content from them recently.'

'Oh, maybe you're right . . . I don't have Instagram, so I kinda miss a lot of stuff . . .' he says.

'That's what it is!' I burst out. 'I—' I say, before stopping myself, realizing how weird it's going to make me sound.

'What?' Henry frowns at me curiously.

'I . . . tried to find you,' I say, covering my face with my hands and peeking out from behind my fingers to check his reaction. When I see he's smiling, delighted, I say, 'I went through all of Luke's followers to see if any of them were . . .'

'Hot gingers?' His blue eyes are dancing in amusement.

151

'Exactly. And some of them were! But none of them were *you*,' I say, which comes out a little bit more sentimental than I had hoped for.

'Well, apologies, I should have told you when we first met that I was an Insta-free zone and saved you the trouble. I'm not, like, *anti* social media, I just feel like I don't really have anything to add.'

'And you're not wildly nosy about the lives of people you meet at weddings?' I say, relaxing now I know he doesn't think I'm a creep.

'Well,' he says, taking a sip of beer. 'I wouldn't say *that*.'

The look in his eye tells me I have absolutely nothing to worry about. It tells me that maybe running out on my wedding was the right thing to do because, within a matter of months, the universe has managed to serve me, *whisper it*, maybe, just maybe, The One.

Once we finish our drinks, instead of staying for another, he says we should be getting back to his so he can make dinner. It's a ten-minute walk from the pub, away from the river and the other side of the main road that runs parallel to it.

We walk up a street of pretty red-brick houses and stop at one. I'm wondering if Henry's secretly rich, when he opens the door and I see the ground floor has a separate internal door and a staircase. We go up the staircase to his flat, which only occupies the first floor. I notice a few pairs of shoes on the landing – muddy, man-size trainers and . . . a much smaller pair. Women's shoes.

'Oh, uh, I should probably say . . .' he says, turning the key and looking over his shoulder at me.

'Going somewhere?' I ask, thinking it's weird he didn't

mention the fact he was moving house. The place is strewn with brown cardboard boxes, piles of books and *stuff* everywhere.

'Uh, no, not me . . .' he says, suddenly inarticulate, standing to one side and gesturing for me to come in. 'My, uh, my ex . . . Melissa . . . is actually in the process of moving out. She's getting there but . . . the stuff remains.'

I take a deep breath. 'I see.'

'I know . . . it's not an ideal situation . . . but,' he says, throwing his hands up in defeat. 'It's sort of taking a while to extricate ourselves from each other. That's where I had to dash off to after the wedding, a Christmas party at her brother's. I wanted to stay and talk more to you, but I knew I had to go. The thing is . . . I really like you, so . . .' He turns back to me.

No, it's not an ideal situation, the spectre of this woman looming over us. And I *really* don't love the idea of him still hanging out with her family. That's kind of . . . a lot, isn't it? But I like him. I really like him. We're standing face to face in his living room, surrounded by this failed relationship. And it doesn't change how much I want him. So, still in our coats and scarves, standing there, staring at each other, the weight of our past lives hanging in the air, I decide to stop waiting for something to happen. I make it happen. I lean forward and I kiss him. At first I expect him to pull away, to say he's making a mistake, to say he can't or he doesn't want to, but . . . he doesn't. He pulls me closer, his gloved hand through my curls, holding the back of my head. The attraction I feel towards him is so unlike anything I've ever experienced before. It feels *real*.

'Well . . .' I say, unable to contain a grin as we pull apart.

'Now that we've got that out of the way . . . I always find

the first one is the most difficult and from there everything just . . . you know, flows,' he says, raising his eyebrows.

He kisses me again, and if we don't have sex tonight I think I will surely die.

We finally take off our coats and he heads into the kitchen. 'How can I help?' I ask.

'You can't,' he says. 'Drag one of the dining chairs in here and keep me company.'

'You're the boss,' I say, duly bringing in a chair and sitting down.

'Time for a little romance, I think . . .' he says, heading into the living room and returning with a laptop, which he balances on top of the toaster, opens Spotify and clicks 'play' on a playlist. The opening bars of Ella Fitzgerald singing 'Bewitched, Bothered and Bewildered' fill the kitchen.

'You like romance?' I ask, smiling.

'I do,' he says, rummaging around in the fridge before shutting the door and turning to me. He holds out a hand. I look at it for a second, then take it, and he pulls me up. He slips his arms around my waist and I rest mine on his shoulders. And there in his kitchen we dance together, occasionally looking each other in the eye and smiling, giggling, kissing. I don't want it to end, which is good because it turns out the song is *extremely* long. But it doesn't matter, we just stick with it. My heart feels so full, like it could spill over. I don't think I could ask for anything better than Henry.

When the song's over, we kiss one more time then he sets about seasoning two salmon fillets before searing them. He pours me a glass of white wine.

'This shouldn't take too long,' he says, sautéing some spinach.

'Are you sure I can't do anything?' I don't *want* to do anything but I fear it would feel rude to just sit here.

'I'm sure,' he says, looking up from the spinach with an expression of pure delight. 'I'm just . . . happy you're here.' He looks back down at the pan.

I study him across the kitchen. I could get used to this. I really could. 'I'm happy I'm here, too.'

'It feels like a nice little twist of fate that we ended up sitting next to each other at the wedding,' he says, which makes my insides melt until I remember that it wasn't fate at all.

'Actually, I did that,' I say, smiling.

'You did?'

'Yeah, I switched the cards to get away from someone who had got on my nerves.' I shrug nonchalantly.

'So you're more powerful than fate,' he says, 'I like it!'

'Phew,' I say, wiping my brow theatrically.

He laughs and starts mixing a sauce for the salmon, swirling it around in another pan. He seems completely at ease. Completely in control of everything. 'Not at all. I don't know if I believe in fate. But I do believe in you, so . . .'

'Well, I'm glad,' I say, taking a sip of my wine and blushing. It's all . . . going rather well.

He plates up and I carry the dining chair back into the living room so we can eat, and something about that shift, back to the room with the boxes, brings me back down to earth. I have this feeling, as we're sitting there, that his ex could walk in the door at any moment. But she doesn't. I wonder where she is, where she's staying. I can't take all of that on, I just have to listen to what he's saying to me. Everything is feeling so good. As the Magic 8 Ball I had as a kid says . . . *All signs point to yes.*

'This is delicious,' I say, 'thank you so much.'

'It's nothing, just a quick little something,' he says, a glint in his eye. 'Wait until I'm really trying to impress you.'

'Oh, is that how it is?' I say, faux-incredulously. 'You don't want to impress me right now? First date's just . . . low-stakes shit to you?'

'No!' Henry protests. 'I just figured you would rather spend more time hanging out than watching me cook . . .'

'I'm joking. It's been perfect. But I can't wait for this gastronomic extravaganza that's on my horizon.'

I can't take my eyes off him as we eat, stealing little glances. It takes a few minutes for me to realize he's doing the same thing for me.

'Busted!' he says. 'I was just checking you out.'

'Did you like what you see?' I ask.

'You know I did,' he says, standing up and collecting my plate. I follow him into the kitchen with our glasses. He puts the plates in the sink, and I reach over to do the same with the glasses. I set them down, and feel his hand around my waist. We're making out so intensely it's almost furious, me pushed against the sink, my arms around his neck.

'Oh my God,' I moan. I can feel how hard he is, pushing against my leg.

'I really want to fuck you right here but . . .' he pants, looking at me intensely and for a horrible moment I think he's going to say he wants me to leave. 'I think the first time should be in a bed, don't you?'

13

And, indeed, the first time was in a bed. As was the second time. And the third . . . The fourth time was on the sofa. Next time . . . maybe in the kitchen? And it's not just about the newness, the not-Alistairness, not-ten-year-relationship-sexness of it. It's true, by the end of me and Alistair, I would sometimes realize I was thinking about a hem of a dress I hadn't got round to finishing, or a work email I had forgotten to reply to, before snapping back to the present moment, guilty and frustrated. But with Henry, there's no room in my brain for it to wander! Nowhere to go! Every fibre of my being is laser-focused on the pure pleasure of being *there*. With him.

It's the last day of the year. I can't believe *all of this* has happened in the past year. This time last year I was still with Alistair, still going to get married in the summer. Now look. There's no doubt in my mind that Henry and I have something special. I just can't get enough of him. And I can't believe I'll be sailing into a new year with Henry in my life.

He's sleeping next to me in the mid-morning light (what can I say, we had a late night . . .) as a text illuminates my screen. It is, of course, from Nicole.

HOW WAS THE DATE

ONGOING

OMG for real? You're still there?

Yep honestly I can't believe it, it's unreal.

FUCK this is so gooooood! I'm obsessed with this!

Me too! It just feels so . . . normal? Like it's just meant to be? No stress or drama?

Does he have a nice 🌶

Firstly, how dare you . . . Secondly . . . yes

Does he have ginger pubes?

Again I say: Firstly how dare you secondly yes looooool

Gahhhh mate I'm so happy for you! Are you going to stay in his warm embrace or do you have plans with someone else tonight OR do you want to come to mine for some drinks later? I fucking hate new year's, so stressful and bullshit. But also I don't want to be on my own!!! Don't worry if you have plans!! I won't cry (much)

That sounds great! Lmk your address and what time etc and I'll bring some 🍷

And all the chat about last night, please

Deal deal deal

I guess I was so fixated on my date with Henry that I hadn't actually thought through the fact that New Year's Eve was literally upon us. Thank God for Nicole swooping in and giving me something to do with my evening. I wonder what Henry's up to tonight. The thought of being apart from him tugs at my stomach a little. But I guess I'm going to have to get used to it. I look around the neat bedroom. My eyes keep getting drawn to the wardrobe. I keep looking at it, wondering about the clothes inside it, wondering about the woman who wears the clothes inside it. I have to fight a compulsion to sneak out of bed, creep over to the wardrobe, slowly, slowly pull open the door and check the labels. I don't know why I care. I don't know why it matters whether she's fat or thin. I don't know what I hope to learn from it. All I know is that I believe I will learn *something*.

Deep in thought, I don't even notice Henry's opened his eyes at first. When I roll over to force myself to stop looking at the wardrobe, I see he's awake.

'Hey,' I say, laying a hand on the soft reddish fuzz on his pale, broad chest.

'Hey,' he says, smiling and sitting up. It's funny to see him without his glasses. It makes him seem vulnerable somehow. He reaches for them on his bedside table.

'You okay?' I ask, feeling, maybe, some kind of atmospheric shift.

'Yeah!' he says, slightly too breezily. 'It's just . . .'

'What?' I feel my heart speed up a little. I don't like this.

'No, nothing, it's just strange to see you here, that's all.'

'In a good way?' I suggest, very emphatically, waiting for him to bail us out.

'Yeah, of course,' he says, putting some boxers on and jumping out of bed. 'I'm going to make coffee, do you want one?'

'Um, sure. Just milk, please, no sugar,' I say.

Fuck. What's up? Maybe nothing's up. He seems okay now, doesn't he? Just a momentary weirdness, now we're back to normal. Coffee is normal! And when he returns with the steaming cups, it *is* normal again. I rest my head against the padded headboard and look at him with such pure, serene joy.

'I make really good pancakes,' he says, blowing on his cup.

'Oh, how interesting,' I say, archly. 'I don't suppose there's a way I could test that claim?'

'I suppose there might be,' he says, before taking a mouthful of coffee. He reaches a hand out and touches the little pool of blonde curls between us from where my long hair hits the bed. 'There's a line about this in a Leonard Cohen song – *your hair upon the pillow like a sleepy golden storm.*'

'"Hey, That's No Way to Say Goodbye",' I say. 'That's my favourite of his, I think.'

He puts down his coffee cup, reaches over and takes mine out of my hands, sets it down on the bedside table on my side of the bed and kisses me. And as soon as he does, I know, I just know that this is the kind of kiss that turns into sex. I suppose pancakes can wait, however impressive he claims them to be. He pulls off the duvet and kisses me in a line from my mouth all the way down my body, and I realize I'm not scared of his assessment of the way I look. I'm not paranoid about what he's thinking of my stomach, my boobs, my thighs.

Maybe it's because I'm more relaxed now that it's today and not yesterday, the pressure of first-time sex now lifted, but when he goes down on me, I find I can actually relax into it. I'm not hyper-aware of everything that I'm doing, that my body's doing, everything that's going on around me. I can just . . . enjoy it. Which means I come fast and hard.

'Fuck,' Henry says, looking up at me all pink-cheeked and starry-eyed. 'You're amazing.'

I lie back, dazed. 'I feel like I should be saying that to you,' I say.

'And now . . . pancakes,' he says, leaping out of bed and heading for the kitchen. I follow him and drag the dining chair back to my position from last night, sipping my now-cold coffee and watching him make the batter.

'First one's always shit . . .' he mumbles as he pours it into the waiting pan. There's something so intimate about this moment that it's almost painful. He's deep in concentration and I'm honestly, truly beyond obsessed with him. It just feels . . . right. When did I last feel like this about Alistair? When did he stop being the subject of all my adoration and love and obsession and start being a very good-looking estate agent who slept in my bed? I'm not stupid, I know that after ten years it's not going to feel the same as on a first date, but surely excitement counts for something? I'm still in my twenties . . . I feel like excitement should very much be on the menu, along with pancakes.

Those we eat at the dining table, drenched in maple syrup.

'So,' Henry says, sawing at one with the side of his fork. 'Do you have big plans for tonight?'

I think for a moment before replying, wondering if this is going to be his way of asking me to hang out with him, that midnight kiss twinkling on the imagined horizon . . . before deciding that would be rude and disloyal to Nicole, however much I fancy Henry.

'I'm having a drink with my friend Nicole at her flat in Stratford. Just the two of us, basically as a way to do *something* for New Year's without having to go out.'

'Going out is the *very* worst,' says Henry. 'New Year's is a special kind of hell, though.'

'At least we don't seem to have acquired the tradition of setting fireworks off in the street,' I say, remembering the terrifying December thirty-first Alistair and I spent in Amsterdam with some old university friends.

Henry shudders. 'I hate fireworks – I'm averse to both loud noises and surprises so . . . it's a lot.'

I smile. 'I'll remember that,' I say. 'I won't plan a fireworks display in an attempt at a romantic gesture. Anyway, what are you doing tonight?'

'We're— I'm— We're—' he stammers, 'going to a party at a friend's house in New Cross.'

I clear my throat a little awkwardly. 'That sounds fun,' I say, trying to dispel the awkwardness.

'Mmm, yeah, it's nice and easy to get to from here . . .' he says. I wonder if he's going with his ex or if the pronoun is just a hangover from the olden days. I don't want to ask.

'Well, I hope you enjoy it,' I say.

'It feels like there's always a lot of pressure on New Year's . . . but this year it feels even more so,' he says, a little sadly. 'All change.'

I don't want to get into the deep and meaningful shit with him right now. I don't want to talk about his old relationship. Maybe next time or the time after that. Because those times will come and I'll tell him all about Alistair and the wedding and I'll wonder what he'll think of me and we'll talk about it and it'll all be okay in the end but I just can't face it right now, not on our first date. Our first date which has been so *utterly* perfect.

After breakfast, I gather my stuff and announce my departure, mortified at the thought of outstaying my welcome.

'I've had the best time,' I say as I step onto the welcome mat on the landing, knowing it's okay to be earnest, that I don't need to play it cool and aloof.

'Me too,' Henry says, holding the door open for me. He looks dazed and happy, his red hair sticking up in little tufts at the back of his head. So cute. 'I can't wait to see you again. I'll text you.'

'You'd better,' I say, advancing towards the landing.

I've barely made it to the top of the stairs when I hear him say, 'Wait! Do you have to go? Or do you have some time today for a . . . well, a second date, I guess?'

I blink, disbelieving. 'I mean . . . yeah? I can stay!'

'Let me get dressed and we can go to the park, just give me two minutes!' he calls to me as he dashes back into the flat. As I'm standing on the welcome mat, I genuinely can't quite believe my luck. After the boring dates. After hearing about flaky men for so long. After *knowing* that Henry was the person I wanted to be with, finding out that all of that was right? It's amazing.

He returns, dressed, wrapped up in a hat and scarf, and we head outside. He slips his gloved hand into mine and I can't help but look at him, smiling. He smiles back, comfortable. We walk to the park and, as we walk hand in hand, I realize that no one can tell we've just met. To the eye of a stranger, we could have been together six months, a year, five years, more. The comfort, the familiarity, it's there, but so is the excitement, the joy of the new.

'So,' Henry says as we're entering the park through a big

black iron gate. 'What's your story . . . relationship-wise? I feel like mine is sort of heavy in the air . . .'

'And now you want to turn the tables,' I say, smiling, although the anxiety is already bubbling up in my stomach at the thought of having to tell him about Alistair and how it ended.

'Sure,' he says, as a child scoots past us at breakneck speed. 'Or at least get to know you a bit better in that regard.'

I sigh. 'I'm not sure you're going to like what you get to know.'

'Try me.'

'Well,' I begin, taking a deep breath of cold December air, wanting to point out the very puffy-furred Pomeranian trotting across the grass but knowing it's not the right moment for it. 'I was with someone called Alistair until a few months ago.'

'And?'

'And what?'

'You trailed it with the implication that there was something salacious and that doesn't sound very salacious to me,' he says, smiling good-naturedly, but I can tell he's curious.

'We had been together for ten years,' I say, not looking at him. 'And we were meant to be getting married, but I couldn't go through with it.'

'You called off a wedding? Brave.'

'Sort of . . .' I say, wondering how to phrase it so he will judge me marginally less harshly. 'I realized that I couldn't do it quite, er, last-minute.'

'How last-minute?' Henry sounds concerned.

'On the day,' I say, not looking at him.

He lets out a whistle. 'Oh boy! That's something, isn't it?' I can't read his tone, exactly.

'Yeah, not my finest hour. But don't worry – I'm very, uh, *aware* of that. I lost friends over it, understandably most people took his side, and my family still don't really understand it.'

He doesn't say anything. He just nods.

'Sorry if that makes me sound like a terrible person.'

He stops walking and pulls me back towards him. He puts his arms around me, our bodies bulky in our coats.

'I don't think you're a terrible person.' He pauses. 'Things are just complicated sometimes.' Although his words are kind and encouraging, something about the way he invoked *complicated* makes me prickle a bit.

'It didn't feel very complicated. It felt like something I had to do. It just turned out that the way I had to do it was very dramatic.'

He nods, and we keep walking. 'Does it still feel like you did the right thing?' he asks. I wish he wouldn't ask me these questions; I feel like whether or not he wants to have a relationship with me all hinges on whether I get the answers right or wrong.

'Yes. I mean, hurting him so much didn't feel right. But it would have hurt both of us more if I had seen it through. If we'd got married.' The thought that I should now be married to Alistair feels funny. Like some other me is off living some other life.

'It's hard, after a long time, to untangle what you want for yourself from what you want for another person.'

I shrug. 'In the end . . . I chose myself,' I say, plainly. I don't want to feel like I have to defend myself to Henry, as much as I want him to want me.

'A fair choice,' he says, squeezing my hand through our gloves.

We stop at the top of the path and I kiss him, because I want to kiss him, because I want to feel the reassurance that he wants me, because I want this to just be one conversation of thousands that we're going to have.

He kisses me back. And then he looks at me, brushes a few stray strands of hair off my face. 'Beautiful.'

'Moi?' I say, fluttering my eyelashes.

'Yes, you,' he says, breaking out into a grin. He fixes me with a look so soft and squishy that makes me feel like maybe everything is going to be okay. 'I love you.'

WHAT?! What? What!

'What?!' I say, because there is nothing else to say.

Henry claps a hand to his mouth, wide-eyed with horror. 'No, wait, sorry, I – I didn't mean that!' He's gone absolutely bright red, I can almost see the sweat forming on his face already. 'Fuck!'

'It's okay,' I say, as reassuringly as I can manage.

'It was an impulse thing,' he says, shaking his head. 'I mean, it just came out by accident because I'm so *used* to saying it . . .'

Just not to me. It's funny, a moment ago I was a little horrified by the whole thing, and now I'm suddenly overcome with resentment at this woman I've never met, being told, compulsively, by Henry, that he loves her. Loved her, I guess.

'I understand,' I say, kissing him quickly on the cheek. 'When me and Alistair broke up it was like the end of a language. Or a culture. Things only we knew or only we understood just ended. Nicknames that would never be used again. Memories that would probably never be talked about with anyone else. Just gone. The end. So I get how you could say it by accident. It's a habit.'

He shakes his head. 'God! It's just so embarrassing! What does it mean?! What am I doing?!'

I start to panic now. 'It doesn't *mean* anything. I'm crazy about you. I'm not put off by it,' I say, my voice rising desperately.

Henry clears his throat. 'Good,' he says.

Under a cloud of awkwardness, we buy cups of tea in the park and drink them on a bench looking down over the town and the river. Henry's restless now, his little slip haunting him. Honestly, if it was me, I would be mortified – I would have rolled myself all the way down this hill and then rolled across the main road and then rolled myself right into the Thames out of pure embarrassment *and yet* I don't want him to have any reason to feel skittish or freaked out so I want, nay, *need* him to chill the fuck out about it. I want things to work out between us and I don't need him having *any* excuse to bail on our budding relationship.

'Fuck,' he says as he tosses his Styrofoam cup into the bin by the bench. 'I really wish I hadn't said that.'

'It's fine. It's really fine.'

'I feel like such an idiot, honestly.'

'Well, you're not,' I say, shrugging. 'Everything is fine.' I take his hand and we walk on, out to the sweeping expanse of Blackheath.

'Where would you live if money was no object?' he asks, shaking off his awkwardness.

I don't even need to think twice. 'There's this huge pink house with a very nice front garden on a corner on this back street in Islington, the other side of the station from where I live. I have no idea what it's like inside but that's my house. How about you?'

'That's a surprisingly specific answer!' he says, delighted. 'I was just going to say one of the nice Georgian houses on the road that runs along the bottom of the park. But now I know I have to be specific I'll say the one with the turquoise door.'

'You know what this says about us?'

'What?' he asks.

'It's that line from *Silence of the Lambs* about how we covet what we see every day, right? We both chose things near where we already live, things we see all the time!' I say.

'I suppose you're right,' he says. 'Do you often look to Hannibal Lecter for wisdom and philosophy?'

'Not often, but sometimes.'

'I liked the book but I liked the film more. Doesn't happen often, does it? There's always *The Godfather*, I suppose.'

'You're telling me you don't think the storyline about Lucy Mancini's enormous vagina was important? You're trying to tell me *The Godfather* is a good film even though it veritably *erases* that key storyline from the book? Are you actually joking?!' I exclaim.

Henry throws his head back and laughs, a gesture so animated and relaxed that it feels like his earlier faux pas is forgotten. 'You're right,' he says, throwing his hands up. 'What can I say, they fumbled the ball with that film and everyone knows it.'

'Thank you,' I say, bowing graciously. 'Hey, it's fucking nice around here, isn't it?'

'What did I tell you!'

I shrug. 'You were right! Living in London is weird. You have all these big dreams and plans for all the fun shit you're going to do and then your weekends just disappear in the blink of an eye and you realize you've spent another one hunched over your sewing machine or going cross-eyed at Netflix and haven't made it further than the petrol station on

Holloway Road. Or, you know, insert local petrol station.'

'Tell me about this sewing machine,' Henry says as we approach a huge, looming church set dramatically on the heath. 'Or rather, tell me about your sewing.'

'Well, I . . .' I begin, thinking about my sewing. I turn to him. 'Okay, so here's the thing. I wasn't always . . . you know . . .'

'What?'

'Well, I wasn't always fat,' I say. He nods. 'And obviously one of the key ways that things change for you when you gain weight is clothes. And I'd learned to use a sewing machine from my uni friend Lola – she's who I live with now actually. But it was only when I kind of . . . gained weight that I really started making my own stuff. It felt like a way of regaining control. Or rather, to not need to rely on an industry that was making me feel more and more . . . alienated.'

'That's really cool! I feel like all our jobs are so . . . intangible, our work only exists on the internet or in the ether, and it's so rare to have a job or a hobby where you actually *make something* with your hands, you know?'

'Yeah! It's true!' I say. I like that he thinks of it like that.

'I still can't believe you made that dress you wore to the wedding,' he says.

'You liked that?' I say flirtily.

'I did. I liked it as soon as I saw it from across the bar when you were talking to that woman with the black hair.'

I blush. 'You saw me?'

'Yeah! I was fucking *delighted* when I saw you were on my table, and even more so when we were next to each other.'

'Huh . . .' I say, smiling. I can't help it. I feel like I'm spilling over with happiness today.

By the time we part ways and I have to make my trek back north, the accidental *I love you* feels like a figment of our imaginations, long forgotten. What remains is the distinct possibility that within four months of running out on my wedding, I've met The One.

14

I go home – charge my phone, shower, change, put on some cute-but-cosy clothes – and then I'm straight back out the door. Thank God, I have been saved from a plan-less evening by Nicole. I'm looking forward to having someone to tell about the *extremely* pleasing Henry situation. Nicole tells me to come at 8:30 and sends me her address, which Google Maps informs me is in Stratford, not too far from the huge Westfield shopping centre.

U nearby? Nicole asks as I step off the Overground.

Just getting off the train

Okay I want to get us some crisps so meet me in Sains in the East Village

I need to buy wine so that's okay

Mate I have so much wine in my fridge don't bother just meet me there

I do as I'm told and stroll the aisles of Sainsbury's in search of Nicole. The mood is high-spirited, everyone picking up drinks for their parties and nights out. I find her exactly where I thought I would – in the crisp aisle.

'I love these cheesy ball things,' she says, holding up a garish yellow bag. 'And onion rings. And those fake Frazzles that they do.'

'So what I'm learning is you like a maize-based snack,' I say.

'Yeah, fuck a potato,' she says, drawing me into a hug. 'How are you, babe?!'

'I'm . . . amazing! Actually amazing! I feel like a whole new person!'

'Isn't it remarkable what sex can do for the spirits?' she says, twirling around ceremoniously.

'I guess! But it's more than that!' I say, relieving her of one of the bags of crisps.

'Don't tell me you're in love after one date.' She eyes me with suspicion.

'No! Not *love*, I'm not fully insane,' I say, feeling like it would probably be disloyal to share Henry's little slip-up on the subject. 'But . . . I really like him. Like, *really* like him. And I have such a good feeling about it!'

'You literally met at a wedding! A cuter meet-cute there never was.'

We make our way to the self-scan checkouts. 'Give it here.'

'You sure? I can get them.'

'I think I can stretch to three bags of maize-based snacks,' she says, swiping the cheese balls through the scanner.

'But then I didn't bring anything!'

'Mate, all I care about is that you're here, I don't feel pressured into going out, I get to hang out with you and hear all about your date with this new dreamboat and we can toast to your success.'

'Okay, if you insist . . .' I say, guiltily.

'Plus you're doing me a favour by forcing me to share the wine I nicked from the fridge at my parents' house.'

'For the greater good,' I say as we step out into the cold night.

'For the greater good,' Nicole repeats. 'That's where I live, right there,' she points up at a balcony maybe five or six floors up in an apartment block ahead of us.

'Oh, fancy!' I say. 'A balcony!'

'We can spy on the fireworks from there if you want,' she says, which makes me think of Henry. I wonder if he's going to the party with his ex, or if he's alone. I hope he's not hanging out with his ex. Or her family. Gah! Early days is hell! But I love it! 'It's fucking nice having a balcony. It's a nice building. It's even got a fucking *gym* as well.'

When we get into the lobby we make a beeline for the lifts and I press the call button. The lift – sleek and silver but pretty small – appears. We get in and, just as Nicole presses the button for the sixth floor, the lobby doors open behind us and a group of three people, two men and a woman, appear, tipsily. One of the men shouts, 'Hold the lift!'

'Ugh,' Nicole says, grudgingly pushing on the 'open doors' button.

We hear the three of them pounding towards the lift. When they get there, bottles clinking in shopping bags for a party somewhere in the building, the woman and one of the men get in but the other hangs back. The woman presses the button for the eighth floor without thanking us for waiting.

'You sure it's safe for me?' the man outside the lift says, smirking.

'What? Come on, Tom,' says the woman.

'Bit of a tight fit . . .' he says, and I feel the instinctive prickle of fear creep across my body. Nicole's body language tightens a little.

'Mate, it literally says right there that it fits eight people,' says the other man, gesturing sloppily at the information panel affixed to the wall.

Tom raises his eyebrows and nods towards me and Nicole. 'Yeah, but what's the weight limit,' he says, finally stepping into the lift.

'You're so bad!' the woman says, swatting the man on the arm as they all laugh.

That prickle of fear turns to pure, hot shame in an instant. I honestly want the ground to swallow me up. It feels as if the journey from the ground floor to the sixth floor takes minutes rather than seconds and I become acutely aware of my breathing, my posture, the sound of the crisp packets rustling together like some kind of evidence I don't want them to find. *Fuck, fuck, fuck why do I look like this, why do I have to live in this stupid fucking embarrassing body*, I think to myself. Nicole quietly squeezes my hand in solidarity.

When we finally reach Nicole's floor, they're blocking the way like fucking idiots when the doors open and, infused with an anger I haven't felt for a long time, I just push past them and Nicole follows in my path. They look at each other indignantly, like I'm somehow the unreasonable one. I feel stupid and self-hating for not saying anything, but I feel pretty sure that I couldn't say anything without crying anyway.

I'm walking down the corridor but I realize Nicole has just stopped in her tracks. She turns around as the lift doors start to close, holds up her middle finger and says, quite calmly, 'You're all cunts and I hope you die alone.'

'Nicole!' I yell, wide-eyed.

'What?!' she says, stalking towards the door of her flat. 'They deserved it.'

'I mean . . . yeah,' I say, still in slight disbelief at her open display of hostility but, fundamentally, realizing she's right. 'They did.'

'What a bunch of dickheads,' she says, shaking her head.

I realize in that moment that there is no part of Nicole that blames herself.

'You can keep your shoes on or take them off, I don't care – my flatmate is mad about it but she's on holiday so I'm the queen of the castle right now,' Nicole says, breezily, like she's already shaken off the unpleasant encounter. She holds the door open for me.

'Wow this is so nice!' I say, looking around, still a little flushed and stressed.

'Yeah, it's not bad,' she says, getting a bowl down from a high cupboard.

'I live in an old conversion, I feel like I never see shiny new flats like this – you know, with lifts and gyms and all that.'

'They didn't upset you too much, did they?' She looks at me with such an expression of concern that I wonder what I ever did without her.

'I mean . . . yeah . . .' I say, beet red with embarrassment. 'A bit. It's hard for it not to get to you, right?'

'It's fucking hard,' she says. 'It's so casual and easy for them and then it just really stays with you, you know. But I need you to know it's a *them* problem not a *you* problem. I properly *need* you to know that.'

I sigh. 'I'll choose to believe you,' I say.

'Good,' she says, setting the crisps down on the coffee table and yanking a bottle of white wine out of the fridge. She pours us two *very* large glasses. 'So, tell me everything about your night of romance! I'm obsessed already, I tell you.'

Is it bad that I already feel a little bit better just thinking about Henry? 'It was so great . . . we had this little stroll and then a drink and then back to his and he made me dinner and then . . . well, dot dot dot.'

'DOT DOT FUCKING DOT is it?! Aaaah, what a dreamy first date!' she says, handing me my glass of wine with an enormous grin on her face. 'Cheers, my dude! To new year, new relationships!'

'Cheers!' I say, daring myself to see it as a budding new relationship. Daring to believe that so soon after Alistair, with so little adventure and rigmarole and bad dates, I've managed to meet . . . can you believe it . . . The One.

'When are you going to see him again?' she asks.

'I don't know, but I know it'll happen. It's weird, feeling so *excited* about it but also like I don't have to worry about it?'

'I've got a good feeling about this one!' she says, looking genuinely delighted.

'It's just a bit weird though, right?' I say, nibbling my lip.

'How so?'

'I ran out on Alistair, what, only a few months ago. That was the beginning of September! It's December now?'

'By a hair,' she says, shrugging. 'So what's your point?'

I sigh. 'I just feel a bit like . . . it shouldn't be this easy. I shouldn't have found it this easy to move on from Alistair. That I should have, you know, suffered a bit more.'

'Quit it with the suffering thing, that doesn't help anyone. And besides, surely the fact that you have met someone new *justifies* the fact that you broke up with Alistair? Use your brain, my dude!'

I smile. I like it when she calls me that. And I've decided to believe she's right. Me meeting Henry is proof the universe was paving the way for it. I couldn't have met him if I had been with Alistair. Who cares that it's only been a few months?

'How's stuff with you? I feel like you're always going on loads of dates but I never hear anything about them,' I say, settling into a more comfortable sofa position and not wanting to talk about myself all night.

'You know, I've got some ongoing stuff, some on-and-off stuff, there's this guy I've been sleeping with for like . . . a year now but still very casual, plus I love a first date.'

'Do you? Really?'

'What?!' She looks horrified. 'Do you think I'm lying?'

'No! But . . . don't you *always* find a first date with someone you've met on the internet scary?'

'I mean . . . yeah, like, it's scary because you might get murdered, but . . . I don't think I'm scared of the date itself any more . . .' she says, thoughtfully.

'For real?' I ask.

'For real! I just try to enjoy it!'

'God, I don't think I was ever going to get there with dates. Good job Henry's come along to save me from having to go on any more,' I say.

'I'm happy for you!' she says, taking a sip of wine.

'So, who's your flatmate?' I ask.

'She's called Jeanne, she's French, she's perfectly nice. She keeps herself to herself, works in some fucking boring finance thing in the City. Remind me, who do you live with?'

'An old friend from uni called Lola. But she's working abroad at the moment. She kind of . . . saved me a bit, when me and Alistair broke up. She never liked him anyway. I mean, no, that's not fair. She didn't dislike him but she didn't like him *for me*, you know? She thought he was kind of boring.'

'Was she right?' Nicole asks with a wolfish grin.

'I don't know . . .' I say with a sigh. 'We were probably not supposed to be together as long as we were. But . . . he was very good-looking. *He* still is.'

'What, like you're not?' Nicole says, rolling her eyes. 'Prove it, show me a pic.'

'You want to see a pic of the guy I unceremoniously dumped at the altar after a ten-year relationship?' I say, smiling.

'Yeah, I'm nosy as hell,' she sits back on the sofa and crosses her legs.

I open Instagram and scroll all the way back. I'm not a super-active user but who doesn't like to post the occasional selfie or dinner photo, you know?

'There,' I say, holding the phone up to Nicole's face.

'Oooooh! He's hot!'

'Right?!'

'Like . . . very *handsome*, you know? Someone that old ladies would like.'

I laugh. 'You're right! They do! All the old ladies in the village got him to sell their houses when they got shipped off to care homes by their kids, it was like they had some kind of old lady group chat where they all agreed this handsome young estate agent could have their business.'

'Show me another,' she says.

'Thirsty!' I say, gleefully. 'Here is your *last* picture of Alistair. After this I'm cutting off your supply.'

'He's so good-looking!' she says, but she doesn't say it in the way that some of the girls I worked with towards the end of our relationship would say it. Like they were surprised. Or disbelieving. 'All I'm saying is, if he's single . . .'

'Nicole!' I throw the phone down on the sofa indignantly. I'm already a little light-headed from the wine. We're making light work of that first bottle.

'Kidding!' she says, wiggling her eyebrows naughtily. It's kind of amazing — her absolute belief that she could date anyone if she put her mind to it. Perhaps one day I'll get there. 'Anyway, he can be as good-looking as he wants but if you don't have that spark, there's no point. Hey, you've got a text,' says Nicole as she gets up and heads for the fridge, the phone screen illuminating on the sofa in her wake.

'You're right, I *do* got a text! And it's from Henry!' I say, clutching the phone to my heart, my stomach doing a gleeful little backflip at the sight of his name in my inbox. It's already starting to feel normal, like part of the fabric of my life. But still heart-stoppingly exciting.

'He's a keen bean,' she says, pulling a bottle of prosecco out of the fridge.

The message hits me like a ton of bricks. The first words make my blood run cold. Hey, Serena, I'm so sorry about—

I close my eyes and stop reading for a moment. I can feel myself shaking with adrenaline nerves already. I can't believe this. I can't. I force myself to read the rest of the text.

Hey, Serena, I'm so sorry about these extremely mixed signals, but I thought it was better to say sooner rather than later that I think we shouldn't see each other. I've been thinking about it a lot today and it just doesn't feel right to me. I think you're great and I hope you're having a fun evening with your friend. Again, I'm really sorry.

I flop back on her sofa and stare at the ceiling.

'FUCK!'

'What?!' Nicole looks at me with an expression of pure horror.

I can't speak. I just hand Nicole the phone.

'What the actual fuck? Didn't you just have the best date?!'

'Yes!' I say in a shriller voice than I thought physically possible. 'I literally don't understand it at all!' I take back the phone and reread the message, attempting to unpick a clue, unravel meaning from a single word.

'Fuck it! Fuck him!' she says. 'Quick, babe, here,' she holds out the bottle of prosecco and I lift up my glass to receive it like it's the elixir of life.

'But . . .' I say, before taking a huge mouthful, followed by another, and before I know I've drunk the whole glass.

'Mate . . .' she says, topping me up. 'You need this. For the shock.'

'It makes no fucking sense!'

She shakes her head. 'Men are properly, properly weird. I literally don't know what to say to you. It sounded like you had it in the bag. Honestly. Like I'm not just saying that − it sounded like you were on to a fucking winner. I don't get it at all.'

I take another swig from the glass. 'I kind of want to kill him? Can I do that? Please tell me I can kill him?'

'Unfortunately after only one date I think the courts would frown upon such behaviour,' she says. 'Not that I don't understand.'

'I know it was only one date but it just felt so *right*, you know? Guys can be so cagey and weird and distant and Henry just *wasn't*, he was easy and calm and fun and kind and now he's just . . . gone? Forever? Doesn't even say he wants to be friends! Nothing! What am I meant to say to him?'

'Nothing,' says Nicole, grabbing my wrist. 'You are not meant to say anything, my dude. Don't even think about replying, especially not tonight. Leave it. Fuck.'

'Fuck indeed,' I say. 'You know he's only the second person in the world I've ever had sex with? Maybe it was that. Fuck! Was I bad in bed?'

'How many dot dot dots did you say there were?'

'Five.'

'Then it's much more likely to be your horrible personality.'

I can't help laughing at that. 'You're the worst.'

'But it made you smile!' She tops me up again, and I'm really feeling light-headed now.

'Do you want to know the stupidest part of the whole thing?' I say, chugging down more prosecco.

'Tell me.'

'He . . .'

'What?' she looks at me, expectantly.

'He told me he loved me!' I say, grimacing.

'What?!' she says again, even more disbelieving.

'Well that's what I said! Obviously it was one of those things that just came out.'

'Like when you call your teacher Mum?'

'Exactly – because he's only just broken up with his ex so it's like a reflex, a thing you say when you're looking at someone and you're feeling all warm and fuzzy inside . . .'

'So he tells you he loves you and then he's, like, oh wait actually no I don't even want to see you again?'

'Nicooooole,' I moan, helplessly. 'What am I meant to do?'

'You're meant to wallow right now, and I mean, *right now.* Because when you wake up tomorrow, you dust yourself off and you make your fucking New Year's resolution to think about *yourself.* You've barely paused for breath since you broke up with your ex, right? You moved to a new city, you were newly single, you started a new job. *And* you put all this pressure on yourself to date and meet new people and sort your life out while it was all so unsettled. It was so much! Like, were you even *enjoying* those dates you were making yourself go on every week? And then Henry came along so soon, all those expectations of how he was *it,* how a new relationship was going to reassure you that it was right to abandon your wedding . . . you need to just cool your jets for a bit. January is Serena Time. Deal?'

Serena Time.

'That sounds . . . kind of nice, you know. Deal,' I say.

'Come to one of my mad exercise classes with me. It's good for sweating out all your rage and fury. Then we can get tacos.'

'Fine, fine . . . at this point I'd agree to anything. I can't believe I'm thinking about tacos at a time like this . . .' I wail, downing another glass.

★ ★ ★

When I wake up the next day, I've got to be honest – that deal is the last bit I remember. I wake up in Nicole's bed in her tidy bedroom, perfume bottles lining a mirrored dresser. She slept in her flatmate's bed.

'I'll Febreze in there and she'll never know the difference,' she says when we meet again on the sofa, my head throbbing.

'What . . . happened?' I ask, squinting in the mid-morning sunlight. I must have slept for hours.

'Well, after the text from Henry you just started caning the wine and at first I was like, wooo yeah go Serena, but then I realized you were going to be fucked by midnight. Which you were. So I tucked you up in bed and watched TV on my own,' she shrugs.

'Jesus,' I say, shaking my head. Which doesn't help.

'Coffee?' she asks. And realizing that it was only *one fucking day ago* that Henry was asking me the same thing makes me want to dissolve into a puddle on the floor. I thought I was sorted. I thought I was set. I thought I was sailing into a new year with a boyfriend I was crazy about. But instead, I'm back to square one. Or maybe square one minus five, because knowing that I've met someone I like as much as Henry but for some reason am not allowed to be with him feels like a kick in the face.

Nicole lets me stay at hers all morning until I feel strong enough to face the Overground in my hungover state. She even makes me an incredible fry-up that could rival Henry's pancakes.

When I do feel up to slinking home, she hugs me tightly. 'Remember your New Year's resolution: it's all about *you*! You've got to wash that man right outta your hair,' she says, ruffling my curls affectionately. 'And that goes for *all* men. No more dates, as much as I personally love them. Just give yourself breathing space, do the things you enjoy, figure out what you're looking for. Figure out your relationship with yourself. And *then* you can see what the world looks like to you after the dust has settled a bit.'

'I promise I'll do some calculated self-care this month,' I say, sighing.

'I don't care if that's a euphemism for wanking or not. As long as it's focused around *you* and not Henry, I'm down with it.'

'Action item one: don't text Henry back. Action item two: kick January in the arse.'

'Starting with a class at the studio with yer old pal Nicole,' she says, raising her eyebrows at me.

I cover my face with my hands. 'I really must have been drunk if I agreed to that. But I'll come.'

As I go down in the lift where I felt so thoroughly humiliated last night, I can't help but feel like the universe has well and truly put me in my place.

And it's only when I'm in the orange embrace of the Overground, the marbles rattling painfully around my skull grateful for the train's smooth movements, I realize it's January. January. That means . . . my self-imposed Alistair radio silence is over! Dare I say it, it might actually be nice to talk to him. Comfort. Familiarity. Kindness. Someone who knows me. I was so certain that I had done the right thing, and now I'm not so sure. But is it really about him? Or is it about me, and my loneliness, and my fears, and my rejection by Henry?

I take out my phone. I start writing a Happy New Year text to him, something about checking in. And then I change my mind. If he wanted to talk to me he would have texted me by now. If meeting Henry was some kind of cosmic proof that I wasn't meant to be with Alistair . . . what does it mean that the very same cosmos has decided Henry *isn't* for me? And what does it mean that the minute I resolve to focus on myself I snap straight back to thinking about myself in relation to men? Nicole is right. It's time to really deal with me. The Serena I have to live with whether I'm single, getting married, sleeping with someone, the Serena that's always been there, that has so much going for her in her own right. I have to learn to love and nourish *me*.

It's Serena Time.

15

Is it possible to sweat out a crush? To become so overrun with endorphins you forget all your woes? Exercise to exorcise, if you will? Let's hope so. Because I've promised Nicole I will go to one of her spin classes and there's no backing out of it now. So, on the first frigid Tuesday in January, full of trepidation, I bring my sports bra, leggings and a vest to work.

'Did you remember a water bottle?' Nicole asks me at lunch-time. 'They're, like, brutally anti-plastic there, if you don't have a bottle you have to buy one of those metal ones for like . . . £500. Or dehydrate, your choice.'

'Yeah, I've got that,' I say, looking in my tote bag one more time just to make sure. It's there. It's there. I will not turn into a dehydrated husk at this class. I simply will not allow it to happen. 'I'm scared.'

Nicole shrugs. 'That's okay, my dude, I was scared too.' I'm glad that she isn't trying to tell me that I shouldn't be scared. I feel like maybe a thin person would do that, but she knows how it is. She gets what I'm scared of. That it's a real thing rather than some intangible anxiety. That I'm scared of going into *any* fitness space with a fat body, that I'm scared of being singled out, that I'm scared of being so bad at it that everyone stares at me.

'But you'll be fine. Anyway, the light at the end of the tunnel is that we're going to eat tacos afterwards. And possibly we could get a couple of beers with lime juice in the bottom and salt around the rim . . .'

'Eyes on the prize,' I say.

'Eyes on the prize,' she repeats decisively. Maybe it'll be okay? Or maybe I'll die. Could go either way. 'The prize is feeling proud that you committed to doing something new that will make you feel great afterwards, just to be clear.'

The afternoon goes by uncomfortably quickly. I'm normally hyped to get out of there because, well, it's work, but today I'm wishing the time would stretch out a little longer. Maybe I shouldn't go? Maybe I should try to get out of it? But then Nicole would think I was pathetic and I actually want her to think I'm cool. Besides, it would probably be good for me and Nicole to do something other than drinking together. Even if that means going to some fancy exercise class which I may or may not survive . . .

'Let's hit the road,' Nicole says, coming up behind my office chair and squeezing my shoulders.

I sigh. 'Is it that time already?'

'Look, if you really don't want to come you don't have to come – plus I won't enjoy it if I have to keep looking over at you to check you're not crying.'

'No, it's fine,' I say, trying to put on my big girl pants. 'I'm up for it. I am.' I shut down my computer and gather my stuff.

'Got everything?' Nicole asks.

'Yeah,' I say, cheerily but with a hint of anxiety, checking

one more time for my water bottle, hairband, sports bra . . .
everything. It's a lot to think about and I haven't even gone to
the class yet.

'Good, now let's make like Tigger and . . .'

'Bounce?'

'You got it.'

Duncan looks up from his laptop. 'What are you two up to?'
He looks vaguely amused.

'Nicole's taking me to her exercise class,' I say.

'Oh really?' says Duncan. 'She must really like you, she would
never let me join her in a million years.'

'I do really like her,' Nicole says, shrugging. 'Take from that
what you will.'

I can never tell if they're flirting or what. Maybe all will
become apparent over tacos. If I'm honest, I'm living for the
tacos.

'Well . . . have fun, girls,' Duncan says with a sly wink. Maybe
he's just flirty in general. It's weird, when you're in a relationship you don't have to be so attuned to this shit and so I sort
of forgot about it.

'Oh, we will,' Nicole says with an eyeroll, taking me by the
arm and marching me out of the office with a backwards, 'Bye
guys!' over her shoulder as we go.

It's only a ten-minute walk to the mysteriously named
The Studio, and when we get there it's all very slick-serene,
neon lights spelling out boss bitch versions of 'Live, laugh,
love'. You know, things like, 'You glow girl' and 'Nama-slay'.
Nicole gives our names at the desk in her usual assertive
tone, like she isn't self-conscious about being here, not one
bit. Maybe she isn't? I mean, I guess that's a possibility?

'Is this your first time?' the receptionist asks me.

'It is,' I say, trying to project an air of confidence and knowing every second that I'm failing.

'What size shoe are you?' she asks.

'Uhhh . . .' I think for a second. 'A seven?'

'Are you sure about that?' she asks with a sugary smile that's meant to conceal what a doofus she thinks I am.

'Yes, sorry, I just hadn't thought about it in a while.'

'And you are . . .' she says, consulting the computer screen for Nicole's size, 'a six.' She turns back to the wall of cubbyholes filled with special shoes, like it's a bowling alley. She takes out two pairs of shoes and hands them over to us. 'The lockers are pretty self-explanatory and I'm guessing your friend can answer any questions but do make sure someone helps you set up your bike. Have fun!'

I feel nauseous. The actual reality of being here is setting in. Setting up my bike! Using a locker! Wearing shoes that a hundred other people have probably sweated into! It's a lot!

We head into the women's changing room where a few decidedly athletic-looking women are changing into sports bras and leggings and I realize I'm expected to do the same. Nicole tugs on the doors of various lockers. 'Ugh, the post-work classes are always so busy. Hey, how about these two?'

'Sure,' I say, but, before I've got the word out, Nicole is already stuffing her normal shoes into one of them and getting changed. I am, frankly, not ready to strip off in front of lots of thin exercise gals yet, so I make an excuse about needing to use the bathroom and slip into one of the toilet cubicles with my tote bag. I know Nicole knows what I'm doing but she doesn't try to stop me.

I change in the toilet as quickly as possible and then rejoin her, shoving my bags into the locker, extricating my water bottle before she demonstrates how to lock it.

'Do *not* forget the code, otherwise you'll have to go half-naked to reception and ask them to open it for you,' she says.

'I won't! It's my—'

Nicole holds up a hand to silence me. 'Don't tell me it's your PIN number because I will remember it and one day I might be tempted to rob you.'

And with that we head out of the changing room. Before we can head down the stairs, Nicole grabs my arm.

'Take those shoes off,' she says, nodding down at the cleated shoes on my feet.

'All right,' I say, shrugging.

'You think you're going to die in the class but the way you're going you're actually going to fall down the stairs and break your neck by wearing those shoes on the stairs.'

'What would I do without you?' I say, yanking the Velcroed shoes off and padding downstairs barefoot.

The crowd waiting outside the studio is almost entirely female. Only a couple of men in tight shorts and tank tops are hopping from foot to foot, brimming with energy they just can't *wait* to release in the class. I can't help but notice the obvious: everyone here is hot and thin. It's just so striking. I think if Nicole wasn't here I would probably have gone home by now. I just feel *so* out of place.

If my body image was, shall we say, *complicated* before this then it's definitely pushing me over into abject self-loathing without much effort. Not to mention being brushed off by Henry, which, although I *know, logically, using my brain*, makes no sense because

I know he fancied me enough to have sex with me multiple times, *and* be seen with me in public. But that familiar prickle of paranoid shame has smuggled its way into my body.

Nicole is chatting away to me but I'm almost overflowing with discomfort and nerves, capable only of nodding and smiling and occasionally interjecting with a 'Yeah' or a 'Really?' I put my shoes back on, and then the doors open.

'We're on bikes number 34 and 35, over by that pillar,' she says, and I head in that direction before she pulls me back by my vest. 'Not so fast, we've got to pick up hand weights first.' So we line up behind the people who would never go to their bike without picking up their hand weights, and Nicole passes me the medium weights. 'Let's go.'

We manoeuvre around the bikes in the rows in front, over to our bikes by the pillar. 'I choose this bike every time because it's near the air conditioning unit,' she says, pointing at the white box on the ceiling and having to shout over the noise of the pulsing music.

'Smart,' I say, copying her by putting my water on the rest on the front of the bike and my weights in the holders under the seat, but she doesn't notice because she's waving her hand in the air to get someone's attention. Attention is the last thing I want. One of the hot, thin employees trots over and Nicole tells her it's my first time and that I need help setting up my bike.

'Welcome!' she says, and makes me stand next to the bike so we can position the seat, and stretch out my arms so the handlebars are set at the right distance. So far, so painless, despite my nerves.

'You good?' shouts Nicole as I try, as elegantly as I can manage, to get on my bike and clip my shoes into the pedals.

My feet keep slipping off, refusing to clip into whatever mechanism is meant to keep our fancy shoes attached to the pedals. Everyone else is very enthusiastically warming up, turning their pedals and lifting themselves up and down on their saddles.

'Mmmhmm!' I say, as brightly as I can manage, attempting to come to terms with the fact this is the first real exercise I've done in years. Finally! One foot clips in! But I don't know how I did it so I can't clip the other one in and end up just spinning one leg while the other hovers off to the side of the bike for a while. I wiggle it with a fierce determination until somehow it slots into place. I'm good to go. Good-ish.

Katie the instructor, a pretty blonde with a Britney Spears headset, gets on her bike at the front of the room. The studio helpers leave, closing the door behind them. The room gets very dark, only occasionally illuminated by coloured disco lights. The music starts pumping even harder. My heart rate increases just a little bit.

'Happy Tuesday, campers! You've made it through the Monday *blerghs*, you've made it through Tuesday and now you're giving something back to yourself here tonight!' Katie calls perkily from her bike while adjusting her headset. 'Let's give a big round of applause to Serena who's joining us for the first time!'

Oh my God how *mortifying*.

'Serena, where are you?' Katie shields her eyes from the light and scans the bikes for me, the newbie.

Grudgingly I raise my hand and everyone turns to look at me while clapping. Great, now they know exactly where to look during the class if they want to feel better about themselves.

Then the real music starts, rather than what I guess was the chill intro music. Everyone lifts themselves out of their seats to a semi-standing position, hovering over their saddles. Shit. I thought I was at least going to get to sit down like you do on an exercise bike.

A mid-tempo dance track with an easily perceptible beat starts.

'One-two, one-two!' shouts Katie from her bike at the front of the room so that we know when to push down with our right leg followed by our left. So far, so manageable. Except . . . it's not. Within a minute of this 'warm-up track' I'm already panting, clinging onto the bike for dear life, mortified at being such a cliché. Everyone around me seems to be bouncing along in perfect time to the music whereas I'm struggling to keep up. Even Nicole is coping with the pace and she's fat too, which means I'm fat *and* fucked.

'You okay?' she calls to me over the blaring music.

'Fine!' I lie, spinning my legs extra hard.

'Give two turns on your resistance dial!' Katie shouts.

I do as I'm told and instantly regret it. What was a struggle before is now excruciating.

'And now we're going to add in a bit of choreography!'

What?!

Katie demonstrates how with each beat she wants us to sort of zig-zag from left to right, from down to up, while our legs keep going at the usual pace. Even though this is pretty straight-forward in theory, I manage to mess it up by zigging when I should be zagging and then getting stressed about it which means I miss the bit where I'm meant to lower my chest to the handle-bars. Fuck. I make it to the end of the track and wonder if that has even killed five minutes of a forty-five-minute class.

'We're going to do some hill climbs now, so I want you to turn your resistance up to fifty per cent of your maximum!'

194

Katie the instructor shouts. 'Your maximum resistance is whatever setting means you literally can't move your legs any more!'

I turn the dial all the way up then back down by half. It feels like my legs are moving through treacle. The song has a heavy beat.

'Remember, this is meant to be mimicking the experience of cycling up a hill so it shouldn't be easy!'

Is any of this 'easy'? I would suggest not.

'Now,' she says, 'when the beat drops, I want you to take the resistance all the way off and to do double time!'

I don't like the sound of it but I don't have long until I find out what double time means – literally just pedalling like mad twice as fast as the beat. And we're meant to go between these punishing high-resistance pushes and these wild bursts of speed? Fuck. I honestly, and no exaggeration here, want to be sick. Even though I can't actually *do* what she's asking me to do in the way she wants me to do it, I still try. I still push myself to do as much as I can and it's absolutely grim. Is it possible I'm having a heart attack? God, what a fucking *cringe* way to go, a fat girl dying at her first ever exercise class. The infamy!

I've never felt like this before in my life, I swear my heart has never been beating so fast, I've never been *sweating* quite so much, my legs have absolutely never in the history of the world burned like this, my lungs have never been quite so on fire. I can feel that metallic taste in my mouth like when I (very occasionally) run for the bus, except this time it's turned up to eleven. When the track ends I collapse onto the handlebars of my bike, gasping for air like someone who's been pulled from a shipwreck.

Oh. My. God.

* * *

At the end of the class, I am broken. A broken husk of a woman. My face has gone from pink to red to purple. My hair is matted to my scalp, as wet as if I'd taken a shower except by no means as clean. So much for Nicole's air conditioner! I stagger up the stairs, wobbling like a drunk, to the changing room, my breath ragged.

'Look,' she says, panting. 'I know it was bad but if I told you how bad it was you wouldn't have come. And now you've done it!'

'I . . .' I say, finally making it into the changing room where I have to queue, puce-faced, for a shower in front of all of these glowing, athletic Victoria's Secret models. 'I . . . literally cannot talk right now . . .'

Nicole grimaces. 'Sorry! But just think! Beer and Mexican food!'

By the time we shower and change and roughly dry our hair, and make it around the corner to La Taqueria, I feel maybe twenty-five per cent back to my normal physical state. That was *intense*. No wonder these ladies pay all that money to go – it must burn about a thousand calories a class. Give or take.

'The thing I struggle with,' I say, taking my seat at the table, 'is being the shittest one there and knowing everyone is looking at me, thinking, *She's so shit*, you know?'

'Okay, so, no offence,' Nicole says, kicking her backpack with her workout kit under the table, 'but no one cares about you. They just don't give a solitary shit what you're doing. No one is looking at you because they've all paid the big bucks to be there and do their workout.'

'Huh . . .' I say, a bead of sweat dripping from my forehead into my eyebrow. I wonder when I'll cool down. Maybe I won't, maybe I'll be like one of those people who gets the hiccups and then just never stops hiccupping for the rest of their life. Except with sweating.

'I'm right,' she says. 'I felt the same way you did when I first went, and then after a few classes of feeling pure cringe, I realized *I* wasn't looking at anyone else during the class, I was just, you know, trying to survive it. Literally!'

I nod. 'Okay, fine, I accept this.'

'Good – the sooner you do accept it the better. So . . . do you think I can tempt you back sometime?'

I think for a moment, because my first instinct is to say no. But really, I do feel pretty amazing right now. And not even in that so-called 'endorphin' way I always hear about. But just . . . because I did it. Because I showed up and stuck it out and did something scary and new and I didn't back out. So maybe it would be nice to feel like this again.

'Sure,' I say. 'Although I kind of liked that I came for free using your plus-one credit.'

Nicole whistles quietly. 'Oh boy, yeah, that's a thing. It's not cheap.'

'Better to find an expensive workout I actually do than a cheap gym membership I never use, right?'

'Right,' she says, perusing the menu. 'Since it's Taco Tuesday, I'm saying . . . one of everything? And then if one is especially delicious, we can order more?'

I pause for a moment. 'It feels kind of weird to do such a crazy intense exercise class and then . . .'

'Does it?'

'Yeah, I guess . . .'

'Huh,' she says, nodding, like she's thinking about it.

I think back to the few attempts I made to lose weight over the past couple of years. The calorie counting, the step counting, the hours spent slinking aimlessly around the gym.

'Yeah, I mean, I've never done exercise without being on a weight-loss thing,' I say, shrugging.

'The two things are sort of unrelated for me,' Nicole shrugs back. 'It's like . . . I exercise because it's fun, I like it, it's probably good for me, it makes me feel good, it feels like a safe way of challenging myself. And it kind of has nothing to do with my body in terms of the way it looks. So food doesn't really come into it. Or rather, it doesn't come into it at all.'

I feel more embarrassed right now than I did for the whole of the spin class. I feel like I've shown myself up in front of Nicole, which is the *last* thing I want to do.

'Yeah, sorry, I . . .'

'It's okay,' she says, squeezing my hand on the table in front of me. 'I get it. It's a process. And I hope you're *in* the process now. Not like a *new year, new me* thing. Unless by *new me* you mean . . . like, more confident in yourself, and in your choices.'

I sigh. A process sounds like a lot of work. But on the other hand, I don't want to be ashamed of my body forever. I don't want to live like that. Knowing the reality of how people view my body is one thing, but that doesn't mean I can't work on how I feel about it myself, on my own terms. Not a Henry in sight. Like Nicole says: it's a process.

'You're cool,' I say. 'I'm glad I met you.'

'I'm glad I met you!' she replies. 'God, I was getting a bit bored there before you showed up . . . You know there are people where you have to mentally prepare before you talk to them and you feel you have to be really *on* all the time, like you're performing or something. That's how I felt in the office, Kirsty trying to talk to me about charging her crystals and whatnot. And Duncan being weird and whatever his angle is. And then you appeared and it was like . . . oh, I can just talk to this person and it's chill and normal,' she says casually, just as the waitress reappears to take our orders, which means instead of thinking of something to say I can just bask in the glow of her approval.

Finally we reach our goal, and are presented with the beer Nicole likes, the one with the lime and the salt.

'Cheers,' I say, holding my glass up.

Nicole clinks her glass against mine. 'To new adventures.'

16

Abandoning the apps and not going on a date a week has left me with . . . well, a lot of free time. I'm trying to find ways to fill it. I go to classes with Nicole, and sometimes I even go on my own. Wholesome things, you know? And, grudgingly, I make a date to see Melanie.

I *know* I should see my sister more often than I do. Highbury to Walthamstow is a dream journey as far as London tube journeys go. And yet, I don't. I'm not actively avoiding her, but I can't say I'm particularly proactive about seeing her. The wedding has made things weird between us, but I don't want that to be forever. So when she asked if I wanted to meet her for coffee and a walk in the cute park near her house one Sunday, I figured, yeah, why not?

'So you're still living in that flat on your own?' Melanie asks. We're in the cafe in the park, sitting outside in the bracing air but under a deliciously aggressive heater.

'Yep! And on mates' rates as well,' I say, sipping my flat white as Melanie nudges the pushchair containing her sleeping baby to and fro with her foot.

'Huh, nice,' Melanie says. 'Would be good for you if she never came back, right?'

'Nah, I liked the company. However short-lived it was. It was hard getting used to being on my own all the time at first. Now I'm kind of okay with it but I'm still looking forward to her coming back in a couple of months,' I say.

'Oh, she's got a return date?' Melanie asks.

'Yep, home in March,' I say. 'How are things with you?'

'Oh, you know, not much to say, is there? Same old, same old. Matt's an angel,' she says.

'Amen to that,' I say, because I've always liked him.

'And she's an angel too, when she wants to be,' she says, glancing fondly at the pushchair. 'It's just hard, isn't it?'

'I wouldn't know,' I shrug gently.

'Well, I assure you, it is.'

'It helps she's literally the cutest baby in the whole world,' I say.

'She is, right?!' Melanie says, her face lighting up. 'I know I'm biased but I genuinely think she might be.'

'I'm marginally less biased than you and can confirm Coco is the cutest baby in the world,' I say. I mean it. I want to nibble her cheeks and her wrists and her ankles, she's simply *too* delicious.

I let Melanie talk to me about the schools in Walthamstow and how hard it is to get a place at the 'good ones' and all her fears for the future, even though I can be of absolutely no help and, besides, Coco can barely talk so why are we worrying about schools? We finish our drinks and start strolling around the park, pretty in the cold, mid-afternoon light and sparsely populated for a pleasant Sunday afternoon.

'So,' Melanie says, maintaining a slow rhythmic pace which seems scientifically optimized to keep Coco asleep in her push-chair. 'Are you seeing anyone?'

'No,' I say, wishing I had a better answer.

'But you're meeting people, right?'

'Yeah . . . I've been on dates,' I sigh, not wanting to give her any evidence that actually being single hasn't remotely been the fun and games I was hoping for at the beginning of this shiny new phase of my life.

'And it didn't work out with *any*?'

'Nope,' I shrug.

'Huh,' she says, nodding slowly. 'What was it about them that was so bad?'

'It varied,' I tell her. 'Sometimes they were annoying, sometimes they were arrogant, sometimes they seemed committed to flakiness, sometimes they were aspiring standup comedians.'

'The worst,' she says, narrowing her eyes at me. Melanie hates standup. Who can blame her?

The one I don't mention is *sometimes I think I've met The One and it turns out they just don't want to be with me.*

'Right?' I say, smiling.

'That sounds like a lot of dates,' she says.

'Clearly not enough,' I say as a guy on a skateboard being pulled along by a labrador on a lead passes us on the path around the pond. The sound of the wheels and the pounding feet make Coco stir in the pushchair but she doesn't wake up, her chubby light-brown cheeks inflating with some half-asleep murmur.

'Do you think that's it?' Melanie asks, sounding genuinely curious.

'Do I think what's it?'

'Do you think it's just a question of not having met enough guys?'

'What do you mean?'

'I feel it's pretty obvious what I mean,' she says, frowning but keeping her eyes trained ahead of her, like a magpie landing on a tree is the most interesting thing she's ever seen.

'No, you'll have to be a bit clearer,' I say, not liking where this is headed.

Finally, she turns and looks at me. 'Come on, Serena, don't you think that the problem isn't all these bad guys? That you're the common denominator here and the reason why you haven't met anyone else is that you really were meant to be with Alistair? Don't you think that's it? Don't you think it's possible you made a mistake?'

Anger starts bubbling up in my chest but I'm hardly going to start a fight with my sister here in bucolic Lloyd Park, rolling around, pulling hair and biting each other like we're kids again. Unless she's up for that.

'I didn't make a mistake. Jesus, Melanie, how many times do I have to try and justify myself to you? Mum and Dad don't fucking *grill* me like this!' I say, but she cuts me off.

'Please don't swear in front of Coco,' she says, sanctimoniously.

'Firstly, she's asleep, and secondly, she can barely talk, I hardly think her first word is going to end up being *cunt* just because Auntie Serena moved to London.'

'Fine, whatever,' Melanie says, rolling her eyes. 'Anyway, just because Mum and Dad don't grill you it doesn't mean they think you were right. This isn't just a *me* thing, you know.'

I flinch. I mean, yes, of course I knew that this was a big surprise to my family, that obviously the way the wedding day went down was sort of a shock to everyone, but I think, maybe naively and without questioning it too much, I just assumed they *all* understood that if I felt compelled to take such decisive and dramatic action then it must have been for a good reason. Was I wrong about that?

'You really think you know better than me about what I should be doing with my life?'

'Why are you being so dramatic?' she says, rolling her eyes *again*. 'You're like a teenager.'

'For fuck's sake why can't you just speak clearly to me about this?' I burst out in irritation and then instantly fear I've woken Coco. But no. She snoozes on, oblivious to the family drama surrounding her.

'Okay, fine,' Melanie says, composing herself so she can come across as the pinnacle of reason against me, the wild, impulsive and foul-mouthed sister.

'I'm all ears.'

'I thought you were making a mistake at the time,' she says, tugging on her knitted beanie hat with one hand while pushing the pram with the other. 'And I still think you were making a mistake. I don't feel like you've shown me that there's anything better out there for you than Alistair, or that your life is any better without him.'

'So what you're saying is you think I should get back with Alistair?'

'Ha!' Melanie laughs. 'As if he would ever get back with you after what you did to him. No, what I think you should do is build a time machine and travel back to your wedding day and fucking marry him,' she says, clearly abandoning her very sincere policy on swearing around her child. 'What was wrong with him anyway?'

'Oh my God, *nothing!* There wasn't a thing wrong with him!'

I say, exasperated. 'But nothing was right either! It wasn't fun any more, it wasn't exciting any more, it, you know, didn't *spark joy*,' to borrow a phrase from Marie Kondo. Even though I *know* it was the right thing to do, having this conversation with her and being knocked back by Henry is sending these unwanted little shivers of doubt down my spine.

I wonder if Melanie can sense my uncertainty when she asks, 'What were you expecting after ten years?'

'You and Matthew have only been together four years, I don't know what you think you know about it,' I say, which I know will wind her up. Good.

'This has nothing to do with me and Matthew! This is about me, your big sister, worrying about the choices you've made.'

'Well . . .' I say, throwing my hands up in defeat. 'I've made them! There's nothing we can do about it now.'

'Would you get back with Alistair if you could?'

'What?' I ask, stupidly.

'If he turned around and said, *You know what, you might have fucked me around and humiliated me in front of all our friends and family, you might have wasted thousands of pounds and years of my life, but, really, we're meant to be together so let's cut the bullshit and get back together*,' she says. 'Would you?'

The answer is no, I wouldn't. But I can't help but think about her little time machine comment. It's not that I want to get back with him, it's just that . . . well, my life *would* be easier if Alistair and I just hadn't broken up. If I was married now. The thought shocks me. I spent so much energy *before* the wedding trying not to think about, well, the wedding and my life *after* the wedding that I didn't ever really fully visualize myself as being married to Alistair. The cottage. The routine. The comfort. The always having someone to go on holiday with. The security, yes, the financial security was nice, I can't pretend it wasn't. People have stayed together for less. People have got married for less. What made me think I was so special that I deserved more than that? What made me think that there was more out there, that it was so obvious to me my life without Alistair was going to be fun and easy and glamorous and full of wonderful men and wonderful experiences that I couldn't possibly have had with him?

Would I get back with him? I don't think so. But right now, after Henry, after all those dates with useless men, would I like to have never intervened in my own future in the first place? The answer to that might possibly be . . . yes.

'No,' I say, resolutely.

'Okay,' she says, nonchalantly. 'I just wanted to make sure.'

'Maybe I should see him,' I say, to placate her.

'Do you think he would?'

'It's worth asking. I mean, it's been four months now . . . it might not be so bad,' I say, hopefully.

'Only one way to find out,' she says.

I take my phone out of my coat pocket and yank my mittens off with my teeth. 'Fine,' I say, through mitten-gritted teeth. I type a message to him.

Hey Alistair, long time no speak. I hope you're doing okay and things are going well with work and everything. I was just wondering if you would want to get dinner sometime? Totally understand if not.

'Look,' she says, gently. 'If the opportunity arises . . . you know, to get back together and get your life back on track . . . I would take it. Don't take this the wrong way but . . .'

Why do I feel she's about to say something that I will absolutely take the wrong way?

'I don't know if you can do better than him. That's all it is. That's why it surprised us all so much – we thought you knew he was . . . well, as good as you were going to get. Frankly, I'm surprised *he* didn't see that.'

'Melanie, what the *fuck?*' I yell, instantly boiling over with fury, a fury loud enough to set Coco off wailing.

'Now look what you've done . . .' she mutters, stopping the pushchair and bending to unclip Coco, herself furious at being so abruptly awoken.

'Me?' I ask in sheer disbelief. 'Just because you're my sister it doesn't mean you can say whatever you want to me and I'll just suck it up! You can call it tough love or whatever you want but it's just plain rude! Nothing you've said today has been remotely helpful, it's just veered between condescending and confusing and upsetting and I've had enough. Coco, I love you,' I say, swooping to plant a kiss on her innocent little cheeks. 'Melanie, don't ask me to hang out again until you've learned how to be less of a bitch.'

I stalk off in the direction of the station, head churning with thoughts and none of them good. *Fuck*, I think to myself over and over. Why did I text Alistair then and there? Why didn't I wait? Me texting Alistair was based on the assumption that my sister was in some way reasonable and correct, and instead it turns out she's just a mean, meddlesome little troll. Maybe she's bored, maybe her life is just so fucking boring now she's not working and she's stuck at home with Coco and CBeebies all day long and she's just going out of her mind and somehow that's ended up biting *me* on the bum. God, Alistair is clearly going to say no, he's clearly going to tell me to fuck off, I'm going to look like a pathetic idiot, she'll go home and tell Matt how *horrible* I was to her today and then this narrative of me being all tempestuous and impulsive and unreasonable will continue when she's having these cosy little chats with our parents about what a perfect beast their youngest daughter is.

Ugh, it's fucking *freezing* and this stupid park is so far from the stupid station and I hope Coco's a proper nightmare for Melanie all afternoon and God is there *anyone* in the world who can wind you up like your family? Jesus. When I finally get to the station and make my way across the piss-smelling bus garage with its blue-light anti-heroin-injecting toilets blaring classical music I'm no less angry than when I set off from the park. I take my phone out of my pocket to touch in at the gate and head down to the tube, when I see a text on the screen.

Sure, I have a work conference in Russell Square in a couple of weeks, would be good to see you again then. It's February 2nd if that works for you.

Okay, so even though I was asking him if he wanted to get dinner, I can't say this is exactly the response I was expecting. Part of me was so sure he would just tell me to go fuck myself and to never contact him again. This has . . . surprised me, I must admit. Fuck, does this now mean I have to have dinner with Alistair even though I know that apparently the leading narrative among my friends and family is that he's vastly out of my league? Oh boy.

Sure, I'll book somewhere for dinner then and let you know.

I stay true to my word. I book dinner at a popular new Italian place in Bloomsbury that Kirsty at work has raved about. Whenever I think about the prospect of seeing him, I can't get Melanie's words out of my head.

'*We thought you knew he was . . . well, as good as you were going to get.*'

Bitch.

But what if the bitch is right?

17

To my surprise, I find I'm actually *enjoying* the date-free life. This time of just being me. Even a few weeks ago I don't think I would have been able to stand up to Melanie, but I feel a little more solid in myself already.

I cook a lot. I read a lot. I go to spin classes with Nicole sometimes, marvelling at the alchemic process of turning my burning leg muscles and screaming lungs into the biggest endorphin rush imaginable. I think about my body more, and worry about it less, although that still feels like a fragile balance that could be disrupted at any moment. I watch a lot of reality TV, even though maybe it's not so great for that fragile balance of body image. I walk a lot, bundling myself up in my leopard-print coat and picking a bakery or a museum or a coffee shop to walk to in another part of town, however far it is. I let myself enjoy the city, from the shimmering skyscrapers to the ragged pigeons, the restaurants with marble facades, to the humming neon lights of a twenty-four-hour cafe in Smithfield. I ring my parents more, even though I don't have anything particularly exciting to tell them, just to hear their voices and let them hear mine. I feel like I keep waiting for *something* to happen. Something tangible that will show me the right way to live, the right way to be, the kind of person I'm meant to be with. Is part of me still wondering if Melanie was right and that's Alistair? Yes. But at least I have our dinner in a couple of weeks to test out that theory.

And, of course, I sew a lot. Today I hopped on the tube and went up to the fabric stall on Walthamstow Market, all the while looking out for Melanie from the corner of my eye, hoping not to bump into her on her turf.

When I'm back with my spoils, I get to work. There's a dress design that's popular with all the cool sewing girls on Instagram and, rudely, the pattern designer hasn't released it in my size. So I'm using all my brain power and experience to figure out how to grade it up to make the perfect fit for my Serena-sized body. Good job I stocked up on a big roll of tracing paper because it's no easy task.

The sound of my phone ringing breaks through my intense concentration and I realize, amid all my hard work, I've completely lost track of time: I'd scheduled a FaceTime catchup with Lola.

'It's you!' I say, elated, at the sight of her on my screen.

'You bet it is! How's my girl?'

'Same old, same old,' I say, even though it's not strictly true. 'You?'

'Actually really looking forward to being home soonish. It's been a nice adventure but . . . there's no place like home. I miss my little routines, the comfort, knowing how everything works. And I miss you, of course,' she says with a smile.

'Of course! The flat is still standing, there are no scary letters from the bank or the council, and I am really looking forward to seeing you IRL soon.'

'What are you up to today?'

I sigh, feeling a little defeated. 'So there's this dress pattern. Kind of folksy-looking, big sleeves, high neckline, really cute.'

'I love it already,' says Lola.

'Well, me too, but the problem is that they don't make it in my size, so I'm sort of . . . hacking it and trying to grade it up,' I shrug. 'It's bad enough knowing that shops don't want to make clothes in my size and then it feels double rude that I'm not even being enabled to physically make them myself because *patterns* don't come in my size either.'

Lola looks pensive, shuffling herself around on her bed and sitting up, leaning her head against the headboard thousands of miles away. 'But you have the knowledge to sort of . . . adapt them yourself?'

'But that's not the point, I shouldn't have to!' I say, frustrated.

'No, no,' says Lola, 'that's not what I mean, darling. What I mean is . . . I feel like you should think about this. There are loads of styles you want to wear but can't, right?'

'Right,' I say.

'And you have, or you could learn, the skills to draw patterns for them in your size.'

'It's a bit of a headache but yeah, essentially.'

'And if we extrapolated from there, you could, shall we say, *adapt* the designs you wish existed in your size into a size-inclusive pattern that you could then sell to other amateur sewists in the same position as you.'

I exhale, exhausted at the thought of how much work that would take, but, at the same time, a little flicker of joy ignites in my chest. 'It sounds like a big challenge . . . but . . .'

'But maybe with the help of your old pal who's an artistic

director of a fashion brand – that's me by the way – who can keep an eye out for trends that your average plus-size brand isn't going to copy . . . maybe it would all be worth your while?'

'Huh,' I say, pensively.

'Look, I'm not saying you need to start some kind of dress-making empire from our flat. Just think about it. Size-inclusive sewing patterns based on real-life trends that people would otherwise be excluded from. It's an idea,' she shrugs.

'It's an idea,' I say, smiling. First Nicole asking if I would consider making something for her, and now this. Maybe I'm better at this whole *thing* than I thought. 'It's funny. You clearly have a lot more faith in me than I would have had in myself. I would never have thought of turning my skills into a side-hustle or whatever you want to call it. But it's not the worst idea.'

'Not the worst idea! Exactly! That's what I aim for!' Lola says, joyfully.

We chat about her frantic pace of work in New York, and how she's already dreading all the prep she's going to have to do this summer for London Fashion Week in September, and before long she's dashing off for a brunch date in Red Hook. Even when she's hung up, I can't stop thinking about her suggestion. The idea of doing better by women who are like me, not accepting the bare minimum, or even being left out completely. It would require a lot of work but, I can't deny, there's something about the idea that appeals to me.

18

'Are you sure about this?' Nicole asks me as I'm twisting my hair into a pretty half-up, half-down style, leaving some tendrils loose around my face.

'Yeah, why not? What's the downside?' I ask, making sure the clip is in exactly the right position.

'I don't know . . .' she says, warily.

Truthfully, I don't know either. For someone I dumped in the most mortifying and humiliating way possible, I'm actually just as nervous about seeing Alistair as I would be about any first date. Looking at myself in the bathroom mirror at work, I wonder what he's going to make of me now, after all these months.

Eventually I shrug, 'I'm just curious, you know?'

'I'm concerned about this . . .' she pauses, '*narrative* that I feel is building for you, about how maybe you made a mistake. I don't like it. I don't think Alistair is the answer to your problems.'

I shrug. 'One dinner isn't going to hurt.'

'I hope not,' she says. 'Speaking of which, Salvatore is coming over for dinner and I said I'd make something elaborate.' From what I can tell, Salvatore is Nicole's favourite of all her casual prospects, so it figures she would be willing to make something elaborate for him. 'Some fucking souffle or something, I don't know.'

'Good luck!' I say, trying to remember why it is that Salvatore isn't her boyfriend, and failing to come up with anything.

'I don't need it, my dude,' she says, winking over her shoulder at me as she holds the bathroom door open for me. We re-enter the office, where Duncan is the only person left, tapping away on his laptop. He nods at us in acknowledgement then goes back to his work.

'All right,' I say, walking over to me and Nicole's desk to pick up my bag. 'I'm off.'

Nicole sits down to send one last email. 'Have fun, but be careful,' she says, pointing one of her elegantly manicured nails at me, palest pink with darker pink glitter scattered at the tip. Extremely Nicole.

I sigh. 'I will, I promise.'

'And once I've sent this email I am going to run into the arms of sexy Salvatore!' She claps her hands together in delight. 'See you tomorrow. But also let me know how it goes.'

She gets to work, and I head out of the office, calling goodbye over my shoulder to her and Duncan. As soon as I make my way down the stairs and emerge from the heavy, industrial front door, I'm hit with a fat raindrop, and another and another. Rummaging around in my bag, I find, of course, that I have no umbrella. Classic. Absolutely classic. Dinner with my ex and I'm going to turn up looking like a drowned rat. Or am I? I let myself back into the office with my keycard and dash up the stairs, hoping that one of the promotional umbrellas Nicole grabbed from a trade fair are still in the stationery/junk cupboard.

When I get back up to our floor, I can see through the

window that Duncan is sitting on Nicole's desk. She's not look-ing at him, she's looking at her laptop. But she's, like, *really* looking at her laptop. Like it's not about what's on the screen, it's about not looking at him. I see him reach out a hand to touch her hair, and push open the door. He springs back from her and leaps to his feet.

'Back already?' he says, a frozen smile on his face.

'Yeah, I was just looking for an umbrella.' As I speak I'm trying to read the scene. 'Nicole, are there any hiding in here? Maybe in a cupboard?' I say, hoping she takes the hint.

'Um . . .' she says, a little flustered. 'Yeah, let's have a look . . .' She slinks past Duncan, who's still just standing there by her desk, watching me.

We walk in silence over to the big cupboard in the corridor near the bathroom.

'What the fuck was that about?' I whisper when the door closes behind us.

'I told you he was being weird with me, didn't I?' she whis-pers back, a mixture of stress and frustration and fear. 'Now you see what I mean! Fuck, I shouldn't have stayed back while he was there. I should have known better.'

'I think it's reasonable to expect you can be in the office with your colleague without worrying,' I say, determined not to let her believe this is on her. 'What was he saying?'

'Just how *nice* I look today and how we should go for a drink sometime and when I said I didn't think that would be a good idea he asked when I'd got so picky.'

'Eurgh, fuck,' I whisper. 'I could tell it was making you uncomfortable, but him trying to touch you was just . . .' I shudder. 'Are you going to tell someone?'

Nicole laughs, bitterly. 'Who? You work here, don't you? There isn't an HR department. There's the fucking accountancy company that do our payroll, and Kirsty does everything else. The blessings of working for a small company, right?'

'Well . . . what about telling Kirsty?'

'Telling her what? That he's coming on to me and I don't like it? I'd be lucky if she even believed me. I honestly don't think Kirsty's brain could compute that *he* could be harassing *me* and that *I* would find it unwelcome. All he would have to do is laugh it off and say he wouldn't be interested in me if I was the last woman on earth.'

'But . . . that's not the truth?' I say, and it sounds impossibly childish.

'The truth looks different when you're fat,' Nicole says, shrugging. She holds my gaze for a moment, before reaching into the cupboard and producing an umbrella. She hands it to me. 'Let's get out of here.'

'If you're sure . . .' I don't want to leave it at that, but I know now isn't the time to push Nicole if she doesn't want to be pushed.

'I'm sure.'

When we emerge back into the main room, Duncan is zipping up his backpack and picking up his headphones. 'Everything all right, girls?' The man knows he's messed up.

'Fine,' says Nicole, coldly.

'See you tomorrow, then,' he says, shouldering his backpack and pulling up his hood before leaving.

We stand in silence for a few seconds, waiting for Duncan to get far enough ahead of us, and then we leave ourselves. I put up the umbrella on the doorstep of the office and we huddle under it.

'Please,' I say, squeezing her hand. 'Can you tell me if anything like that happens again? Even if you're not going to tell Kirsty or Anjali, can you please tell me?'

'Yes,' she says, nodding. 'I promise I will.' She puts her arms around me. 'Have a good time with Alistair.'

'You have a nice evening, too,' I say, and I hope she can.

As I make my way towards dinner, I feel chilled not just by the rain but by Nicole's words. The idea that even for someone as confident as her, as unbothered by her body, as empowered, that there are still limits she's forced up against, borders that have nothing to do with confidence or self-love, that are imposed on her by other people. That even Nicole – beautiful, dynamic, unstoppable – is left feeling like decisions are made for her because of the way other people look at her body. It's a thought I know will hang over me.

When I get to the restaurant, I try to put those thoughts out of my mind and focus on the task at hand: projecting an image of pure radiance, grace and elegance to Alistair. I'm surprised to see he's already there. He looks great: put-together, but not too smart, relaxed but not complacent. I wonder what he's thinking, if he's here out of curiosity, if he's thinking maybe we could get back together.

'Conference ended a little early and I didn't want to get trapped in a pub scenario with the guys from the Clapham office,' he says, standing up to greet me, and just for a moment it feels like we're meeting for dinner like any couple would, like we're still woven into the fabric of each other's lives, time-tables, plans. 'It was actually useful to have an excuse not to go with them.'

'Oh, well, it's nice to see you,' I say, shattering the illusion that this is just business as usual for us.

'You too,' he says. When he sits down, he holds his tie against his chest so it doesn't drag in his water glass, and something about that gesture I've seen a thousand times makes me want to cry. We grew up together. We know each other so well. Why wasn't that enough for me? Is it really gone, beyond recognition, beyond the point of no return? Or could we go back there?

'You look good,' I say, looking at him over the top of my menu. It's true. He's found the optimal length for his thick, dark hair, and has transitioned from grey suits to navy blue. The colour suits him. He's always been good-looking – Nicole wasn't exaggerating. Tall and slim but not too lanky, hanging onto the sharp bone structure he had when we met. Which is more than you can say for me, I suppose.

'So do you,' he says, smiling kindly, which makes me feel like shit.

I don't reply, pretending to study the menu. I was thin when we met. A thin eighteen-year-old girl. And now I'm not. I guess it just happened. And sometimes I'm more okay with it than others. Right now I don't feel remotely okay with it.

The waitress takes our order and then all the distractions are gone and it's just me and him.

'So,' he says, 'how have you been?'

I put on my best smile. 'Yeah, good, busy.'

'How's London life? I bet you're loving it,' he says.

'Yeah, it's great!' I say, wondering what my London life is actually made up of. 'So much to do all the time!'

'And work's okay?'

'Work is actually . . . pretty good, you know?' At least that part is true.

'I bet Coco's a teenager by now,' he says, gently. He only met her a few times but he was always delighted by her, gently squeezing each of her tiny round toes, mesmerized by her black, fuzzy hair and her impossibly long eyelashes.

'She's a delight but my sister's a nightmare as usual,' I say with a laugh that comes out a little more harshly than I meant it to.

'Oh, Melanie's all right . . .' Alistair says, taking a sip of wine. They always got on well, which probably explains why she was so against us breaking up.

A burrata appears, the waitress setting it down in the middle of the table.

'You still like this, I assume?' Alistair says, cautiously.

'I do,' I say, delighted.

'I thought it was safe to order one to share,' he says, chopping it in half and scooping it onto his plate before pushing the remaining half towards me.

'You would be correct. So, how are you? Any news?'

'Not really . . .' he says, thoughtfully, furrowing his brow. 'Obviously it's been a bit of a strange time.' He balances a bit of the burrata on a slice of bread and smushes it down with the back of his fork.

'Yeah,' I say, nodding, wondering what to ask next, what would be polite to ask about and what would be too far, insensitive, unkind of me, the questions that would suggest I expected him to be sad or lonely after I ended things the way I did. 'I'm still sorry about it. The way it went down.'

He shakes his head, his face unreadable. 'It's okay, you know? I mean . . . it's not. But . . . yeah.'

'Yeah.'

'So,' he says, looking up at me, fixing me with a serious gaze. 'What is the nature of this meeting?'

'What do you mean?'

'Well, I assume you didn't just ask me here to hang out?'

'Would it be so weird if I did?'

'A little bit, yeah,' he says, frowning. 'Surely something moti-vated it.'

'Well, no, not really. I suppose I just wanted to see you. It's been strange, you know, for you to just walk out of my life after so many years, just gone.'

'I don't think it was me who did the walking out,' he says, wearily dragging his remaining burrata through the oil on his plate.

'Don't you think I know that?'

'I don't want to turn this into a fight. I just thought maybe you wanted to tell me something or you had news or . . . I don't know.'

'No, not really,' I say, feeling hot with embarrassment.

The waitress reappears and scoops up our plates.

'Look,' Alistair says, unbuttoning his collar and loosening his tie a little, sitting back in his seat. 'I may not have approved of your methods, but . . .' He swallows, trying to find the right words. 'I can't say, now, with hindsight, that you were wrong to put an end to it.'

'Oh!' I say, a little taken aback.

'I'm not saying it's impossible to stay in love with someone for ten years or more – God knows it's possible, my parents are proof of it – but I just don't know if we *were*, you know?'

'Yeah, I do.'

'So, I guess, thank you for being brave enough to end it,' he says, with a sad smile.

'I didn't feel very brave,' I say. 'I felt awful.'

'I do wish you'd done it a little sooner,' he says, looking up at the waitress who's appeared with our main courses. Fish for Alistair and some kind of aubergine pasta for me. We sit in a tense silence until she leaves.

'I honestly, truly, can't apologize enough,' I say once she's gone.

'It's . . . it's fine, it's over,' he says, throwing his hands up in the air. 'We have to be honest about the fact that the spark was gone, we just weren't attracted to each other any more, those days are over. It's all behind us, and now we have the rest of our lives to live, you know?'

Even though I *knew* it would be wrong for us to get back together, even though I *knew* I was making the right decision when I ended it – however brutally – it still makes me want to curl up in a little ball of embarrassment at the thought I'd entertained ideas of us being together again. Of course he wasn't attracted to me by the end. Jesus. Who would be? No wonder all my dates suck. No wonder Henry didn't want to be with me. What on earth do I have to offer anyone?

'Yeah!' I say as enthusiastically as I can muster. 'Totally!' I twirl some pasta onto my fork and lift it to my mouth. Unfortunately somewhere in between, it manages to un-twirl itself and flops down onto my collar, leaving a vivid red mark.

'Oh,' says Alistair, 'you've got a—' He points at the stain.

'I know,' I say, quietly, dabbing at it with my napkin. There's nothing to be done about it. I am simply a mess. I go to dip the napkin in my water glass but in my flustered state I manage to knock it over instead. 'Fuck!' I say as the whole restaurant turns around at the sound of breaking glass. In that moment I'm not only embarrassed for myself but also for Alistair for having to be seen with me. Poor guy.

'It's okay,' he says, looking pained at my embarrassment. 'It's okay, baby, don't worry about it.' He sounds so sincere, so gentle that it breaks my heart. 'Sorry, I didn't mean—' he says, shaking his head. 'Force of habit.'

We both know I'm not his baby any more.

'Thank you, sorry,' I say to the waitress who's clearing up my mess. 'I'm just going to go to the bathroom for a second,' I tell Alistair.

I feel like everyone in the restaurant is looking at me as I make my way to the toilet. I lock myself in a cubicle and sit on the seat, before realizing I've left my phone in my bag back at the table so can't talk to anyone. I compose myself, accepting that there's nothing I can do about the garish stain on my collar, and nothing I can do to un-break my water glass, and nothing I can do to stop me and Alistair from knowing we are not meant to be together.

When I finally go back to the table, Alistair is eating with one hand and texting with the other, eyes down on his phone. As soon as I scrape my chair out, he locks his phone and puts it down on the table. In the seconds before the screen goes dark, my eyes are drawn to his screensaver. Alistair and a pretty, thin, glamorous brunette. So that's that. I feel a little light-headed at the thought of it, even though I know perfectly well I have no right to feel anything at all about it. Nothing at all.

He hasn't brought her up, so I don't bring her up either.

'Sorry about that,' I say, brightly, as I sit down.

'It's okay. It's all okay, please don't worry about it,' he says.

'Hey, how was Thailand?' I ask, smiling.

'God, that feels like a long time ago!' he says. 'Thailand was . . . fucking boiling. You would have hated it.'

'I'm sure I could have suffered through it,' I say, glad to be on some kind of solid ground.

'But yeah, it was strange to be on a solo honeymoon, but other than that it was pretty great, so, uh, thanks for letting me do that,' he says, grinning at me. 'I think it was exactly what I needed. A change of scenery until things blew over.'

'I'm happy to have been able to help,' I say. And I mean it.

Fortunately, the rest of dinner is uneventful and when we part ways after he's insisted on paying, we hug and it, finally, feels like a real ending. He's met someone else. That's all there is to it. So no more kidding myself. It's all over.

19

'I'm baaaack!' Lola trills from the hall. I shuffle in from the living room to help her with her stuff.

'I missed you!' I say, drawing her into a hug.

'Relieved to see the place is still here,' she says, looking around. 'And it's clean!'

'I'm not a complete animal,' I say, smiling, carrying her suitcase and hand luggage into the living room where she flops onto her preferred end of the sofa. She lets out a groan as her head lolls back onto the sofa cushions I puffed up especially for her return. 'So . . . how was it?'

She sighs, kicking her shoes off and putting her feet up on the coffee table. 'It was great but hectic. I'm glad I went – it was a cool opportunity and all that and I'm *honoured* they thought of me – but I don't really feel like I stopped working the whole time I was there.'

'So it wasn't all rooftop cocktails after all?'

'Alas not. I assume nothing too dramatic happened here otherwise I'd have got an emergency phone call in the middle of the night?'

'Only the break-in where they stole all your jewellery,' I say, grinning, 'aside from that, nothing much to report. Oh and I threw the KitchenAid out of the window.'

'The jewellery I can accept but the KitchenAid is a step too far,' she says with her eyes closed.

The feeling is bittersweet to see Lola again after all these months. I'm happy to have my friend back but what kind of progress have I made since she went away? What do I have to show for all that time? I mean, sure, I haven't lost the job she helped me get, in fact, I seem to be doing pretty well at that if I do say so myself. Plus there's Nicole, and without her I would be *very* bored. But . . . beyond that? I don't feel like I've moved forward at all. I felt so optimistic when I moved here, so ready to be charmed by London, to make the most of this new freedom of mine. Dating has been a total bust. I'm possibly *more* confused about Alistair than I was when she left. Pathetic. She's been living it up drinking cocktails on rooftops in New York and I've been hiding under her expensive Hudson Bay Company blanket, trying not to get pasta sauce on it while I watch old episodes of *Keeping Up With the Kardashians*. Once more I say: pathetic.

'I have a game plan for today,' says Lola.

'Oh yeah?'

'I'm going to put my washing on and then sleep for a bit because I didn't manage to on the flight and I honestly feel like I'm dying.'

'You do look a bit . . . deathly.'

'Cheers,' says Lola with a wry smile. 'But then maybe later we can go for a drink at the Lamb or something? When my brain is working a bit better?'

I'd sort of assumed the opposite – that she would want to

go to bed early and I would be free to hang out with Nicole. Oops.

'Um . . .' I say.

'Oh! Unless you're busy? Sorry, I shouldn't have assumed you'd want to hang out with me!'

'No, it's not that! I'd made plans with my friend Nicole but if you're okay with having to chat to someone new on your first day back then I'm sure she would love to meet you.'

'Sure!' Lola says, gamely.

'Okay, I'll tell her to come to the Lamb at, what, eight?'

'Sounds good! And if she's awful at least I can claim jet lag . . .' Lola hauls herself to her feet and starts rummaging through her suitcase, gathering up laundry and ferrying it to the washing machine in the kitchen.

'I assure you, she's the opposite of awful,' I say, picking up one of Lola's stray socks. I hope they get on. I think they will, anyway. 'So, what's your goss? Any drama, intrigue, romance, nonsense?'

She slams the door of the washing machine shut then leans on it to make sure it locks. 'It was . . . a lot. Who knew that this accent was catnip to the queer women of New York?! Suffice to say, I had a lot of fun.'

'So Cinzia is just fully gone, done, old news, out of your mind?'

'Who?' Lola says, squinting at me theatrically. 'Just kidding. But yeah, nothing so useful to help you get over one woman as getting under another. And another, and another . . .'

All I can say is I'm glad that she's had a more eventful few months than I have. Not that that would be hard. 'I'm delighted to hear it.'

'Right . . .' she says, clapping her hands together. 'I'm going for a nap. If I'm not awake by seven, come and gently rouse me from my slumber.' She carries her considerably lighter suit-case out into the hall and up the stairs to her room.

I flop back on the sofa. How will I explain Henry to her? It sounds like nothing to an outside observer but it feels like *so much* to me. How I met someone that I thought was going to be, like, *the one*, or at least *a* one, who I fell for fast and hard, and who then backed away with no real explanation.

I text Nicole.

Sorry for changing plans but turns out my flatmate actually wants to go for a drink tonight. If you're up for it please still come? She's super nice, I promise! The Lamb on Holloway Road at 8?

Ugh fine I guess I'll still come . . . jk, sounds great, I look forward to meeting her.

In the spirit of being a good flatmate, I head out to buy ingredients to make some mozzarella and chorizo baked gnocchi for me and Lola's dinner later. It's a slightly grey, cloudy day, a day that makes you feel a little out of sorts, like you can never guess what time it is by the light outside. I want to breathe some fresh air, so instead of going to Tesco down by the station I decide to walk up to Highbury Fields, see if there are any cute dogs about and cross the green down to the Sainsbury's on the other side of Highbury & Islington tube.

I grab a bag for life out of the bag full of bags for life that hangs in the kitchen, and stomp up to Highbury Fields. I'm snaking my way across the green, admiring a large black poodle trotting away on the path, when I hear someone call my name.

'Serena?' I stop, wondering if I'm imagining things. Maybe it's the wind. 'Serena?' I look around.

'Rachel!' I shout back, spotting her on a parallel path further up the green. We walk towards each other, me with my hands stuffed in my pockets, her swinging a large pink gift bag as her fine, dark hair blows in the breeze. 'What brings you to my neck of the woods?'

'I completely forgot you lived here! I almost forget you don't still live in your village any more, let alone so close to me! I'm going to my colleague's baby shower.' She rolls her eyes. 'Every weekend a new hen do or baby shower, right?' she says, as if I'm definitely going to be able to relate.

'Right,' I say, smiling. 'How's married life?'

'A whirlwind! Wedding then Christmas then honeymoon.'

'I saw the photos! Mexico looked incredible,' I say, thinking of my own missed honeymoon in Thailand. I wonder if I'll ever make it to Thailand in my life. Maybe I should have seen the wedding through just for the honeymoon, and *then* done a runner.

'It was incredible! Thank you so much for coming to the wedding, by the way, it was really nice to see you, even though, God, it's such a weird day – it just slips away from you and you don't get to talk to everyone you invited!'

'Don't worry about it,' I say, gently. 'I don't think anyone expects one-on-one time with the bride.'

'Well either way, I heard from Susie that you and Luke's mate Henry were hitting it off at the dinner?' Rachel says, her blue eyes aglow with delight.

I blush, wondering how much she knows. I assume if she's

only heard it from Susie then she doesn't even know we went out at all. For her it can exist in the realm of cute, fun fantasy, rather than the disappointing reality.

'Yeah, it was nice to chat to him,' I say, trying to keep it neutral, not give away *quite* how taken I was with him.

She cocks her head a little, a look of sympathy clouding her features. 'Henry's great. I mean, duh! Luke would be dead without him! But yeah, he's a good guy. Shame he's so on and off with his ex,' she shrugs. 'I feel like he's never going to make his mind up and they're just going to be dancing around each other forever.'

Oh. I see.

'Mmm,' I say, nodding like this is purely small talk for me. Like I'm not thinking about all those boxes piled up when I went to his flat, stepping around piles of women's shoes, her presence so felt in its anticipated absence. 'Nice guy.'

'Anyway!' Rachel says, perkily. 'I'm going to be late for the first round of Guess the Baby Food. But let's get dinner soon now things are a bit more back to normal after the wedding? '

'Sure!' I say, trying to match her perkiness. 'Text me!'

I make my way around Sainsbury's like a zombie, focused totally inward on my thoughts. I even nearly buy low-fat mozzarella, a certified crime against humanity which would get me barred from entering Italy for the rest of my life, but manage to catch myself in time. So now I know what happened, I guess. Henry got back with his ex. I was a fun little diversion for him. That's all there was to it in the end. And I had to hear it from Rachel.

★   ★   ★

Lola wakes up just before seven so I don't have to take on the unenviable task of rousing a jet-lagged person, and we eat dinner together before meeting Nicole at the pub.

When we push open the door to the Lamb, the buzz of conversation and music envelops us like a hug.

'Hey!' Nicole says, looking over her shoulder from the bar.

'Nicole, this is Lola, Lola, this is Nicole,' I say, doing my mutual friend duties. They hug politely.

'I just ordered you an IPA, but tell me what you want, Lola?'

'Oh, no, you don't have to!' Lola says.

Nicole swats her away. 'Come on, just tell me what you drink.'

'I'll have a glass of rosé, please,' she concedes.

'I should have guessed that,' she says, shaking her head like she missed a trick. 'You have the look of a rosé drinker.'

We pick up our drinks from the bar, sipping so we don't spill them, and sit down at a table in the back illuminated by candlelight. It's kind of romantic and mysterious. Would have been nice to bring Henry here sometime.

'I'm glad we're meeting somewhere so dark because I got my fillers done again today and I'm looking a little bit, well, to quote from *When Harry Met Sally*, baby fish mouth,' Nicole says, shielding her lips.

'Fuck!' I say, delightedly, 'I literally thought you just had incredible lips! Like I've always thought you had amazing lips and I thought you were just born that way.'

Nicole rolls her eyes. 'As if,' she says. 'I pay good money for these and I don't want anyone to forget it.' She purses her lips into a pout.

'Honestly, they look great,' says Lola.

Nicole clinks her glass against Lola's. 'I'll drink to that.' She takes a sip of her pint. 'So, our mutual friend Serena says you've been off gallivanting in New York for months?'

'True,' Lola nods. 'I work for a designer and I was doing some work in the New York office.'

'Which designer is it?'

'Mirabeau?' Lola ventures, picking up her wine glass. 'It's sort of pastel, gauzy, puffy things.'

Nicole rolls her eyes. 'I know what it is. I also know that they don't have any interest in being size-inclusive so, until then, will never get my hard-earned coins.'

Oh no, the sparks are flying already, why didn't I think of this before?

But instead of being defensive, Lola puts her glass down, sighs and says, 'You know what, you're right.' She shakes her head. 'I can't say there's any particularly compelling reason why we make such a limited size range. It's embarrassing.'

'I'm sure there's—' I say, but Nicole cuts me off.

'Damn right it is! I mean, unless you think there's something *wrong* with my body? Undesirable?' Nicole says, tossing her hair over her shoulder.

'No, no, not at all!' Lola says, wide-eyed with horror. 'You're totally right, I'll try to fix that . . . sooner rather than later.' She looks properly embarrassed.

I mean . . . yeah, I've always thought it's kind of sucky Lola's company doesn't make clothes that fit me, but I kind of figured . . . you know, they're not *for* me. But maybe I was wrong.

'That's what I like to hear,' says Nicole. 'No time like the present!'

Lola looks keen to take the spotlight off herself. It's funny, she's usually the boss in social situations, so it's oddly delightful to feel like maybe she's met her match in Nicole.

'So if you work with our darling Serena then that means you work with Anjali, right?' she asks Nicole.

'I do indeed! Do you know her?'

'We were at Saint Martin's together,' she says, smiling warmly. 'Is she a good boss? It only occurred to me after I recommended Serena for the copywriting job that I have absolutely no idea what it's like to work for her.'

'She's a great boss. Very hands-off, trusts you to know what you're doing.'

'That's true,' I say, even though I hadn't thought of it until then.

'Rest of the office is kind of *meh* except for this one,' she says, cocking her head towards me.

'She's not so bad, right?' Lola says, delighted.

'If only we could sort out her love life,' says Nicole, pulling a cartoonishly sad face.

'Yeah! I don't really get what's going wrong there, you know?' Lola furrows her brow at me.

'Handsome Henry was the wrongest of the lot, it turned out,' Nicole says drily.

'Huh?' Lola says.

'Yeah, about that . . .' I shift in my seat. 'I didn't actually mention Henry to Lola. . .'

'Why?!' they both ask in unison.

'Because I was so hyped to have good news to tell her and then when it all *failed* I couldn't face talking about it!'

'Well, fill me in now!' she demands, banging her hand down on the table so the candle shakes.

'I met him at a wedding.'

'Ugh! The perfect meet-cute!'

'And he actually asked me out! Can you believe it?'

Lola frowns at me. 'Yes, I can believe it.'

'Well, I couldn't. Anyway, we had a couple of great dates . . . well, one date spanning two days, if you know what I mean. But then he just really pulled away from me and that was that, over. Apparently he got back with his ex, which would explain why he was so weird and cagey with me when he had been so keen at first. And even though in my brain I *know* it's not that, I can't help but be scared it was just a sex thing for him. But it just didn't *feel* like that. But now I'm so confused about it all that it *could* be that!'

'Oh. I'm sorry,' she says. 'It sucks when that happens. And it's not like you've met anyone *else* good online, right?'

'I've been trying!' Nicole says. 'Gently encouraging her to go on dates and stuff.'

'And?' Lola asks.

'I have been!' I protest. 'I told you, I did the one date a week thing!'

'Wait,' says Lola, draining her glass and leaping to her feet. 'I'm going to buy us all another drink and we can try and get to the bottom of what's going wrong here. Same again?'

'Yes, thanks pal,' I say, a little wearily.

'Sure, thanks,' says Nicole, and Lola strolls off to the bar. 'So, what's her story then?'

'Lola?'

'Who else?' Nicole says, watching Lola walk away.

'Oh!' I say, understanding what's happening here. 'I didn't know you . . .'

'You never asked, my good bitch,' Nicole says, smiling. 'But yeah, I don't have a particularly fixed policy on who I date.'

'Ugh, I'm such a rubbish friend, aren't I?' I moan.

'May this be a lesson to you. Anyway, this ain't about you – tell me about Lola before she comes back.'

'Well, yeah, I mean, she is gay so that's a good start.'

'And is she single? Is she ready to mingle?'

'Yep, she was in a pretty serious relationship until last year but they broke up . . . she was kind of hung up on that for a while but she was literally just saying today that New York was good for putting all that behind her. So,' I say, shrugging. 'I can't promise anything but it seems like you're not, well, barking up the wrong tree.'

Nicole nods slowly. 'We shall see.' I can't help but marvel at Nicole's approach, her absolute belief that the only thing that stands between her and Lola is whether Lola is single. I can't imagine seeing the world like that.

Lola returns with the drinks and maybe it's because Nicole already said something, but I suddenly notice how skittish Lola is, not her usual composed self. Nicole has made her a little flustered and off her game. I smile at the unintended side-effect of this casual drink in the pub.

'So,' Lola says, sitting up straight on her bar stool, setting her shoulders back like she's preparing for a very important interview, 'tell me everything.'

20

'And you didn't sleep with *any* of them?' Lola asks. She sounds more than a little incredulous.

'Aside from Henry, no. So basically, no, nothing.'

'And exactly how many dates have you been on?'

'Like . . . a lot. As per my goal, I was going on one a week until I got too depressed and gave up. Wasn't I, Nicole?'

'I can confirm the truth of that statement,' she says, drily.

'Certainly enough that I should have found someone nice to sleep with at least one or more times. And instead, nothing. It's kind of frustrating.'

'I'll bet it is,' says Nicole, picking up her pint glass.

'That too,' I say, thinking how much easier my life would have been if I could have just kept having sex with Henry.

'I feel like it shouldn't be this hard for you to find people to bone. It doesn't sound like you're trying to find some long-term relationship . . .' Lola says.

'No! Not at all! I mean, I wouldn't have said no to Henry, but . . .'

'Henry's gone, Henry's dead, we can't think about Henry any more,' Nicole swats the air as if to physically push his ghost out of the way.

'He's not actually dead,' I say to Lola, quickly. 'This is just Nicole's way of being supportive.'

'Got it,' Lola nods, clearly a little confused by it all. 'Anyway,' she says in an attempt to get the conversation back on track.

'My point is, you know, I was putting the effort in, I was sending the messages, the smoke signals, I was out there, talking to guys, going on dates, showing up, you know? And it was just not getting me anywhere,' I say, a little pathetically. Taking time out from the apps has been good for me, yes, but I really *would* like to meet someone. I'm not too proud to admit that.

'So . . . what's the beef?' Lola asks.

'Come on . . .' I say, a little awkwardly. 'I feel like it's pretty obvious what the problem is . . .'

'What?' she asks.

'I mean . . .' I say, looking to Nicole for backup but she's just waiting for me to speak. 'It's a body thing, right?'

'You think these guys didn't want to sleep with you because of your *body*?' Lola asks.

'I mean, I didn't want to sleep with them in the first place,' I say. 'But . . .'

'Wait, so . . . I don't get it . . . what's the problem?' Lola frowns.

'Hold up,' says Nicole. 'You want to have fun, you want to date, you want to sleep around a little bit, hop into bed with some nice men. You say you're putting the effort in, and all that. But you're meeting up with guys you don't fancy? Did you know you didn't fancy them before you went on the dates?'

'No!' I say, instinctively defending myself. But . . . wait. What if I did know that?

Lola and Nicole are looking at me intently.

'I mean . . . maybe . . . yes . . . but like . . .' I cast around, trying to explain it. 'Not actively, you know? It's not like I was seeking them out because I didn't fancy them . . .'

'You're so weird,' Nicole says, eyeing me suspiciously. 'I wish I could see inside your little noggin.'

'What, why?' I don't feel like I'm particularly interesting, or mysterious, for that matter.

'It's just . . . you're funny,' she says, smiling. 'I feel like I have no idea on what basis you were going on dates with these guys at all?'

'They seemed . . . nice?' I say, which is true. They didn't seem like literal serial killers. They had faces. They could hold conversations.

Nicole is looking at me, gently amused, like she's trying to figure me out. 'Do you think, maybe, what you were doing was looking at these men and thinking "Would this person fancy me?" when what you should have been thinking was "Do I fancy this person?"'

'I . . .' I say, as her words sink in. 'I mean . . . I hadn't thought about it that way. I hadn't thought that was what I was doing. But . . .' I look down at my pint in my hand and then back up again to Nicole, Lola just observing, quietly. 'You know what . . . I think that, yeah, that's exactly what it was.'

'Okay! Now we've figured this one out, it means your life is going to get marginally easier!' Nicole says, slamming her hand down on the table.

'But how does it help me?'

'How doesn't it help you?'

'Well . . . because I guess I just don't know if . . . if I really believe that it's possible for men to really fancy me,' I say, shrugging as if I haven't just shared my most sincere self-limiting belief, and one that I don't really even admit to myself. And besides, Melanie basically came out and said it, too. 'I feel like I was, you know, *lucky* to have got Alistair and then I threw all that away because it didn't feel right. And now I'm not sure why I thought I would ever have been able to do any better.'

'Because you're fat?' Nicole asks.

'Yeah! That's a pretty good reason!' I say, throwing my hands up.

'But . . . how do you explain the fact that I'm, you know, merrily boning my way around London, going on dates, having fun, basically doing what you want to do and we're pretty much the same size?' Nicole asks me, incredulous. 'Look, I get it, bitch, I get it. The world is fucked up and hostile and hateful to fat bodies. I'm not going to tell you that's not true, because it fucking is true, but that doesn't mean you have no power at all. It just doesn't.'

'Yeah but . . . you're you! You're pretty and glamorous and whatever. Groomed. You get your lips done!'

'Babe,' she says, looking at me like that's the most ridiculous thing she's ever heard. 'You go and get your lips done, I'll give you my girl's number. And you can get a blow-dry and a mani-cure. But I guarantee you that will not make your dates any more fun if you're still only meeting up with weird scrubs that you think will like you because you don't think *you* get to be the one that chooses.'

I just sit there. I don't know what to say. I genuinely don't know what to say at all. I could keep arguing with her about all the reasons that she manages to have a good time dating, fucking, all that, but in the end . . . I think she might be right.

'You decided that it was your body imposing limits on you but really it sounds like it was your mind,' she shrugs.

'Fuck,' I say, laughing.

'You know I'm right,' she says, narrowing her eyes and pointing a shiny candy-pink nail at me.

'Fuck!' I say again, laughing a bit louder.

'Did I just witness a huge breakthrough?!' Lola finally pipes up, knowing this conversation was very much not for her.

'I think so!' I say, feeling some kind of psychic pressure lift off my head. 'I mean, look, I don't think I'm going to be laying waste to the men of London tonight . . . but . . .'

'Well,' Nicole says, pouting a little. 'I think you should.'

'Baby steps!' I say. 'I feel like at least it will prevent me from actively wasting my own time on any more dates with random men that I've decided would deign to fancy a fat girl.'

'Right?! Look, pal, I think you just need to sort of . . . present yourself to the world with the belief that you deserve good things. That you deserve to be happy. That you deserve to fuck who you want to fuck. Even if that's not true yet.'

'Fake it till you make it?' Lola ventures, tentatively.

'Exactly,' Nicole says, winking at her. Lola's eyelashes flutter involuntarily and when I look at her out of the corner of my eye she's got a little smile dancing on her mouth.

'Okay, right . . .' I say, furrowing my brow in concentration. 'So I just have to sort of . . . project confidence. Act like I believe in myself.' It's not that I don't believe in myself so much as my ability to believe in myself has become so inextricably linked to my weight that I can't untangle the two. I need to untangle.

'Yeah! Don't be surprised when someone likes you. Or at least, don't act like you're surprised! It's totally and completely fine to not be a hundred per cent at peace with your body. It's hard, man. It's really hard. You need to control your own narrative. And if you tell people – and I don't mean literally tell them, I mean if that's the vibe you're putting into the world – that you're not worth their time or you don't deserve to fuck who you want or whatever, then people will start to believe that. But if you're walking around like you're the queen of fucking everything, then maybe they'll be like, *Oh, Serena? Yeah, she's hot.*'

'I've got to say . . .' Lola says, 'I think this sounds like good advice! I mean . . . people do kind of believe what you tell them.'

'Exactly!' says Nicole, enthusiastically. 'And this isn't just a dating thing, you know.'

'What do you mean?'

'It's an everything thing. Stop slinking through the world like you're lucky to be there, or like you're waiting to be found out, exposed for having a fat body.'

I blush, knowing she's right. I do that. 'Like where?'

'Like at spin class! Just walk in like you own the place! Sure, we're the only fat babes there, but we deserve to be there as much as everyone else!'

'I guess . . .' I say, wondering what it would feel like to do that. What it would actually feel like to walk in there with my head held high, not wondering how long it's going to be until I'm somehow found out. Focusing on myself for the past couple of months has felt really good, and finally, I feel like this is the last little push I needed to take it to the next level. Just a few words, just a few questions to help me see that maybe I'm looking at things all wrong. If I'm always wondering what

244

people are thinking of me, whether they think I'm attractive enough to be there, whether I deserve their time because I'm fat, what kind of choices does that leave me? Certainly not empowered ones. After spending time alone, away from the hamster wheel of dating, I feel more able to identify people that I think I would be a good match with. And now I have the motivation to try and make it happen.

'Look,' she says, gently. 'You don't *have* to change your body. You just don't. And you don't have to prove yourself to anyone. You don't have to prove that you love your body or whatever, you don't owe that to anyone. But I just know that if you act like you're the queen of the fucking universe then you'll find it easier to navigate this shitty world.'

'Okay,' I say, taking a deep breath. 'I think maybe you've just changed my life a tiny bit.'

21

'There you are!' Nicole says, stretching her arms out to me outside the studio, as if she didn't see me a mere twelve hours prior. 'I thought you might stand me up.'

'Never,' I say, when in fact she's right – after my pints last night with her and Lola, hauling myself to an exercise class was the last thing I wanted to do.

'I had fun last night,' she says, pushing the heavy glass door open. 'Sorry if I got too intense and fucking . . . wise old owl, you know? It's just, I've been where you are and I know the grass is much greener over here.'

'No,' I say as we join the short queue to check in and get our shoes. 'It was amazing. Thank you.'

When we reach the front of the queue, I give our names rather than hiding behind Nicole. When we get into the bustling locker room, I find us two lockers together rather than waiting for Nicole to do it. I pick up towels for us before the class. I chat to her outside the spin studio as we're waiting and, instead of wondering what everyone around me is thinking about our bodies, I just let myself focus on our conversation. I set my bike up confidently, and when the class starts I realize I'm sitting on the bike differently, my spine straighter, my pose more determined. The class is still so hard it almost feels impossible, but I know that I deserve to be there as much as anyone else. It doesn't matter that I suck! I'm not the instructor, it's not my job to be good. It's just my job to show up and try my best and that's exactly what I do. And as I'm frantically turning the pedals, engaging my core and pushing myself harder than I've ever pushed, I realize Alistair was never going to save me. Even Henry can't save me. No one I match with on Tinder can save me. I can only save myself. Nicole gives me a sweaty high-five at the end of the class, by which point I'm soaked to the skin, my breathing ragged, and amazed with myself at being able to see it all through to the end.

'You're making such good progress!' Nicole says as we drag our weary bodies towards the showers.

'It's still fucking hard though,' I say, trying and failing to catch my breath on the stairs after such an intense class.

'You did it, that's all that matters,' she says.

After we shower, I don't scurry off to the toilet cubicles to get changed, as much as every fibre of my being is crying out for me to do that. I push on. I dry myself off without worrying *too* much if someone catches a glimpse of my fat, pale, decidedly unathletic body. It turns out no one is really paying me any attention at all. They're just trying to get dried and dressed and blast their hair with the hairdryer and do a quick face of makeup and then get on with their Sundays. Just like me.

'Want to get coffee?' I ask Nicole as she swipes some mascara onto her lashes.

'Sorry,' she says, grimacing, 'can't. I'm having lunch at my brother's because I haven't seen the girls since Christmas.'

'That's okay!' I say. Maybe I'll go get a coffee on my own. Maybe that would be kind of nice. 'I saw you last night, I'm seeing you now, and I'll see you at work tomorrow. I'm pretty sure I can survive one flat white without you.'

'Hmm,' says Nicole, squinting at me, swirling her damp hair into a high bun and pulling a few strands loose. 'If you don't come into work tomorrow I'll know why. It was because it turns out you *couldn't* survive the flat white without me.'

We hug goodbye and, true to my word, I do go to the cafe down the road on my own. I try not to waste too much time being paranoid that I nearly knock the sugar on the next table over with my bum while taking my seat. I try not to think too much about the way my thighs spread against the bench underneath me. I try to focus on my book rather than wondering if everyone I in the cafe is looking at me and quietly laughing at the fat girl on her own. On balance? They're probably not. They're probably reading their own books, drinking their own coffee, scrolling through Twitter, reading the newspaper.

Endorphins: they're a real thing, huh? I feel . . . optimistic. I feel light in my chest. I feel a bit like I want to hug the world. And I *really* want to text Henry, not because I'm sad and I miss him, but because I'm happy. I want to have a chance to get to know him properly. I want *more* of the good stuff I already saw in him. I want, at least, to see how things play out. But when I take out my phone I can't bring myself to do it. I would simply feel like too much of a dickhead if he was, like, *I THOUGHT I MADE MYSELF CLEAR!!!* It's not worth it. Let's take these endorphins home.

★   ★   ★

On the bus home, I check my emails on my phone, and amid the '25% OFF LIMITED TIME ONLY CODE' emails about makeup I don't need, and NatWest telling me my 'statement is ready to view online' – no thanks – is an email from my sister. That's a name I don't see in my inbox too often. The subject line says only 'Hello'. I wonder if she's been hacked and it's some kind of phishing thing. Warily, I open it . . .

Hey Reenie, can we meet for a drink please? I feel like we need to talk. One night next week? I can come to you. Xx

Intriguing. I'm a bit fed up of stewing over what was said all those weeks ago, so I reply and say yes, offering next Wednesday night. On my sporadic phone calls with Mum she's always on at me about making up with Melanie, and I can only assume Melanie's been on the receiving end of the same.

I'm sufficiently caffeinated but absolutely starving and wondering what I'm going to make for lunch when I get home. When I push the door to our flat open, the smell of warm, savoury food, of garlic and onions and richness, hits me like a tidal wave.

'Thank God you're here!' says Lola when I appear in the kitchen. 'I've made so much risotto I thought I was going to have to eat it all and risk an untimely yet delicious death. Please help me?'

She's stirring an enormous simmering pan on the hob and is dressed in some kind of old-fashioned gentleman's silk dressing gown over her pyjamas. The colours of it remind me of the print on some mid-weight cotton poplin fabric I bought up the road the other day, and something about the way the collar falls helps me settle on making it into a jumpsuit. Possibly a little afternoon project?

'I would literally love nothing more – I feel weak like a tiny baby after that class.'

She stirs in some perfectly green garden peas and crispy pancetta that's sitting, waiting, on a plate to the side.

'Oh, is that where you've been?' she asks. I nod. 'With Nicole?'

'Yep!' I say, about to change the subject.

'It was nice to meet her last night,' Lola says. I clatter about retrieving bowls and knives and forks and laying the table, but I notice something weighing in the silence after Lola's words.

'Oh yeah? She's cool, isn't she?'

'Yeah,' Lola says, a little too nonchalantly. 'Really cool.'

I smile, remembering what Nicole said about her last night and wondering if maybe, just maybe, the feeling is mutual.

'What?!' says Lola, herself breaking out into an irrepressible smile. 'Why are you smiling like that?!'

'Why are *you* smiling like that?' I ask as she scoops the risotto into the waiting bowls.

'I'm not smiling like anything!'

'You're literally smiling right now, I can see it with my eyes! My own eyes!'

'I just thought I was getting a vibe, that's all . . .' she says. We sit down at the old gnarly oak dining table, full of cracks and bumps that I've learned to navigate over the past months – where not to put your glass down, where crumbs are likely to escape through.

'And would it please you if I was to confirm that, indeed, you did get a vibe? Or would that be purely academic information?'

'Well . . .' she says, stirring some more parmesan into her risotto which is so hot that it melts the cheese instantly. 'Everyone likes to feel special, don't they?'

251

'So what you're saying is that you think Nicole is cool and maybe you would like to hang out with her sometime?' I blow enthusiastically on my forkful of risotto.

'I guess I am,' she says, dropping the coy act.

'I love this for you!'

'I love this for me too!'

'It's funny,' I say, 'I wouldn't necessarily have put you two together . . . but I feel like it works?'

'Serena, my friend,' she says, resting her fork on the side of her bowl and looking at me with an incredibly serious stare. 'Romance works in the most *mysterious* ways.'

22

Maybe Nicole is magic. Literally magic like a witch or something. It's just a working theory. Or it could just be she is really
fucking wise. Either way, I've felt . . . different this week. I
haven't been dwelling on why things didn't work out with
Henry. I haven't felt bruised by Alistair's comments. Maybe I'm
faking it until I make it, and it's doing a good job of tricking
my brain either way. The combination of having time to myself
plus Nicole's radical confidence tactic has really *worked*. I'm
back on the apps, but I've been looking at the dudes of the
online world with new eyes – *mine* rather than theirs. Maybe
I'll choose to meet someone, maybe I won't, but just taking
that step feels good to me. I just feel *ready* for the world. I feel
now the way I wish I'd been able to hold onto back in September
when I first moved to London, that excitement, that feeling
that everything was possible, that I could do anything I wanted
whenever I wanted, that I could be anywhere, that some kind
of infinite possibility was out there.

So after a week of feeling just that little bit better, a little bit
less flat and lost, I decide to enjoy a Saturday of solo adventure.
I take Duncan at work's advice and decided to attempt to get

a day seat for a production of *Hamlet* that's on in the West End which he recommended. I've kept an eye on him since the Nicole situation happened and there hasn't been anything untoward so I'm *hoping* that was the end of it. And even if the production ends up being bad, at least I'm *going* to the theatre. Doing something, actually taking advantage of living in London.

I walk up to Holloway Road station and take the Piccadilly line to Piccadilly Circus, which stresses me out because I *never* choose the right exit, no matter how clearly signposted they are. When I get to the theatre on Shaftesbury Avenue, a short queue has already formed for day tickets. Maybe I'm too late. Oh well, in which case I'll just stroll around the West End, maybe go to the cinema. The world is my oyster! I need to embrace that, rather than fear it.

I duly join the queue with twenty minutes to go until they open the box office, slipping in my little earphones so I can listen to some true crime nonsense podcast while I wait. I've only listened to a couple of minutes when I feel a tap on my shoulder. I slip out my earphones as I turn around.

'Oh, I'm so sorry, I couldn't see you were wearing headphones!' an older American man says, incredibly apologetically. 'I just wanted to know if this was where I should line up if I don't already have a ticket.'

'No, it's okay! You just surprised me, that's all! Yes, this is the day ticket queue,' I say like I'm some kind of expert and didn't just join the queue myself.

'Great, thank you so much, I'm so sorry to have bothered you,' he says. As I look at him I notice that he's really not *that* old, he just has very grey hair. Tanned skin, sinewy arms, a collection of black tattoos below the elbow, wearing a denim shirt with the sleeves rolled up and khaki trousers with desert boots. He's . . . kind of handsome. On second glance, he's *really* handsome.

'It's no problem at all,' I say. 'I hope we both manage to get tickets.'

'Yeah, I tend to have pretty good luck with this stuff. It helps when there's only one of you.'

'That's good to know,' I say, smiling at him. Why shouldn't I smile? If I act like a hot girl, I might be perceived as a hot girl. He seems like as good a place as any to start. 'I don't do this so often.'

'You should! It's a smart idea if you wanna see stuff but you suck at planning,' he says.

'Yeah, I always feel like by the time I hear about something I want to see, it's sold out. Anyway,' I say, not wanting to wear out our conversation to the point of awkwardness, 'good luck.' He thanks me and I turn back around and put my headphones back in. But I make sure I stand up a little straighter, make my posture that little bit more confident. Finally, the queue starts moving and when I get to the front of the line it seems like it's been a pretty good day to try my luck, since there's the matinee and evening performances on a Saturday. The box office guy assigns me the best available ticket of the remaining day seats and sends me on my merry way until the matinee. The American guy from the queue is at the ticket window next to mine, so at least he's been lucky too.

I spend the rest of the morning wandering around the National Gallery. Of course it's packed, what with it being a place you can see priceless works of art for *free* with no thought or planning required. I sit in front of the huge painting of the execution of Lady Jane Grey, which, it turns out, is literally called *The Execution of Lady Jane Grey*. There's something about her fumbling, uncertain posture under that blindfold that breaks my heart. As I walk around the different galleries it strikes me that even though I don't really know anything about anything I'm looking at, it's still just fun to be here, among all these people, all these paintings. When I get hungry, I roam the streets of Chinatown in search of something cheap to eat, settling on a huge, puffy white cha siu bao sold from a window. It's steaming hot and as big as my hand. As soon as I finish it, I regret not buying another. I walk around the Chinese supermarket on Gerrard Street, wondering if I should buy something, then feeling overwhelmed with choice and leaving without buying anything at all. Next time, I tell myself. Because next time could be any time I want it to be. This is my life now.

Eventually it's time to head back to the theatre, which is a hive of activity. I show my ticket to the usher, trying to shake off my innate self-consciousness about being on my own (what, can't the fat girl find any friends to hang out with her?) and making my way to my seat in the front row of the circle, one seat in from the end of the row. The seat is . . . a little small for my bum, but I just have to hope that whoever's sitting next to me isn't a jerk. The seat to my left is occupied by a middle-aged woman deep in conversation with someone I assume is her son, but the seat to my right is empty. Long may it continue. I suppose I can't hope for it to be empty since the performance is sold out, but maybe whoever bought the ticket is ill. Or dead?

But no, someone squeezes along the row towards the seat.

'Fancy seeing you here!' It's the American guy from the queue.

'You said you had good luck,' I say, meaning that I knew he would get a ticket, but as soon as I say it, I realize it sounds like I think he's lucky to be seeing me again. Cringe. But I'm going to own it.

He takes his seat and says, 'Hey, not bad!' admiring the view out onto the stage.

'Not bad at all,' I say.

He smiles, and it's so composed and serene that it's like he has a secret. 'I'm Sam,' he says. 'I figure I should introduce myself since we've been thrown together like this, not once but twice.'

'I'm Serena,' I say, trying to take him in. I mean, yeah, he's definitely, like . . . in his fifties. But he looks good. Really good. And nothing at all like Alistair. 'So you're not from around here?' I ask but, to my mortification, the lights go down as soon as I get the words out.

The first half feels interminable — not that I'm not enjoying it! I am! It's great! But part of me just wants to take another look at his face. I feel distracted. I feel like I've got half my attention on the stage and half on Sam's body language next to me, whether he's enjoying it or not, what he's responding to. His long legs are crossed into the aisle next to him and his hands are folded in front of him. I don't know what I'm meant to learn from that, other than that he appears to be capable of paying attention. At least the play isn't boring, though. But I am kind of looking forward to the interval. Although . . . I wonder, as someone gives a soliloquy that I'm only half-listening to, what I'm actually expecting to happen. Some more nice conversation? A little light flirting if I'm lucky . . .

When the lights come up, he jumps to his feet to stretch

his legs. I stand up too, to let the middle-aged woman and her son pass.

'So, what do you think?' I ask Sam, not wanting to venture my opinion first, because I'm a coward like that.

'Pretty great! I like what they've done with the set design and the costumes.'

'And he's great,' I say, meaning the guy from the thing.

'Yeah, I liked him in that cop show,' Sam says. 'But you were asking me if I'm from around here, right?'

'Oh yeah!' I say, faux-nonchalantly as if it had slipped my mind.

'So, no, I'm not. I'm over from the States on a sort of work-slash-vacation.'

'What's your work?' I ask, as a couple more people squeeze past me to get out of the row, Sam gallantly standing aside so they can scramble out. I can't take my eyes off him. There's just something extraordinarily magnetic about his face. The wild grey hair, the vibe of a former punk, the tan, the long limbs. Just magnetic.

'I'm a photographer. I work mostly in LA, but sometimes I get sent on assignments. And when I do, I like to, you know, make the most of it,' he says, shrugging, like that's just normal and not extremely glamorous.

'Oh, that's cool,' I say, nonchalantly. 'What do you take photos of?'

'People, places, things,' he says.

'Huh . . .' I say with a smile. 'So you must be pretty good at it if someone's going to the trouble of flying you all the way over when I assume we're not short of photographers here?'

He looks a little embarrassed. 'There's no accounting for taste.'

'Well, congratulations on your illustrious career,' I say, and I wonder exactly what I see in this man, where this attraction has come from. But it doesn't matter. It just *is*. And yeah, maybe some of it has something to do with the fact that in the queue earlier I thought he was handsome in a way I didn't fully understand, and then the charming fate of running into him again here, that feels like maybe the universe is trying to tell me that I'm not completely worn out: that I am capable of feeling attracted to someone.

He holds my gaze for a moment, like he's trying to figure something out, then he looks over his shoulder at the usher at his stand. 'Say, can I buy you one of those tiny ice creams?'

'Yes!' I say, quickly, knowing the interval won't last forever. What the fuck is going on? Is this what life is like outside of a long-term relationship? Men hitting on you in the theatre? Or is this extremely rare? Or was Nicole right about vibes? Is this a single vibe thing? Or a newly confident vibe thing? God! Vibes!

'What flavour?'

'Chocolate, please,' I say.

'Coming up,' he says, reaching into his back pocket for his wallet. 'Don't go anywhere.'

I'm so confused. Is this really happening?

He returns quickly and hands me my ice cream. We eat in companionable silence even though I want to ask him a ton of questions.

'So, if you'll pardon me using the oldest phrase in the book,' he says with a wry smile that makes me feel a bit gooey inside, 'do you come here often?'

Instinctively my eyes widen and my eyebrows shoot up. 'Oh!' I say, hoping I haven't completely misunderstood him.

'Sorry,' he frowns, 'too far? Did I make it weird?'

'No, not at all . . . I just wasn't sure if you meant it like *that* or if you were just asking . . .'

'Would it be okay if I meant it like that?'

I almost literally can't believe it. This is too weird. I can't wait to tell Nicole about this.

'It would,' I say, nodding slowly.

'You're really beautiful,' he says, which instantly makes my cheeks flare up like a traffic light.

My hands fly to my face, covering my eyes. 'God!'

'Did I say something wrong?'

'No!' I say as the bell to mark the end of the interval buzzes and people start crowding back into their seats. 'Not at all, I'm just *extremely* flattered,' I say. People are already treading on my toes so I shimmy my way out and stand next to Sam until they're all safely installed in their seats and well away from my toes.

'Flattered?' Sam says, delightedly. He towers over me, even though I'm not particularly short.

'You're very handsome,' I say.

I look up at him and he looks down at me and finally, after nearly thirty years on the planet, I understand the weird, inexplicable, indefinable quality of sexual chemistry. It's not rational. It's pure instinct. And that instinct is kicking in as we stand there, just looking at each other, like we're playing chicken. All of a sudden an usher is telling us to sit down, so we do, but before the lights go down on the second half Sam leans down a little in his seat and says, 'My hotel is not far from here. I will be going back there after the play. If you would like to join me, then no pressure, but I would love that. Think about it until everyone on stage is dead. Your choice completely.'

I nod. I don't say anything. I can barely concentrate on the play. Thank God day seats were only twenty quid. I'm almost buzzing with attraction to him. It's like my mouth is watering except it's my whole body. Fuck. Who *is* this guy?

When the lights go up I put my hand on his arm on the armrest between us.

'Let's go,' I say, and he leaps to his feet. We don't talk as we make our way out of the theatre, shuffling slowly down the red-carpeted stairs. I start to wonder if he's changed his mind.

It turns out he wasn't joking about the hotel being nearby. We wind through a couple of streets off Shaftesbury Avenue and we're there, him nodding at the doorman authoritatively. We press the button for the lift and it seems to take an age to arrive, but as soon as the doors close behind us, we take one look at each other and that's it. It's on. We crush our bodies together in the lift, our lips against each other's like it's life or death. Of course, in no time at all we arrive at his floor, and he drags me by the hand down a corridor with botanical drawings for wallpaper, down to his room.

He closes the door behind us then before I know it I'm up against it. He reaches for the button on my jeans.

'I haven't shaved my legs . . . sorry . . .' I say.

He laughs, but not unkindly. 'I can't say that's ever been something that's put me off wanting to fuck a woman.'

'Oh, okay . . . good . . .' I say, breathlessly, feeling a little stupid for even bringing it up.

He unbuttons my jeans and reaches his hand inside. I let out a sigh like a cry you can't stifle any more, but instead of carrying on he leads me over to the bed. We undress in a hurry, clothes thrown across the floor. Of course, his body is nothing like

Alistair's. Older, tanned, skinny, marked with tattoos. But the sex is nothing like with Alistair either. It's not ten-years-into-a-relationship sex. It's sex that reminds me why people have sex. It's earth-shattering. I've got to say . . . it's not much like sex with Henry either. It's more intense, more purely physical, rather than the sensation of being a perfect match.

If this is a consolation prize then consider me consoled.

'I've never done this before,' I say, when we're lying in his soft, cloud-like hotel bed afterwards.

'Oh please, you don't have to tell me that.'

'Really.'

He rolls onto one side and props himself up with his arm, his bicep flexed so a tattoo of a bull's skull is warped out of shape. 'Don't tell me you were a virgin before this because . . . well, I'm not gonna believe you,' he says.

'No!' I say, swatting at him with the back of my hand. 'I mean I've never met someone and just like . . . had sex with them pretty much straight away, based on very little at all.'

'Look, it's not like I'm just fuckin' . . . you know, picking up girls left right and centre, though believe me in my, shall we call it, misspent youth that was pretty much the name of the game. But now I'm . . . more discerning.'

'Well, I'm glad.'

'If you've never done this before, I'm glad you made an exception for me,' he says.

'You're not married, are you?' I ask, just to make sure.

'Don't you think it's a little late for that?' he grins, infinitely amused. 'But no, I'm not. I have been. A couple of times.'

'Oh, cool,' I say.

'Why, are you?'

'No! Jesus, no,' I say, and even though I *know* I don't need to tell him anything, something about him makes me want to. 'I was with my boyfriend for ten years and he was the only person I'd ever slept with until very recently. You're . . . the third,' I say, shrugging.

Sam raises his eyebrows, the contours of his face transforming into pure intrigue. 'Is that so?' he asks.

'That is so. Is that . . . weird? Have I ruined it?' I say, instantly regretful.

'Jesus, no, it's a fucking honour,' he says, rolling over and picking up the phone next to the bed. 'Can I get some room service, please?' he says into the receiver before turning back to me. 'What do you want, cutie?'

'Oh, uh, I don't know . . .'

'The chicken schnitzel is good, that's what I always get anyway,' he says, so I give a thumbs up. 'Two schnitzels please, and some of your wonderful shoestring fries, thank you.'

'So, to return a question you asked me earlier . . .' I say, shaking out my hair and sitting up against the headboard. 'Come here often?'

'When I come for work I always end up staying here. Best schnitzel in London.'

'That remains to be seen,' I say.

'I would never, and I mean *never*, lie about something as important as schnitzel. Say,' he says, which I'm learning is his preferred way of beginning a sentence, 'I'm not keeping you from anything, am I?'

I shake my head then catch myself. 'Or wait, was I meant to say that I need to dash off for some black-tie dinner tonight?'

'I guarantee you will have a better time hanging out with

me eating room service and watching . . .' he says, picking up the remote and aiming it at the TV. A nondescript superhero film from a few years ago appears on the screen. 'Whatever this fucking garbage is.'

And he's right. He gets dressed to answer the door and I pull my T-shirt over my head for the sake of modesty as a sharply dressed young man sets our dinner down on a valet stand beside the bed.

'Would you be able to sign here, Mr—' the guy says and I listen so *so* carefully for his last name but I just can't tell what it is. Carnes? Carn? Karn? I make a mental note to Google variants in pursuit of his identity.

We eat off pillows on our lap, some kind of high-stakes intergalactic battle happening on the screen in front of us that neither of us are following.

'Good, huh?' Sam says, offering me another fry, which I duly accept and dunk in the flawless mayonnaise.

'Very,' I say, realizing he's still looking at me. 'What?'

'What is this what? You're beautiful!' He leans over, careful not to disturb the plates, and kisses me and I'm a hundred per cent sure that once these plates are cleared it's time for round two.

I am not proved wrong.

By then, it's dark outside. 'I should get going,' I say.

'Are you sure?' he asks, and it actually sounds like he means it.

'Why, do you . . . want me to . . .?'

'Stay? Sure, why not?'

'Really?'

'Why do I get the feeling you've been burned by some flaky assholes?' Sam is frowning at me. 'If you want to stay and sleep in this fucking fancy hotel bed with me, I would be happy for you to do so. If, however, you want to go, please feel free to leave at *any* time. I have a car picking me up in the morning for the shoot, it's kinda early, that's the only thing.'

'How early?'

'Like, six,' he says, grimacing.

'Damn! That's harsh,' I say. But I stay. We order wine and get a little tipsy and have sex for a third time, and then we fall asleep. When his alarm goes off at stupid o'clock, I feel like I'm about to leave a soft, safe cocoon.

'You want me to order you breakfast?' he asks.

'It's okay, I'll pick something up on my way home,' I say as I get dressed.

'Say,' he says, scribbling something on a hotel notepad, 'I'm not here a huge amount but if you're ever in LA, here's my number. Maybe you can drop me a text so if I'm next in your fair city and I don't sit next to a pretty girl at the theatre I can text you and complain about it.'

I can't help but smiling. I don't care if he means it or not – we both know this was a one-time thing. And it's kind of perfect that way. I drop him a text anyway, just to keep up the ruse. I hear the phone vibrate as the text comes through.

'Well,' I say.

'So long, Serena,' he says, smiling kindly.

And as I make my way home, the city is waking up. The streets are being cleaned of the night before, deliveries arrive at restaurants, and it isn't just that I'm not usually wandering central first thing in the morning but London looks different.

Soho feels new. Shaftesbury Avenue more sparkling. Piccadilly Circus feels fresh somehow. Is it possible being single isn't *so* bad after all?

23

Whatever she wants to say, however she wants to defend herself, whatever family drama is about to pop off . . . I feel ready to see Melanie. Maybe a few weeks ago I would have still half believed she was right about me and Alistair, that I was lucky to have him and that it was ridiculous of me to end our relationship. But now I just don't buy it. She can't bring me down! It cannot be done! I am un-bring-downable! I slide into a booth at the Horatia, just around the corner from our flat. Melanie stomps in a couple of minutes later and buys me a drink without even asking what I want because she's my sister and she instinctively knows. She sets the drinks down on the table and sits at the opposite end of the curved booth to me.

'Hi,' she says.

'Hi. Thanks for the drink,' I say flatly.

'How are you?' she asks, shrugging off her jacket.

'Fine,' I say, taking a sip. I feel childish pleasure at not making this easy for her. 'You?'

'Good,' she says.

'And Matt?'

'He's good, too. Coco's been crawling uncontrollably, she won't stop, she's like a machine.' I do miss Coco. It would be worth enacting some kind of truce with my sister just to be able to hang out with my niece again.

'Sounds cute,' I say, more warmly than I intended to.

'Look,' Melanie says with a sigh. 'I don't want to beat about the bush. I wanted to apologize. I've felt really bad about how it seems like I took Alistair's side.' She pauses for a moment, and her cheeks redden. 'And what I said to you in the park.'

'Oh have you? Why?' I take another sip.

'Because it wasn't fair. It wasn't right for me to be worrying about Alistair after the wedding when obviously everyone was rallying around him. I should have been checking in with you, even if I didn't understand why you did what you did. I still think it was very extreme of you and obviously it would have been better if you'd resolved it all *before* the wedding day—'

'Do you think I don't know that?' I say, exasperated. 'Of course it would have been better if I'd known in advance! But I didn't! Or at least not enough. The only reason it played out the way it did is because I felt like that was my only option, my last chance. That's why it happened in such a stupid, dramatic way! I didn't have anyone I felt I could talk to, confide in, express my anxieties to. That's why it all erupted on the day.'

'I wish I'd been there for you more. I wish you could have talked to me about it,' she says. She sounds so sad, so deflated by it all. 'And I don't know why I said that you were lucky to have Alistair and that you probably wouldn't meet anyone better. I guess . . .'

'What?' I ask, genuinely curious.

'I guess I felt like you didn't understand the consequences

of your actions. Like you were just little Reenie tripping off merrily into the sunset, leaving all this carnage behind you, and you didn't understand how great Alistair was.'

'And now?'

She casts about for the right words. 'And now I see that was stupid, and that you're an adult and you're capable of making decisions for yourself and I can't imagine the courage it must have taken to do what you did. It would have been easier for you to go through with it, even if it wouldn't have been right.'

'Thank you,' I say, softly.

'And of *course* Alistair is great, and kind, and good-looking and all of that. But if that's not enough to keep you with him, then he's not the person for you. And you are more than capable of meeting someone else because you're brilliant and beautiful and thoughtful and talented. I'm sorry I ever suggested otherwise.'

I rest my head against the back of the seat. 'It really stressed me out, you know,' I say. 'I'm not trying to guilt-trip you or anything, but it did put a bee in my bonnet about the whole thing. I even wondered if we should get back together, not that Alistair would have ever gone for that after what I did. But that made it even worse – the idea that he was, actually, the best person I would ever meet, and that I'd thrown it all away and couldn't get it back. I know now that you're wrong, and I'm glad that you do too, but I can't pretend it didn't affect me.' I feel that heat rising in my face, prickling at my eyeballs, and even though I absolutely do not want to be crying in the pub, I am, unfortunately, crying in the pub.

Melanie slides her hand across the table and squeezes mine. 'I'm really sorry. I've been a really bad sister. Really bad. I'm on your side. Promise.'

'It just feels as if you think you can say anything and do anything and I'll understand it's well-intentioned just because you're my sister. But it doesn't work like that. We're still people, you know?'

'Yeah . . .' she sighs. 'Maybe I do do that.'

'I forgive you,' I say. And I do.

Which leaves the rest of the evening free for us to gossip about the less shiny sides of motherhood, my recent sexual adventure, Lola's idea for our future business, an old schoolfriend of Melanie's who's just popped up in a new Netflix drama, and more and more and more, until we are interrupted by the sound of the skinny girl in the vest behind the bar ringing the bell for last orders.

24

Good sex: there's something so *sustaining* about it. It reminds you it's possible. The past couple of weeks since my . . . encounter, shall we call it? Well, they've been delightful. It's partly knowing that sex, or rather, my own desirability, doesn't always have to come bundled up with some kind of anxiety or complication. And it's partly because I feel like I'm slowly but surely entering the 'make it' phase after dabbling with the 'fake it' phase.

'You wanna have a little post-work pint with yer old pal?' Nicole asks me on a Friday afternoon.

I shake my head ruefully. 'I have a date,' I tell her.

'Oooh! And is it with a horrible troll-man? Or someone you actually fancy?'

'Those days are over, my friend. This guy is a hot Norwegian academic in town for a conference,' I say.

'Is this your new thing?'

'Is what my new thing?'

'Out-of-towners. Tasty little treats for a one-night thing.'

'Huh . . .' I shrug. 'It could be! But I don't know if two guys make a pattern.'

She sighs. 'Would be nice if this one was as charming and delightful as the last, though.'

'It really would,' I say, smiling.

'I feel like you wouldn't be sacrificing a Friday night for this if it wasn't a legit prospect,' she says.

'True. You wanna see him?'

'Always,' she says with a heavy sigh, like it's the stupidest question in the world.

I show her his profile. 'Cute, huh?'

'Hello Arne!' she says approvingly. 'Those eyes! Piercing! Yes, my dude, *this* is what I want for you!'

'Part of me is worried he's a catfish,' I say, grimacing.

'That sounds like Old Serena talking if you ask me,' Nicole says.

'What if I told you . . . Old Serena and New Serena are the same person?'

'You know what I mean,' she says impatiently. 'This guy is exactly on your level. There is nothing inherently superior about him. He's good-looking, you're good-looking. End of story.'

'I know, I know . . . it's just . . . hard to get used to thinking like that *all* the time. Sometimes the mask slips and I'm back to square one.'

'That's okay! It's a process! But I assure you: this is what you should have been doing all along!'

'And *who* I should have been doing, more to the point,' I say. 'Hey, is it Anjali's birthday drinks next Monday or Tuesday?'

'Monday, why? You got another date?' Clearly Nicole thinks my schedule is as packed as hers. Alas, no.

'No, I just didn't write it down,' I say, putting it into my phone calendar.

'Can't miss the boss' birthday drinks, even if they are on a Monday,' Nicole says, shaking her head.

'I wouldn't dream of it,' I say, turning back to my computer to write the next week's promotional emails. 'You know what? I can have one drink before my date.'

'Atta girl!' Nicole says, clapping her hands together victoriously.

This concession to Nicole's desire for a post-work drink is why I've ended up mildly buzzed by the time of my date with Arne. Date number . . . well, I don't know any more, because my January break with dating sort of derailed my quest a bit. And besides, who cares what number it is? When I embarked on this challenge it was very much about quantity. But now I know myself better, know my worth, know what I'm looking for . . . it's time for quality, baby.

The Bricklayers Arms in Fitzrovia is packed with a high-spirited Friday evening crowd, but Arne's managed to secure us a cosy corner table upstairs.

'Well done!' I say, delighted, sitting down opposite him. 'I thought we were going to be standing!' I'm sliding in with a confidence I haven't felt on my previous internet dates, largely because I actually *am* happy to be here. I'm happy to be having a few drinks with a really hot guy who I may or may not get to have sex with later.

'I hit it lucky,' he says, with a smile that produces two perfect dimples, giving a sweetly child-like quality to his handsomely chiselled face. He has the perfect amount of dark blond stubble and a thick sweep of hair, bright blue eyes like a husky, and when he jumps to his feet to buy us a drink I see that he wasn't lying about his height on his profile. 'What can I get you?'

'An IPA? But I can get them . . .' I say, wondering how much researchers into geological phenomena get paid.

He waves me away and says, 'You should see what drinks cost where I'm from . . .'

As I wait for him to come back, I remind myself that I deserve to be here, I shouldn't feel *grateful* that he chose to meet me. There are thousands of girls in London and I'm sure I'm not the only one who would want to meet him for a date on a Friday night. That's it, that's the end of me questioning it. No more.

When he returns with our drinks, I sit up straight and put my shoulders back, the picture of confidence.

'Thanks,' I say.

'No problem – cheers. So, has anything exciting happened to you today?'

I like the cheerful musicality of his accent, it feels sweet and puts me at ease when my natural inclination is to be intimidated by how good-looking he is.

'Oh! What a question!' I say, thinking. 'No . . . I don't think so! I was just at work.'

'What do you do for work?'

'I write all the copy for a jewellery brand. So, like, emails and the website. Stuff like that.'

'Do they treat you good?'

'Yeah! I have no complaints. What do you do?'

'Let's say it's stuff with rocks and earthquakes and leave it at that,' he says, smiling.

'Your English is so good . . .' I say. 'I studied languages for years at school but I don't feel like I really got anywhere near fluency. It always makes me wonder how people get so good at speaking English.'

'Oh, yeah, they call it cultural imperialism,' he says, laughing gently.

I blush, feeling a little stupid. 'I guess so.'

'But really, I was super into The Smiths when I was a teenager so I learned a lot of my vocabulary from Morrissey.'

'Look, at least you got in before—'

'The mad nationalism? Yeah, he sucks.'

'But I'm glad you managed to squeeze something useful out of him before that!' I say, taking a sip of my beer.

'I'll always remember learning the word *loutish* from—'

'"I Know It's Over",' I say.

'Yeah!'

'Who among us *didn't* go through a Smiths phase as a teenager?'

'For our sins,' he says, smiling.

'So, tell me about Norway,' I say.

'What do you want to know?'

'Well, where are you from?'

'Oslo. But I live in Bergen.'

'Okay, what's Bergen like?'

'Pretty but fucking rainy. Lots of nature. A mountain. Sea air. We're an outdoorsy people.'

'There's a mountain in the city?'

'Yeah, I like to walk up it for exercise. It gives you a nice view of the city,' he says. 'The city's tiny, nothing like London.'

'Yes, we don't have too many mountains here,' I say.

'True but you can eat out more than once a month, should you so wish,' he says, smiling. 'That's a definite upside of London, even if you probably think it's expensive here.'

'Good to know,' I say, although it seems unlikely that I'll end up in Norway any time soon. 'So, what's your review of the ladies of London?'

He picks up his drink and looks at me. Takes a sip like he's buying time.

'My review is that they're damn cute.'

'Oh?' I say, trying to interpret that answer.

'I mean, you're the only one I've met this trip but if you're a representative sample then . . .'

I feel the blush rise in my cheeks but I stay calm. 'I can't say for sure whether I am or not. But I'm glad you're not disappointed.'

'Disappointed? No way – you're actually prettier in person,' he says, and I'm about to launch into something about how as a fat woman you're never sure whether you're accurately representing your body, when I decide, no, Arne doesn't need to hear that. Save it for Nicole.

'Thank you,' I say, confidently, like people tell me that all the time. 'You're not so bad yourself.'

'Oh, really?' he says, raising his eyebrows.

'Really,' I say, meeting his eyes.

'Well then . . .' he says, not taking his gaze off me.

We chat easily over our first drink and then I buy us another round. As I sit back down, sliding his pint towards him, I realize: I really have nothing to be worried about. This isn't a high hurdle to jump. Not a high bar to clear. This is someone who's in town briefly, who's here, now, for a drink with me, who I already know thinks I'm cute. I deserve to be here. There is no reason why I shouldn't. There's no more to it than that. There's no need to overcomplicate things by throwing whatever old anxieties I might have about my body into the mix. They're not relevant. They don't matter. He has not given one shred of a suggestion that they matter.

'Hey,' he says, noticing that the sofa area is emptying. By this time it's eight o'clock and while one side of the floor is still packed with what looks like an after-work-drinks situation, lots of colleagues squished tightly together in one area, the other side has thinned out considerably. 'Wanna move to somewhere a little more comfortable?'

'Sure,' I say, demurely. We move our stuff over to the sofa.

Now we're here we don't know what to say to each other. We just look at each other, a little embarrassed.

'So . . .' I say.

'So . . .' Arne says, smiling a wolfish smile.

Emboldened by being halfway through my third pint, I say something I don't think I've ever said before. 'Do you want to sleep with me?'

'I don't know,' he says, to my horror. 'I haven't kissed you yet. Can I kiss you first and then let you know?' Maybe the horror was a little premature.

'Sure you can,' I say, fluttering my eyelashes a little. Of course there was a reason we moved onto the sofa. He leans forward and kisses me, moving an arm around my shoulder in the process that doesn't move away when we move apart. 'So. What's the verdict?' I say, grinning uncontrollably.

'Yeah,' he nods, slowly, like he's making a very scientific assessment of the situation. 'I want to sleep with you.'

We still have half our drinks left, so we make our way through them, interspersing our conversation with making out.

'You're so handsome,' I blurt out. We've nearly finished our beers and then it's back to mine.

'Who, me?' he says, coyly.

'Yeah, you,' I say, because I can. Because I'm in a safe pair of hands. Because I know we're going to have sex and there's basically nothing that can derail it. 'Don't tell me you don't hear that all the time.' I kiss him again.

'I'm really feeling your confidence, you know,' he says. 'I feel like a lot of women I meet are very . . . I don't know, they want me to make the first move or something, like that's very important to them. But with you, you just do it. I like that.'

Which means . . . it's working! It's really working! I have moved beyond a need to go on dates with – what did Nicole call them? Horrible troll-men? Yes, no more of that. Just certi-fied hotties like Sam and this gorgeous Viking dude. Whoever next? The world is truly my oyster!

I drain my drink. 'Shall we go? We can walk up to Warren Street and then I live a few stops from there,' I say, slipping on my now-beloved leopard-print faux-fur coat.

'Nice coat,' he says. 'Lemme feel it.' He slips an arm around my shoulder. 'Oooh, soft! Is it real leopard?'

I look up at him standing next to me with his arm around me. He really is *incredibly* handsome. He kisses me again, because he can, because this is a one-night thing and he doesn't have to worry about whether or not I get attached, or whatever it is men worry about that stops them from forging relationships with women. Making out with a hot guy in a pub: decidedly new territory for me and I like it. As we move towards the door, he slides his arm down my back from my shoulder to my waist. I look over my shoulder to check I didn't leave anything on the sofa and, as I'm turning back, for a split second I lock eyes with . . . Henry?

I feel like I'm at the top of a cliff and looking down. Vertigo. He's been there the whole time. The dizziness swirls around my brain, my heart hammering in my chest, all from a few moments of wordless eye contact. The last few months of changing things up, trying to shake up my mindset, they've felt like a long time. But it all comes back. The confusion and disappointment, that desire for him, and the bitter regret that he didn't want me. Those feelings are still there.

I can't stop myself from glancing back again one more time before we slip out the door and down the stairs, and I see he's still looking at me just as Arne plants a kiss on my crown. Good. Let him look. I don't care.

The closer we get to the tube station, the further Henry gets from my mind. He's not welcome tonight. And by the time we get to my flat, he's basically all but disappeared, so delicious is the prospect of sex with Arne.

'Hey!' Lola calls from the living room where she's watching *Goodfellas*. The only thing she can do when she finally gets home from work every day in the lead-up to Fashion Week in September is lie motionless on the sofa and watch films. It's the scene *before* the scene I like where Lorraine Bracco runs away from Robert DeNiro when he's trying to make her look at the designer clothes. Ordinarily I would stay and watch with her, but . . . well, I'm busy. 'Oh, you have company!'

'Lola, this is Arne,' I say.

'Nice to meet you, Lola,' he says, shaking her hand confidently.

'Aren't you handsome?' she says gleefully.

'I keep hearing that tonight . . .' he murmurs.

'Well . . .' I say, a little awkwardly. 'We will leave you to *Goodfellas*.'

'I should think you will!' Lola trills. As I step to the side to let Arne out of the room, I see that she's mouthing, 'He's so hot' at me.

I lead us into my bedroom and turn on the bedside light. He's pulling his T-shirt off over his head, revealing a soft, broad chest. I see we're getting straight down to business. As I'm dragging my tights off, I realize I'm not remotely nervous. He has given me no reason to be nervous, so I won't be.

Before I know it, I'm in my underwear and he's . . . well . . .

'Ha!' I say, clapping a hand to my mouth.

'What?' he says.

'I mean . . .' I say, literally speechless for once. 'You . . . literally have the biggest cock I've ever seen?'

'Oh, yeah,' he says, running a hand through his hair and looking a little awkward. 'Is that a problem? I understand if it is . . . but I did bring my own condoms, I've got it under control.'

I laugh again, sort of deliriously. 'That's sort of a joke among women, how men are always like, *Oh I can't wear condoms, I'm too big*, and there you are, proving that's utter bullshit.'

He shrugs, smiling. 'It's my cross to bear.'

I sit down on the bed and pull him towards me. I take him into my mouth and he moans appreciatively, but after about thirty seconds my jaw tenses up.

'Hey,' he says, gently touching my hair. 'You don't have to do that, you know.'

'Are you sure?' I say.

'I'm sure,' he says, pushing me onto my back, slipping his fingers inside me. And after a while he says something that strikes fear into my heart. 'Sit on my face.'

Oh God. No. God. Why? What if I literally kill him? Hasn't he noticed that I'm fat? I could break his jaw, Jesus!

'Are you sure?' I say.

'Don't you want to?' he asks, looking stricken.

'I'm just . . .' I feel like I'm visibly sweating. 'What if I crush you?'

Arne smiles, amused. 'Are you serious?'

'I'm just scared, you know?'

'You're absolutely not going to crush me. And if I think you're going to crush me then I will let you know.'

Fuck this! At moments like this I think to myself, *What Would Nicole Do?* and I know for a fact Nicole would a hundred per cent sit on the man's face.

'If you insist,' I say, unable to control my smile. I'm kind of obsessed with Arne so I'll pretty much do whatever he wants me to. And so I hop on! It takes me a while to loosen up and just let myself feel the feelings, but then I do. And boy do I.

And then . . . the box of appropriately sized condoms makes an appearance. The intensity of the pleasure-pain feeling is absurd, and I never want it to end.

But when it does end, and we're lying amiably in my bed before he leaves for his Airbnb in Dalston, there's something about the way he's looking at me. Just pure desire, like there's still a deep pool of it left over even after sex.

'You don't care that I'm fat, do you?' I say, more as a statement than a question. He shakes his head. 'Do you prefer it?'

He looks thoughtful for a moment. 'I can go either way. I mean, I have had sex with thin women. But I probably prefer it, yes.'

'Huh,' I say.

'Does that surprise you?'

I'm about to say yes, that it does surprise me, give into my old way of thinking, when I make a conscious decision not to.

'No,' I say, shaking my head. 'I'm just interested.'

'People make out like women are mysterious and men are very straightforward but I think men are fucking weird,' he says, his accent landing particularly sweetly on *fucking weird*. 'About bodies, I mean. Just such an arbitrary thing and they make out like it's so important.'

I smile. 'I guess so.'

When Arne's gone and I'm back in bed, alone, basking in the palpable good vibes of fucking a gorgeous man, I find Henry's pushed my way back into my thoughts. I can't help it. I know he's what I want and I know he's what I can't have. The decision was taken out of my hands. I didn't even get a chance for him to prove we weren't the perfect match. I just have to believe that we weren't. Seeing him today, I wanted to run over, talk to him, ask him how he is, how things are going, but, from what Rachel said when I saw her the other week, he's back with his ex. And even if he's not, it doesn't change the fact that he doesn't want to be with me. Lucky for me that there isn't a shortage of guys that do!

Date Number: WHO'S EVEN COUNTING ANY MORE?

With: Tommy Who-Likes-Fat-Girls-But-In-A-Chill-Way

After we've been engaged in polite first date chat for an hour or so, Tommy fixes me with an intense gaze, which is hot, because he's hot. He's hot even though he's wearing a padded jacket that's a bit horsey. He's tall and blond and has a pretty, full-lipped face and a sharp jawline. 'What are you looking for?'

'Oh! Um . . . I don't really know? I'm in an exploratory phase at the moment . . . just trying things out. Trying to just go where the wind takes me or something,' I say. I really genuinely want to have sex with this guy so I don't want to give a wrong answer. That's what it feels like a bit – that it's a test and I might give a right or wrong response.

He nods, thoughtfully, his hair flopping down over his eyebrow. 'That's cool. I'm into that. Dating in London is kind of a lot, right?'

'That's one word for it.'

'You having a bad time of it?'

'No, no,' I say, smiling. 'Not any more. But when I first started . . . I don't know . . .'

'What?' He looks up at me and his green eyes are really very pretty.

'I was making kind of bad choices.' I grimace.

'Bad like . . . serial killers?' He tosses his head back and the lock of hair returns to its designated place.

'No, not that bad! I'm still here, thankfully. But,' I sigh. 'I was meeting kind of random guys because I thought I wasn't allowed to meet guys I actually fancied.'

'Oh?' he says. 'And why was that?'

I swallow, wondering how best to answer. The answer is because I'm fat, but I don't want to say that in case he hasn't noticed, but that's stupid because of course he's noticed and, besides, there's nothing wrong with it anyway, but sometimes my old brain plays tricks on me especially when I'm confronted with a hot guy I definitely want to sleep with.

I decide on honesty. 'Well, I got it into my head that the fact I'm fat is kind of a . . . barrier to entry?'

Tommy smiles, blushing a little. 'Well, that's not a problem for me.'

'No?'

'No. I actually prefer it.'

'You prefer—?'

'Yeah, I just prefer bigger women to . . . smaller ones?' he says, smiling.

'Oh, cool,' I say, because it is cool. It's extremely cool for me.

'That's not a problem, is it?'

'That you're more likely to think I'm hot?'

He laughs. 'Yeah, I guess that's what it is. Some people are a bit funny about it, though. Like it's a fetish or something.'

I shrug. 'Who cares if it is? As long as you understand I'm an actual person, I'm not going to judge your preferences.' Also I really want to sleep with you.

'Okay,' he says, looking relieved. 'Well, my preferences are for really gorgeous plus-size women so . . . if you're not completely against the idea, I was wondering if you want to go back to mine? Assuming you don't think I'm one of the random weirdos of Tinder?'

I do want that. A lot.

Date Number: Quality Not Quantity

With: Jamal the Insomniac

'So . . . is this how you normally meet women?' I ask, as the bell's ringing for last orders in the pub where we've just sat down. An hour ago I was in bed, in the flat, in my pyjamas, chatting to a guy cute enough that I could forgive him for being a finance bro.

I say 'chatting' but it was most definitely flirting. Heavy flirting. And now I'm . . . here? In the pub, with Jamal, the finance bro cute enough to drag me out of bed at 10 p.m., slap some makeup on my face and hop on a bus down to Old Street. I feel very animated by a renewed optimism in dating these days, like maybe it's actually . . . fun? Anyway, here I am, meeting this guy for a drink that will absolutely a hundred per cent lead to sex, which I am absolutely a hundred per cent okay with.

He looks a little embarrassed. 'The thing is, I work late . . . usually until about nine or ten, and I don't sleep so . . .' He shrugs. 'I end up wanting to do things kind of late. Which, er, doesn't suit everyone.'

'Hence meeting someone for a date at last orders,' I say, clinking my glass against his and taking a sip.

'Exactly. I hope if it was really inconvenient for you that you would have said.'

I shrug. 'It's fine. I'm giving into new experiences at the moment.' Does that sound wanky? Maybe! 'So . . . you said you don't really sleep?'

He shakes his head, furrowing his black eyebrows. 'Not much.'

'Is this, like, a new thing?'

'I wish. It's been going on for years. I've been to all types of specialist, taken any legal medicine I can get my hands on, some *illegal* too, tried meditating, pillow spray, sleep hygiene, all of it. It just doesn't work for me. So I'm just going with it for now.'

I nod. 'Huh, well, that sounds terrible and I'm sorry about it.'

'I like that you haven't tried to give me advice. Most people can't resist it. My favourite was a colleague who recommended just a touch of heroin.'

'That sounds like a . . . bad idea?' I say, tentatively.

'Look, it's not the solution for me,' he says. 'Anyway, enough about my shitty sleeping habits. So you're a writer?'

'Not really,' I say, blushing. 'I write copy for a jewellery brand, do their emails and website, stuff like that.'

'Wait, so, in what way is that not writing?' He looks genuinely curious.

'I mean . . . technically it is? But I'm thinking more and more about doing something with clothes. Making them, I mean. I have a couple of friends that I think would be up for it.' I haven't said this out loud before, so why am I saying it to this guy? I guess sometimes it's easier to talk about big things with someone you don't know than someone you do. No preconceptions.

'Oh, cool! Well, I like what you're wearing,' he says, gesturing at my yellow gingham top tucked into a heavy navy linen skirt.

'That's a good start,' I say, smiling.

'You're really cute,' he says. 'I like your smile.'

'You move quickly,' I say, blushing.

'Sorry, I didn't mean—'

'No, it's good! I didn't really come out of the house just for an eleven p.m. drink, right?'

'Well, I hope not, but I don't like to assume . . .'

'I think we can safely say we're on the same page about . . . the purpose of this drink.'

Jamal smiles. 'That's up to you. I live over there,' he says, nodding past some black railings. 'I would rather you joined me, but no pressure at all.'

'I think I would definitely like to join you,' I say. It's amazing how scary the idea of sex with someone new felt before I started, well, having sex with someone new! And now it's not scary at all.

'Only thing is,' he says, as we start walking in the direction of his flat. 'With the whole no sleep thing . . . I don't really like people staying over. It just doesn't work.'

'Okay,' I say, because, well, it is.

'So if it's okay with you I'm totally happy to get you a cab, you know, when we're . . . done?'

'Yeah, sure,' I say, smiling. I don't know why it's so funny, but there's just something about how straightforward the whole thing is. I expect everything to be buried under layers of meaning and intrigue and people not saying what they really mean when it comes to dating but . . . often they just do?

'I feel like a dick about it but I figure it's best to be honest,' he says, shrugging.

'Look, I have no interest in you watching me sleep all night.' I laugh.

Well, it turns out there wasn't much sleeping to be done anyway. When I finally leave at some mysterious, bleary-eyed time between three and four o'clock in the morning and hop into the Uber that Jamal summoned for me as promised, I find that I kind of like the clean break. Variety is the spice of life, right?

25

'Talk about an early birthday present!' yells Anjali, gleefully. I've barely got through the office door and she is dashing after me, brandishing a magazine. It's a copy of *Vanity Fair*. She whacks it down on the central desk and screams, 'Look at that!'

'Huh,' Duncan says, picking it up and inspecting it in great detail. It's amazing how quickly he's descended from 'pretty cute' to 'actively repulsive'. At least Nicole hasn't mentioned any further unpleasant encounters with him since then. 'Nice fucking job!'

He tosses it to Nicole, who likewise peruses the cover then flicks through to a fashion shoot halfway through. 'Fuck, this is great!' she says. 'These photos are incredible as well.'

'Right?! We couldn't have *paid* for better publicity.'

When Nicole passes the magazine to me, I see a pair of our iconic squared hoop earrings dangling from the ears of a young British actress, star of the new Ryan Murphy vehicle which dropped on Netflix this weekend. Inside, as I flick through the shoot in reverse order, I see they've used the gold pavé lightning bolt earrings, the large medallion necklace and the curb chain bracelet in the shoot. An early birthday present indeed.

'The fashion editor owed me a favour and *man* did she come through,' Anjali says, sitting down at her desk and twirling around in her chair.

'Happy fucking birthday to you, Anjali!' says Nicole. 'Double reason to celebrate later!'

'Thanks, Nic!' she says. We all wish her a happy birthday and settle in for a day of good vibes.

'Fuck, I thought traffic was up massively yesterday!' Duncan says, shaking his head in disbelief. 'Now I know why!'

But the real disbelief is mine. Sitting down at my desk I finally make it back to the first page of the feature, and I see it. *Photos by Sam Kahan.* I just know. To make sure, I google him, and yep, unmistakably, there is the man I slept with. I don't delve too deeply but can't help a glance over to the right-hand panel where I can learn that he is fifty-five, and has been married to one contemporary artist and one character actress he divorced two years ago, both appear to be his own age. Thank God I'm not a complete hypocrite after complaining about men who *only* want younger women.

'God, I just love those photos! I always feel so delighted by his shoots,' Nicole says, leaning over my shoulder and gently stroking the pages. I let out a little laugh as I put my phone away.

'What?' she says, looking at me curiously.

'Well . . .' I say, blushing a little.

'What?!'

'You remember the old guy? The American?' I say.

'Who you boned? How could I forget!'

'Well . . .' I say again, holding the photo spread up to Nicole. She just looks at me. 'Are you fucking kidding me? Sam Kahan? The old guy was Sam Kahan? Like, are you actually joking?!'

'No,' I say, laughing, 'I'm not joking! I know it sounds like I am but I'm not! This must have been what he was in London for!'

'Fuck!' Nicole says, possibly more joyful than I've ever seen her. 'And you literally had no idea who he was?!'

'Nope! Just some weirdly charming tattooed guy with grey hair who picked me up at the theatre,' I shrug.

She shakes her head. 'Wow. Well. Respect, my guy. He's like . . . *hot*, you know. Hot hot. Not just old-man hot. And it's even hotter that he knows a babe when he sees one.'

I smile. 'I guess he does.'

'Hey, so your Danish guy was a good time?'

'Norwegian. And yes,' I say, wondering when things got so fun for me. Of course, it was Nicole's pep talk in the Lamb. 'Are you going to make a move on Lola?'

'Actually . . .' she says, looking unusually serious. 'I was going to talk to you about that . . . I, uh, slid into her DMs . . .'

'Oh is it?! She kept that one quiet . . .'

'It happened last night!'

'A *late-night* DM slide, I see . . .'

'Yeah, so, anyway,' she says, trying to refocus my attention on the matter at hand. 'I did kind of ask her out . . . so . . . if that's okay with you, we're going out on Friday night? It was the only night this week we could both do, what with us being busy metropolitan millennial elite and all,' she says, shrugging casually. 'But only if it's okay with you of course.'

'Mate, I'm delighted by this unexpected turn of events!' I say.

'I feel like today is full of unexpected turns of events . . .' she says, scooting her swivel chair back to her desk.

I raise an invisible wine glass. 'To unexpected turns of events!'

Nicole raises an invisible wine glass of her own. 'To you being a sly fox and sleeping with famous photographers, among others!'

As I'm tap tap tapping away at my keyboard all afternoon, I feel my mind drift towards Henry. A little tug of dissatisfaction. The problem was, I just *liked* him. It wasn't complicated. I wasn't projecting onto him, imagining some perfect life with him. I just . . . liked him. He made me feel comfortable but excited at the same time. Happy, and hopeful. And it didn't work out. Good job I've had some non-Henry men to remind me it's not all awkward conversations and bank transfers for a glass of wine.

Anjali declares us to have finished work at 5 p.m. on the grounds that it's her birthday and we're celebrating the huge amount of orders generated by the magazine coverage. We slam down the lids on our laptops ecstatically and Nicole, Anjali, Duncan, Kirsty and I head out to the pub.

'This is literally just a chill post-work drink and not a mad rager – I'm having dinner at seven with Marco,' says Anjali. 'So I was thinking we could go to that little bar round the back with the courtyard bit?'

'Ah yes, Shoreditch's prettiest smoking area,' says Nicole flatly as we walk. Spring is decidedly in the air, the long winter slowly melting away and being replaced with the optimism that comes with lighter, longer evenings.

'I don't think I've been there,' I say.

'I feel like we're not drinking as much these days,' Kirsty says, a little sadly. 'Back in the day it was Friday night drinks every week.'

'We're busy bees now!' Anjali says. 'No time for drinking!'

'By that she means she was a party animal until she met Marco and then it was cosy nights in forever more,' Nicole murmurs to me. 'You should have seen her a couple of years ago, it was hard to get her to go home before three a.m.'

I notice that Duncan is walking a little slower, more in step with me and Nicole than with Kirsty and Anjali. He's wearing a beanie hat which looks slightly dim.

'Hey, Duncan,' I say.

'Hey, ladies,' he says. 'It feels like a bit of a waste doing this on a Monday, doesn't it?'

'I guess so!'

'I'm kind of happy about it,' says Nicole. 'Means it's probably not going to turn into a mad one.'

'You've changed your tune,' says Duncan with a short laugh. He turns to me and says, 'She used to party with the best of them.'

'Oh did she now?' I say.

'You know, I've had my fun,' she says, airily. A little too airily. Maybe I wouldn't have noticed the slight edge to her voice when we first met but, after months of friendship, I can pick it up instantly. I check my phone and see there's a text from Tommy. Hot Tommy. Want to come over later? Yes, Tommy, yes I do. I reply saying so, trying not to be self-conscious about an instant reply.

We're the only people at the bar, and Duncan insists on buying the first round.

'Cheers!' we all chorus, clinking our glasses together so enthusiastically that beer spills over the sides.

'Happy birthday, Anjali!' 'Happy birthday!' we all say on top of each other, before gulping down the drinks.

Even though we're the only people there, we've somehow

conjured up such a giggly, convivial vibe that it doesn't feel at all bleak. Anjali seems to be having a good time, and insists on buying us drinks to celebrate the *Vanity Fair* coverage even though it's her birthday.

'I'm your boss! You shouldn't be buying *me* drinks!' she maintains. So we let her. By the time she goes off to dinner with her boyfriend, she's pretty tipsy, but so are the rest of us.

'Another?' Kirsty asks, slamming her hands down on the table.

'Sure, why not!' I say, enthusiastically. Duncan and Nicole agree, and Kirsty returns with four pints pulled by the very bored, very young-looking bartender. Who wouldn't be bored? It's Monday night, there's hardly anyone here – only one other table has appeared since we arrived.

Duncan and Nicole are chatting on the other side of the table, Nicole looking slightly distracted. I, on the other hand, have somehow got embroiled into a conversation with Kirsty about tampons.

'I mean . . .' I say, not having had to defend my tampon use before. 'I just figure that given I'm literally putting something in my vagina, it should be something I'm comfortable with?'

'But have you *tried* a Mooncup?' she asks, wide-eyed.

'Yeah, once,' I say, shrugging. 'I didn't really like it, though.'

'Did you know women throw away over a hundred kilograms of sanitary waste in their lifetimes?' she says.

'No, but—'

'It's just so *amazing* to learn the way your body functions, you know? To have that kind of relationship with it, with your period,' she's nodding emphatically at me.

'Personally, I see my period as an unpleasant inconvenience

in my day-to-day life,' I say with a smile.

She shakes her head. 'It's one of the most amazing parts of being a woman, that collective experience, how we're all going through the same thing . . . and I just feel like cups help you *really* understand your flow.'

'I'm pretty sure it made my period pains worse . . .' I say, even though I know I'm not going to be able to convince her I know what I want to put in my own body. 'And anyway—' I begin, about to tell her that not only is it *not* an amazing part of being a woman, it's not even actually part of being a woman since it's the twenty-first century and surely we all know better by now than to do biological essentialism in the pub. But she cuts me off.

'Really? Are you sure that wasn't psychological?' Kirsty is looking at me with the utmost scepticism. 'Corporations make *billions* off convincing us our periods are dirty, shameful things.'

'I'm . . . I'm aware of that . . . but I'm also aware of my own personal comfort levels . . .' I say, desperate to extricate myself from this conversation. I jump to my feet, which makes me realize just how tipsy I am. 'Another drink? Kirsty? Duncan? Nicole? How about you help me carry?'

Nicole looks up from her conversation with Duncan. 'Sure, I'll join.'

I collapse onto the bar, my head in my hands. 'I didn't necessarily *need* another drink but I needed an escape hatch – Kirsty was talking my ear off about—'

'Don't tell me,' she interrupts, holding her hand up, drunkenly. 'Menstrual cups?'

'Yes!'

'Been there, done that,' she says.

She duly helps me carry the drinks back over to the table. Is this many drinks a good idea on a Monday night? Probably not. But I'm so rarely induced to do office socializing that I might as well go along with it just this once. All the drinks are catching up with me and I realize I'm absolutely desperate for a wee.

'Want to come out for a smoke with me, Serena?' Nicole asks.

'No, I'm gonna run to the bathroom,' I say. She shrugs and heads for the courtyard while I head for the toilet.

I'm washing my hands at the sink afterwards when I hear voices float through the window above the sink.

'It's not going to happen.' It's Nicole. I freeze just before I put my hands under the dryer, suddenly curious to hear the rest of the conversation.

'Come on . . .' A man's voice. Duncan. 'You were flirting with me back there and now you're giving me the brush-off?'

'I . . . I'm sorry if I gave you that impression . . .' The usual confident Nicole is gone, and there's a note of fear in her voice.

'You think I enjoy sitting in the office listening to you talk about all these different guys you're fucking and then you brush me off like you're so *fussy*?'

'Look, I'm sorry . . . I'm sorry if you thought I was flirting with you,' she mumbles.

'Come on, just one kiss . . .'

'Please, let me go back inside.' She sounds . . . scared?

'You might like it, you won't know until you try,' I hear him say as I'm pushing my way out of the bathroom, through the bar where Kirsty's looking bored on her own and into the smoking area, my heart racing.

I can see through the door to the courtyard that Duncan is blocking Nicole's way, an arm across the corner she's standing in, cigarette in hand, eyes full of fear. As I push open the door, Duncan whips around and fixes me with a look of anger.

'Hey Nicole,' I say, confidently. 'Is everything okay?'

'Why wouldn't it be?' Duncan says over his shoulder.

'I'm not talking to you, I'm talking to Nicole,' I say.

'What are you so worked up about? What's the problem?' He turns to look at me, leaving Nicole behind him.

I swallow, knowing it would be easy to extricate Nicole from there and leave without a confrontation. And maybe a year ago I would have. I'd have just done what I needed to do and got out. But now? I want him to know he's fucked up. That we see him and we know him and we're sick of it.

'The problem is that you're harassing your colleague. The problem is that you're trying to force her to kiss you. The problem is that you're trying to shame her into it. There are just, like, a *lot* of problems,' I say, breathlessly, my voice shaking.

'That's a bit much,' he says, throwing his hands up and taking on an expression of disbelief. 'I'm not a fucking . . . I'm not a *rapist.*'

'I hope not. But that doesn't make this right.'

His face changes to pure fury. 'So what the fuck are you going to do about it then?'

'I'm going to tell Anjali that one of her members of staff is harassing his colleague. Sorry, I thought that was really obvious,' I say, with a confidence I don't feel.

Duncan rolls his eyes. 'As if anyone's going to believe that *I* was coming onto Nicole.'

'Well, good job I recorded it then,' I say, quickly. 'You can hear every word when you're in the women's toilets.'

He looks stunned. He doesn't know it's a bluff. He takes a

deep breath, points at me, says, 'Fuck you,' before turning to Nicole, 'And fuck you as well, you stupid fat slut.' He pushes past me and out of the courtyard, the door swinging behind him.

'Fuck!' shouts Nicole, slumping onto the bench.

'Are you okay?' I sit down next to her and put my arm around her.

'Fuck!' she says, shaking her head.

'I should have come sooner, I heard what he was saying to you but I just froze . . .' I say, apologetically.

'No, fuck, it's fine,' she says, her breathing fast. 'Obviously I knew he was a creep but I didn't know he could be this scary about it.'

'God . . . I'm sorry.'

'Did you really record it?'

'No,' I admit, smiling a little. 'I just knew it would freak him out if he thought I did.'

'He's a complete fucking creep. Ugh, I hate him!'

I think back to my first day, what Duncan said about her. It was like he was trying to stop me from being her friend. Trying to isolate her.

'Are you going to tell Anjali now?' I ask her. I don't want to push her, but I figure it's at least worth asking.

'I mean . . . I want to . . . but, like, would anyone else believe me except you? Or is the idea that he would be harassing a fat girl just too impossible for anyone to believe?' she says, slowly, but just then Kirsty appears through the door.

'What the fuck happened with Duncan?' she slurs. 'He just stormed out?'

'Nothing,' I say. 'He'd just had too much to drink. I think

Nicole and I are going to make a move.'

'Oh,' she pouts, clearly wanting to stay out.

'We'll see you tomorrow, though,' I say. I can tell she wants to know more, why I'm sitting with my arm around Nicole, why usually chatty Nicole isn't contributing to the conversation.

She shrugs. 'Okay, so I guess I'll see you tomorrow then.'

We head inside after her and collect our things. 'Let's get a bagel,' I say, decisively.

'All right,' Nicole says, smiling weakly, like she's just so tired of the whole thing. I hate that he has the power to do this to her.

We walk quietly over to Brick Lane. I buy us two salt beef bagels, one with pickles and mustard for her, one with pickles no mustard for me, and we sit on the benches opposite the cinema to eat them.

'I don't want to go to work tomorrow,' she says, chewing thoughtfully on her bagel.

'It's so fucked. He's a creep . . . it's nothing to do with you. I mean, it's nothing you did. It's him.'

'Ugh! Why! Why, why, why!' She shakes her head emphatically.

'Are you going to tell anyone?' I ask.

'Even if we had an HR department I don't even really believe they would help,' Nicole sighs.

'I would hope they *would*?'

'That's not what they're there for. They're there to protect the company, not, you know, the actual people. Actual people are an inconvenience to them. What do you think would happen if I told Anjali?' she says.

'I have no idea, honestly. I mean, I would like to think that she would do *something* but . . . I don't know.' I've existed in the world long enough to know that even in a situation like this where there's a clear aggressor, people can circle the wagons effectively enough that the story becomes murky, dubious. 'I'll back you up, a hundred per cent though.'

'You will?'

'Of course I will! Jesus!' I say, trying not to choke on a chunk of salt beef.

'Let me think about it. Anyway, I'm bored of talking about him. What's your chat?'

'No chat,' I say, wondering if she's in the mood to hear about my impending encounter with Tommy, but also unable to stop a little smile creeping across my face.

'Oh my God, stop, you can't lie to me!' she says, indignantly. 'Obviously the thing with Duncan was shit but you know the best way to cheer me up is with good chat!'

'So,' I say, bending to her wishes. 'I had a date the other week with this really cute guy and he texted me asking if I wanted to come over again tonight.'

'Why are you still here? Go!'

'No! I told him I would be round late, it's fine.'

'Who is this juicy little morsel?'

'His name is Tommy—'

'And he's, like, six foot three with an angelic little face, bedroom skills and kind of posh?'

I gape at her, open-mouthed. 'How did you know?!'

She grins wolfishly. 'I don't see him that often but when I do!' She kisses her fingertips like a cartoon Italian chef.

'So you've slept with him?' I say, trying to figure out if I feel weird about it or not. Is it a bit weird to sleep with the same person your mate sometimes sleeps with? Maybe? But I guess if we have to endure the world of dating as fat women, then I would like as many of us as possible to benefit from the good bits. Sex communism or something.

'I have indeed, my friend. I'm not always sold on the idea of the penis but his is particularly nice.'

'You're right!' I say.

'You need to keep me updated with, like, *every* guy you sleep with so we can compare notes. This shit is my lifeblood. It sustains me.'

'I solemnly swear,' I say, holding up three fingers in a Brownie promise.

We gossip about Tommy a while longer until it's time for me to hop on the bus to his. We hug goodbye and I don't bring Duncan up again, but before I head for the bus stop, Nicole exhales loudly. 'Okay,' she says, after a long pause. 'I've thought about it. Let's do it.'

26

The next morning, with the residual glow of a night with Tommy, I sit nervously at my desk while Nicole and Anjali go for 'a walk'. Not as nervously as Duncan, though, who came in with coffees for everyone and is full of inane chatter. Now he's shifting uncomfortably in his seat, throwing glances at the door every thirty seconds. When they come back, Nicole slips quietly into her seat, mascara slightly smudged.

'Duncan, can we have a chat?' Anjali says quietly to him. There's nowhere to talk privately in the office, so they have to go for 'a walk' as well, leaving me, Nicole and Kirsty in the office.

As soon as the door closes behind them, Kirsty explodes. 'Can someone tell me what the fuck is going on? I feel so left out!'

I look at Nicole, knowing it's not my story to tell.

'Duncan was harassing me at the pub last night. It wasn't the first time either. He keeps trying to touch me or make me kiss him and I'm sick of it.'

'You mean he assaulted you?' Kirsty says, her mouth staying open.

'Not exactly, although he's come close. Fucking close,' Nicole says, shaking her head bitterly.

'So what has he done then?' she asks, folding her arms across her chest. I flinch at her tone. This isn't the reaction I was expecting, to be honest.

'Kirsty, can you just back off, please?' I say.

'I just don't really get what's happening? You two have some kind of problem with Duncan and now you're trying to get him in trouble?'

'*In trouble?*' Nicole says in a deeply mocking tone. 'What, are we at school? Fuck no, I don't care about getting him *in trouble* as you so kindly put it, I'm interested in being able to come and do my fucking job without having to look over my shoulder.'

'Just feels like a witchhunt, that's all,' Kirsty says, staring at her screen rather than looking at us and clicking around on her trackpad.

'Fuck you,' Nicole says, wearily. Kirsty doesn't reply, just sneers disapprovingly.

Eventually Anjali reappears with Duncan. She sits down at her desk, while he stands by the door, looking awkward.

'Nicole,' he says, 'and everyone else in the office. I just wanted to apologize for my behaviour last night.' He clears his throat. 'And in the past. I understand it was wrong. It won't happen again.'

Nicole nods, keeping her eyes constantly moving. Within a few minutes, an email arrives from Duncan, who's literally sitting metres away from everyone he's emailing, saying his contract is up at the end of next week and he won't be staying on. Kirsty lets out an indignant huff, but Nicole and I just look at each other wide-eyed over the tops of our computers.

The office is deathly quiet for the rest of the day, but Nicole and I are frantically instant messaging each other in disbelief. Nicole says that Anjali asked if she would be okay with it if Duncan was let go, but Nicole didn't think Anjali was actually *asking*. At least she believed Nicole. It feels a pathetic thing to feel grateful for, and yet I am grateful for it.

'You want to get a drink?' I ask Nicole when everyone's quietly slinking off home. I can sense that she doesn't want to have A Big Talk but I wonder if she could do with a little distraction. 'Just one, just a lil pint before my date?'

She sighs. 'Not today, Satan. I think I just want to go and smoke on my balcony and order Chinese,' she says. 'But thank you for offering.'

'I hope you're feeling more sprightly by Friday night,' I say, raising my eyebrows suggestively.

At that, Nicole's face brightens. 'Oh, I *will* be. I'm not going to let that dickhead get in the way of me finding true love with Lola.'

I can't help but smile. 'You think it's gonna be good?!'

'Oh, I think so,' she says, confidently. 'Anyway, who's your date tonight? I feel like you're on a roll at the moment.'

'I hope you're right! He looks pretty cute . . .' I say, and maybe even a month or two ago I would have added, *Maybe too cute*, but now, I just own it. Why shouldn't I be meeting a cute guy? Nicole's right – I kind of am on a roll. Although no boyfriend material just yet, Nicole's advice to heart has definitely translated into some confidence-boosting encounters. I actually feel like I've sort of . . . achieved what I set out to do with this whole thing? Have fun, meet people, boost my confidence, reassure myself that leaving Alistair wasn't a huge mistake, have slept with more than one person in my life, you know the drill. Maybe tonight's date will end up being boyfriend material? David is tall, dark and handsome, pouty lips, thick, curly deep brown hair, bright blue eyes. Delicious. . .

'Show me!' Nicole chirps.

I duly dig out my phone and bring up his profile. I show it to Nicole, who flicks through the photos approvingly. 'Hot! Hot as hell! I'm almost jealous that I've never seen his profile because . . . I *would* be asking out this man.'

'I'm glad you approve!' I say. 'I fancied him, so I swiped right. I didn't reject him on the grounds that he's hot.'

'Good! God, I can't believe you lived that way for such a long time!' she says, shaking her head as she forensically examines his photos. 'Can you imagine if you hadn't boned famous photographer Sam Kahan or seen a dick the size of a baguette because you thought you didn't deserve it? Oh, I think tonight's hottie just messaged you.'

My heart sinks. Obviously he's cancelling. But when I check the message, I see he's actually confirming. **Still good for later? 7 at the Owl and Pussycat?** I reply saying Yes, I'll be there.

'Well, good luck with this absolute fucking *babe*, my dude, I have no doubt you're going to knock his socks off,' she says, squeezing me tight.

I shrug. 'Maybe I will,' I say, smiling naughtily.

I leave the office with an hour to kill before my date, so I start off on a slow stroll towards the pub. Within a few minutes, my cute and extremely date-appropriate pink slingbacks that I'd only worn briefly before today are starting to rub the backs of my heels. I abandon the walk plan and take the bus a couple of stops to Shoreditch High Street, where I sit in a Pret a stone's throw from the pub with the fizzy grape and elderflower drink I like. Jesus, I was around here only last night and what a mess *that* turned into. Hopefully tonight will be about a thousand times more peaceful and less dramatic. And more than anything, I'm hoping my treacherous shoes are the worst of it. Fucking shoes, who needs them anyway?

Just before the appointed time, I walk s-l-o-w-l-y over to the pub. As I'm pushing open the door to the pub, I look over my shoulder to see if anyone's coming in after me, and . . . they're not, but I catch sight of a man across the road. The man looks an awful lot like David who I'm meant to be meeting, except he appears to be hiding behind a post box. Hiding like a rather incompetent spy. Is it him? I try to get another look at him but he's . . . well, he's still crouching next to a post box . . . I decide to make my way into the pub. He can join me when he's good and ready.

I don't have long to ponder the mystery of the crouching man because also there, at the bar, is Alistair. Yes, him. Real, actual Alistair, my partner of ten years, jilted fiancé. Looking decidedly dressed down, on his way to growing a beard, which is an absurd thought, but undeniably Alistair. He spots me instantly.

'Serena!' he says, delightedly. 'What are you doing here?!'

'I have a date!' I say. Amid my surprise and confusion I'm genuinely glad that I can say that to him.

'Oh, wonderful!' he says, in a tone that's only *slightly* patronizing.

'What about you? What brings you into the big city?'

'I had annual leave to use up so me and Sophie decided to

come for dinner at Boundary. It's the place across the road,' he says, nodding out of the window.

'Yeah . . .' I say, waiting to see if he's going to elaborate on who Sophie is, or if he thinks it's pretty self-explanatory.

'Oh, there she is now,' he says, beaming. The elegant brunette from his phone background is teetering towards us on a pair of high heels. He stretches an arm out to her and slinks it around her tiny waist. 'Babe, this is Serena.' At first I want to correct him – *You mean, this is Sophie* – but then I realize I'm not his 'babe' any more.

'Sophie. Nice to meet you,' she says, offering a manicured hand. She turns back to Alistair. 'How many Serenas do you know?!'

'Why?' I ask, a little bemused.

'Isn't that your ex's name?' she asks, brightly.

'Babe . . .' Alistair says, quietly, as my cheeks go beet red.

'What?' Sophie looks at him inquisitively. Then back to me. Then back to him. The penny drops. 'Oh.'

'Guilty as charged,' I say, jovially, raising my hand and instantly feeling like an idiot, like someone's dad making a stupid joke. I bet Sophie never has to make stupid jokes. I bet she gets to feel perfectly assured that everything is going her way a hundred per cent of the time.

'Great!' Sophie says. 'What are you up to this evening, Serena?' Her tone is excruciatingly polite.

'Serena is meeting a gentleman for a date,' says Alistair. 'So we should leave her to it. Here,' he says, handing her a glass of rosé.

'Oh, well, good luck,' she says, smiling encouragingly, like she thinks I'm going to need it.

'Thanks,' I say. 'See you, Alistair.' I knew it was over months ago. I knew it was over the day I dumped him, unceremoniously, on our wedding day. Of course I did. But I can't pretend it doesn't tug on my heart, just a little, to actually *see* him with someone else. Someone so groomed and glossy and . . . I can't avoid the thought . . . thin. No, Serena, keep it together, I tell myself. Don't slip into thinking like that. Being thin won't solve your problems, you'll just find a whole load of new ones.

He nods at me and they head to an empty table. I just stand there for a moment, wondering if I should sit down or wait at the bar. I mean, I know my date is around here – I saw him. I saw him hiding behind a fucking post box – but I saw him with my own two eyes nonetheless. He can't be far behind me – once he's finished . . . whatever he was doing. So I wait at the bar, uncomfortably aware that Alistair and Sophie keep glancing over in my direction, waiting for my date to arrive. Believe me – *I'm* even more desperate for him to turn up than you are, my friends. At least when he shows up it'll prove to Sophie that even though she clearly thinks I'm some kind of disgusting goblin person who could *never* have had a relationship with Alistair, I'm perfectly capable of getting a date with an attractive guy.

Except . . . he isn't here. And I've been standing here for ten excruciating minutes, trying to avoid the bartender's eye, trying not to look at Alistair and Sophie's table, trying, more than anything, not to cry with embarrassment. Why did I come inside? Why didn't I loiter outside? As I'm refreshing my Instagram feed to give me something to do, I see another Tinder message pop up from David.

So sorry, something super urgent came up at work, not going to be able to make it.

I stare at the message, growing increasingly hot and dizzy. And then he blocks me. In a way, in a horrible, sad, way, I can't believe it's taken this long for it to happen, for a guy to arrange a date with me, take one look at me and decide to do a runner. Because that is what obviously happened – he was hiding from me, behind the post box. I feel sick with humiliation. All the working-on-myself, all the confidence, all the *knowing* that I'm brilliant, beautiful, worthy of love and affection in the world can't protect me, at this moment, from feeling like shit.

I need to get out of here. I need to get out. I need to go home and wail at Lola about what a *horrible* evening I've had. The painful shoes seem like such a minor complaint now that I've been stood up *and* humiliated in two separate acts. But the painful shoes remain and fuck me if I can be bothered to walk from the station stop in them. I can't wait to throw them in the bin. I can't wait to get home and hide under the covers and eat a net of twelve Babybels (six would be fine in the face of a normal inconvenience but to be stood up means I require twelve).

I open Uber. It feels so extravagant to take an Uber to somewhere I could easily take the Overground but, honestly, the thought of walking up Holloway Road is making me feel sick. I don't know if I could even make it up the stairs and out the station, especially not with such a depleted spirit. I hover over the button before deciding a Pool is a good compromise. No walking but less extravagant than taking a whole car to myself. As I watch the driver's icon get closer and closer to the pub, I try not to cry. I was doing so well. I felt on top of things. I felt like I deserved romance, happiness, all of that. I felt like I deserved to make choices. Hold it together, Serena, for God's sake! What would Nicole say? Probably something along the lines of *He's a pathetic worm and you are better than him*. But if that was true then why wasn't it me running away from him?

No, come on. It's okay to feel down about this. I've been treated badly by someone. It's okay to acknowledge that. But it is not going to set me back, send me spiralling into researching juice cleanses and getting slightly *too* into going to classes with Nicole and accepting dates with losers I don't fancy just because I believe life would magically improve and men would magically be less shitty if I was thin. I am angry, but I'm not defeated.

Finally, the car arrives outside the pub. I dash to the exit without wanting to deal with Alistair and his babe, but – evil cosmic justice – the slingback strap on my shoe finally breaks. I trip, only briefly, but by the time I'm on my feet Alistair is there to steady me.

'Woah, you okay?'

'Yes, just leaving.'

'Don't tell me he stood you up?' he says, with a kind smile.

I know Alistair is joking and I know he feels terrible the moment he sees the tears well up in my eye. Could it get any worse? Well, Sophie lets out a great big laugh and then covers her mouth when she too realizes it's true. It's true! HIS FAT EX HAS BEEN STOOD UP ON A DATE!

I literally dive out of the pub. The shoe is dragging off my heel. I yank the cursed object off and throw it in the gutter as I clamber into the waiting car. I know, I look *pathetic*. I look crazy. I'm already regretting that it's a Pool as by this point I am properly bawling. To compound this misery, there is not one but two other passengers. I cover my face, pitifully, from the skinny stranger in a suit who's shifted across to the middle seat and is staring straight ahead. At least the passenger on the other side is occupied with a big box file on their lap so less likely to pay attention to my misery.

The car pulls away. By this point I'm hot, I'm flustered and I am well aware I should have just sat in the front next to the driver rather than squishing in the back here with these randos but I'm here now and the tears are just getting worse. Every time I think I've figured it out, something like this happens and shows me how fragile it all is. How I really haven't got it together at all. How I entirely am *not* on a roll. Fuck that there are people in this car with me. I just let out some big heaving sobs.

'Are you okay?'

Can't you have a breakdown in an Uber Pool in peace any more? I turn to the man next to me but he's staring straight ahead. It's the other guy who spoke, the one with the box file on his lap.

'Are you fucking kidding me?' I say, and I don't know if that comes across as happy or furious.

It's Henry.

27

Hot, ridiculous tears keep-a-coming.

The driver is checking the rear-view mirror, almost as if he thinks he might need to intervene. But he clearly decides this isn't going to kick off and turns his eyes back to the road.

I was all geared up for not letting today get the better of me, but it finally, truly, has.

'What are you even doing here?' I ask, sniffling.

'We're moving offices – just off Brick Lane – and I've said I'll take some stuff back to my flat,' Henry says, looking at me, bewildered, which is perfectly understandable because he's being asked to account for himself by a crying girl.

'But you don't live near me?' I say, but it comes out like a wail. I wipe away my tears with the sleeve of my leopard-print coat.

'I didn't want to stay in that flat any more,' he says, shaking his head. 'I moved to Stoke Newington with Malcolm. This is Malcolm by the way,' he says, gesturing to . . . I suppose I have no other choice than to describe him as Malcolm in the middle.

'Hi, Malcolm.'

'Hello,' Malcolm murmurs, staring ahead, looking like he is trapped in a unique kind of hell and cannot bear the thought of getting dragged into whatever nonsense is going on either side of him.

'Malcolm and I work together. We got lumbered with moving this, it's just flyers and stuff. But what about you? What's the matter?' Henry looks genuinely concerned. And who can blame him.

'I'm just having the worst evening,' I say, laughing wetly. 'I'm sorry, I don't mean to cry – I fucking hate crying. It's just been a lot.'

Henry shifts the box on his lap more to the right and holds onto it with his right hand. He reaches his left around the back of Malcolm's headrest and tries to stroke my shoulder.

'Please,' I say, shaking my head. 'This isn't what I need from you right now. Everything about this evening has been so humiliating. So you being nice to me because I'm so pathetic isn't going to help.'

'I don't think you're pathetic,' he says, frowning. He strokes the back of my neck. I liberate an arm that's going a bit dead squished up against Malcolm's. I reach behind my seat and lay my hand on Henry's against my hair.

We just sit there in silence for a moment, my tears drying up, my breathing returning to normal. I withdraw my hand and put it back on my lap.

'You were possibly the last person I wanted to see tonight. It's been the worst. The proper, actual worst. Sorry, Malcolm, I know this is probably an odd conversation for you to be in the middle of.' I turn to the strange man sitting next to me who just looks at me out of the corner of his eye and nods imperceptibly. I switch my attention back to Henry. 'And now you're here. You made me feel *so rubbish* back at New Year.'

Henry sighs. 'I'm sorry about that . . . but you never replied to me so I thought you just . . . weren't bothered, I guess?' We round a corner and he takes his hand off my hair to hold onto the box with both hands.

'Are you serious? I was *so* bothered, Henry,' I say. 'So fucking bothered.'

'Well . . .' he says, a little uncomfortably. 'I know I messed up. I missed my chance, and . . . I get that.'

'What?'

'You've got a boyfriend now, right?'

'No, I don't?' I say, trying to figure out what's going on in that ginger head of his.

'That guy in the pub, the tall, blond guy.'

Oh! Does he mean Arne? From when we saw each other in the pub?

'He's not my boyfriend! He was just a casual thing,' I say. 'I really wanted to text you that night. I lay in bed just like . . . really wanting to talk to you, really wanting to see you again. But you were, you know, done with me.' I feel like I've got nothing to lose at this point. 'And I figured you'd got back with your ex. It seemed like you weren't ready to move on.'

We sit in silence, Henry and I, and Malcolm. The driver looks back at us, almost disturbed by the quiet after the crying followed by the constant back and forth.

Frankly, I'm feeling a little overwhelmed by it all. Finally, it's Henry who breaks the silence.

'You want to know what it was?' he says, shifting the box on his lap, squaring his shoulders and looking straight ahead. 'You want to know what it was? It was that I couldn't deal with the fact that after all that back and forth with Melissa,

315

after all that pain and putting each other through such a fucking long and torturous breakup, I'd actually met someone I liked as much as you. I mean, you saw it,' he says, gesturing as if we're still in his flat, as if it's still months ago. 'She wasn't even gone when we met! I felt like I . . . I felt like I owed it to her to *suffer* and to withhold happiness from myself for her benefit. It didn't feel right that I met you when I did, it didn't feel right for me to be as happy with you as I was. Her stuff was barely out the door! You saw it! Still in boxes in my living room! And I was already moving on?'

'I guess I thought you'd got back together with her . . .' I say, thinking of my conversation with Rachel, how I took for granted that their on-and-off relationship was on.

He shakes his head. 'No. It just felt wrong, somehow. Unkind.' He pauses for a moment. 'Not that how things worked out with you felt particularly kind either. I felt like such a dick for texting you but . . . once I got it in my head I couldn't get it out.'

I shrug, not knowing what to say. 'I don't know if there's some kind of romantic egg timer for this stuff.'

He sighs.

'Did you cheat?' I ask him.

He looks at me like I'm mad. 'No! Jesus!'

'Well then . . . fuck, I mean, I literally *left my fiancé at the altar on our wedding day*. How fucked up is that? Isn't that just the worst thing you could do? Does that mean I should never be happy again?'

'I don't think so,' he says, shaking his head.

We're at the turning for my road. I'm just going to get out and leave Henry behind.

My heart's pounding as I try to find the right words. The least mortifying way to express how much I wish we were together, how much I feel like we're the right fit.

'I just feel like we're not done. Me and you,' I say. It's the best I've got.

We're pulling up. Henry hasn't said anything. He's just looking stressed and overwhelmed and honestly . . . who can blame him? I open the door and step out remembering that, yes, I am wearing one shoe and that this is probably not an especially alluring look. I accept defeat, even though my head is full of the sweet moments that have kept buzzing around my memory for months now, that little electric charge I felt when we first met at the wedding, looking up at the painted ceiling, kissing him in his kitchen, staying for pancakes. Those things I can't forget. I slam the car door behind me. The poor driver will be getting a big tip. I rummage around in my bag for my keys, waiting for the car to drive away. But it doesn't. Instead I hear another door slam shut. Henry.

'I asked Malcolm if he wouldn't mind dropping the stuff at my flat without me,' he says. 'I'll be buying him a lot of lunches to make up for . . . *that*.' He's shaking his head like he can't quite believe what he's doing. He crosses his arms across his chest and looks at me intently. 'So, who's been making you cry?'

'Aside from you?' I say, and despite the absolute chaos of the last half an hour, I can't help but smile.

'I would never,' he says, frowning. 'Not on purpose anyway . . .'

I exhale loudly, trying to expel all the bad feelings from inside my body. 'Some guy I was meant to having a date with just took one look at me and stood me up *and* all this happened in front of my ex and his new girlfriend!'

Henry looks at me, open-mouthed. 'Shit . . . that's dark. Extremely dark.'

'I know!' I wail, but the wail turns into a laugh and Henry's laughing too. 'So in a way I wasn't even *surprised* when you turned up because it just seemed so completely obvious that the universe is trying to shit on me today!'

'You want me to hop back in the Uber and track the guy down? Kick his butt?' Henry offers.

'I can kick my own butts, thank you very much,' I say, which is very clearly not true because I've just been weeping in the back of a car.

'You should have kicked mine,' he says, before averting his gaze away from me.

I sigh, feeling completely defeated and wondering what the point of this conversation even is. 'I didn't want to. That was the problem. I just liked you so much and when you dropped me and backed off all of a sudden I wasn't even angry. I just felt sad.'

He chews his lip.

I continue. 'It just felt very . . . right, meeting you. Uncomplicated. And then . . . it *became* complicated.'

'Look, if we'd met some other time . . . I can't help but think it would have worked out,' he says, throwing his hands in the air. I don't want to accept that there isn't a chance for us. Timing isn't a good enough reason.

'I'm not good at timings,' I say. 'I think I made that pretty clear when I abandoned my wedding. But that doesn't mean it wasn't the right thing to do. For me and my ex. The thing was more important than the timing.'

He looks pensive. Like he's really thinking. But he's not saying anything. Part of me doesn't want him to say anything, so I don't get knocked back once again. Not today of all days.

'Don't you think there's a reason that we keep running into each other?' he says, finally. My heart is racing. A glimmer of hope.

'No,' I say. He looks a little hurt. 'No, I don't think there's a reason. I just think they're coincidences. I think the reason we should be together is much more straightforward than that. No cosmic intervention needed. The fact is, we're a good match. I fancy you. You fancy me. I'd feel like that if I met you on Tinder, I'd feel like that if you chatted me up in a bar, I don't need all the coincidences to tell me.'

His eyes light up. 'I guess . . . you're right,' he says, a huge smile breaking across his face. 'I guess I got caught up in the . . . romance of it all . . . but really, that's all secondary. Fuck, I'm just crazy about you. Every day since I sent that text I've regretted it. I thought I had to suffer and delay . . . being happy, I guess. But maybe I don't.'

I shake my head. 'You don't. You really don't. How about if we'd met this evening. In that car. How about if I'd never switched the name cards at the wedding and we'd never met before, if you'd never asked me out and we'd never gone to the Painted Hall and you'd never made me dinner and we'd never known that we *worked*, and this was the first time we were meeting. Would now be the right time?'

I want him. I'm allowed to want him. I'm allowed to take control of this situation. I deserve to be happy. I deserve to live the life I want.

'Now . . . feels like exactly the right time,' he says, smiling, a dazed expression on his face. 'But first you need to tell me why you're only wearing one shoe.'

'Shut up and kiss me.'

And he does. After the weirdest of days, I get to kiss Henry again. The thing I've wanted to do over and over again since the first time. The thing I want to do forever. Walking straight into the rest of my life: with no illusions and no more running away from the altar.

28

I don't know exactly what I thought my life would look like a year on from my wedding-that-wasn't. I don't know what I was hoping for. Maybe I hoped I would have met someone else nice, that I wouldn't have given up on living in London. But I don't think I ever imagined that I would have become stronger, more confident, more able to know what I want, what I deserve, how to be a better friend, how to be fully present in my own life. A year ago there was no Nicole and no Henry, which is equally hard to believe, given what outsize positions they both occupy in my heart.

Five months isn't a lifetime. I know that. Five months is not even close to ten years, but . . . with every passing day it becomes obvious that my feelings for Henry when I met him were not the romantic delusions of a schoolgirl crush. Not one thing about Henry has been disappointing. He's the real deal.

I laugh out loud every day. I have never made my own cup of tea in his presence. I walk the streets of London with him, seeing things I'd never notice on my own. I never worry that my friends will think he's boring or not good enough for me, or too good for me, because I know for sure we are a perfect match. Every kiss feels like a first kiss. And if it had worked the first time around? Well, I don't know if we would be here today. Yes, Henry wasn't ready for another relationship, but neither was I. I thought meeting him was the solution to all my problems, all my insecurities, my uncertainties around leaving Alistair. But it turns out that I was the solution to all my problems. All I needed was to give myself space to figure myself out, to be daring, to show myself that I didn't need to be in a relationship to know I deserved fun and happiness. Just having chemistry isn't enough. There has to be a solid foundation, too. Not *needing* a relationship made it even clearer that what I *wanted* was Henry.

And, ever the romantic, he's looking me right in the eyes, holding a bottle of beer in one hand and a microphone in the other, singing 'This Must Be the Place' by Talking Heads in the karaoke booth at Nicole's twenty-ninth birthday.

Although Lola is here, her and Nicole are officially extremely unofficial. By that I mean, every few weeks I wake up and Nicole is in the living room, but broadly speaking they are involved only in the loosest terms. Besides, I think Lola has something going on with one of the plus-size models that her brand cast for their next campaign, after listening to Nicole about being more size-inclusive. And maybe Nicole, Lola and I are working on a little something together on that front, but it's early days and I don't want to get my hopes up about cool clothes for fat babes.

And Nicole? Well, she's in high spirits, that's for sure. She's already blasted through some Celine Dion, Whitney Houston and Cher and I have no idea where she can go from there. It turns out karaoke is one of her great loves, hence why we're sweating ourselves dry in a karaoke booth in Soho on the hottest day in August. It just goes to show that I would *truly* do anything for her.

She slides up next to me on the sweat-slick vinyl bench that surrounds the room, a *very* full glass of prosecco in her hand, liquid sloshing over the top.

'He's a good egg,' she says, nodding at Henry. This isn't the first time she's said this. She uses that expression a lot, but only ever in conjunction with Henry.

'The best egg, I think,' I say, smiling, as he does his best approximation of David Byrne despite being chunky, sweaty and ginger, and not the lead singer of Talking Heads. 'Hey, twenty-nine is not so bad, right?'

'Not bad at all,' she says, shaking her head and looking around the room, so packed with various friends, family and lovers that the sweat is starting to condense on the ceiling before, presumably, falling as some kind of gross, indoor rain. 'Thirty next year, innit.'

'You're not stressed about it, are you?'

'Me? Stressed? I'm looking forward to it, mate. Imagine all the fun I'm going to have between now and then!' Nicole of the eternal optimism. Nicole of the indefatigable spirit. Nicole of the boundless confidence. Thank God for her.

We clap as Henry's song ends. I leap to my feet and throw my arms around his neck, kissing his sweaty face.

'I love you,' he says.

'I love you,' I say back. It's funny, the fact he said it the first time was enough to freak him out and convince him he wasn't ready to meet someone else but, in a way, it's made things much easier for us now. It's not looming over us like a huge milestone. It's just there, in the atmosphere, loving and being loved.

He hands the microphone to Nicole, and she in turn thrusts the microphone at me.

'I don't know what to sing!' I say, shaking my head, my general human instinct not to sing in front of people taking over.

'Right then, I'll just choose a random number from the book and you can sing that,' she says, decisively. 'There's no escape!' She turns to the screen and punches in some random numbers. The universe has managed to surprise me so much by this point that I'm not even taken aback when the karaoke-fied intro music that fills the room is 'Everybody Wants to Rule the World' by Tears for Fears. It's like I'm right back there in the back of that taxi on my wedding day. The thought of it makes me feel dizzy at what could have been, everything I would have missed out on. Can I sing very well? No. At this moment, do I care? Not one bit. I take a deep breath, and hit the first line with carefree abandon.

Acknowledgements

Thank you above all to Natasha Bardon, for encouraging me to write for adults in the first place, not to mention for ushering this story into the world. This has been my first book with Rachel Mann as my agent, and I can't thank her enough for giving me the best guidance and encouragement, and for being someone I can rely on. I am forever grateful for the mind and heart of certified creative genius Paul Haworth, who's always asking how I can make something sillier, weirder, more fun. Thank you once again to Alice Slater, Beth John and Jenny Tighe, cheerleaders par excellence, and would like to add Alex Smyrliadi to my customary list of names. A special thanks to Harry A for the consistent support for my books, and for being an extraordinary person. I am always grateful for the love and support of my family, all the Rutters and anyone Rutter-adjacent, especially my parents and my brother. A final thank you to everyone at HarperCollins who has already worked on this book and to anyone who will work on it after I've written these acknowledgements – I appreciate every one of you.

And if you loved
Welcome to Your Life,
look out for Bethany's next hilarious,
uplifting, sexy rom-com

BIG
DATE
ENERGY

Serial monogamist Fran has waited years for her chance to be single, and now's her time to shine. She wants to date as much as she can. She's got Big Date Energy.

But her Mum has other ideas. She's desperate for Fran to find *real love* and nominates her for a new TV dating show, Date My Mate, which promises to pair people with their perfect match.

And when Fran walks onto the set, hoping for a bit of a laugh and a story to tell, she's confronted with Ivy. Her first love, her high school romance. And the one that got away...

COMING
2024